GASLIT HORROR

Stories by
Robert W. Chambers,
Lafcadio Hearn, Bernard Capes,
and Others

EDITED BY HUGH LAMB

D1297634

DOVER PUBLICATIONS, INC.
Mineola, New York

Bibliographical Note

Gaslit Horror: Stories by Robert W. Chambers, Lafcadio Hearn, Bernard Capes, and Others, first published in 2008 by Dover Publications, Inc., is a new anthology of thirteen stories reprinted from *Gaslit Nightmares: An Anthology of Victorian Tales of Terror,* edited by Hugh Lamb, published by Futura Publications, London, in 1988, and *Gaslit Nightmares 2: An Anthology of Victorian Tales of Terror,* edited by Hugh Lamb, published by Futura Publications, London, in 1991.

Library of Congress Cataloging-in-Publication Data

Gaslit horror : stories by Robert W. Chambers, Lafcadio Hearn, Bernard Capes, and others / edited by Hugh Lamb. — Dover ed.
    p. cm.
  ISBN-13: 978-0-486-46305-6 (pbk.)
  ISBN-10: 0-486-46305-2 (pbk.)
   1. Horror tales, English. 2. English fiction—19th century. I. Lamb, Hugh.

PR1309.H6G375 2008
823'.0873808—dc22

2008009991

Manufactured in the United States of America
Dover Publications, Inc., 31 East 2nd Street, Mineola, N.Y. 11501

To Delphine

Acknowledgements

I must acknowledge, as usual, help received from Sutton Public Library who keep tracking the books down for me, and from Mike Ashley and Richard Dalby, who help me with the background details when I've got hold of the books. And John Jarrold, who thought it was all a good idea.

Contents

Mrs. G. Linnaeus Banks

In her introduction to *Through the Night* (1882), Isabella Banks remarked on the strange anomaly "that the era of hard science and scoffing unbelief should have given so many mystic and ghost stories to our literature." And she was right, of course; the hard-nosed Victorian age gave birth to a host of spectral tales. Mrs. Linnaeus Banks was merely echoing the bewilderment of so many authors who found an avid market for their collections of ghost stories.

Mrs. Banks' *Through the Night*, subtitled *Tales of Shades and Shadows*, was based on her own experiences and contact with others who had, as she put it, been "visited by apparitions." Isabella Banks, however, came from a most unfanciful background. Born in Manchester in 1821, she was the grand-daughter of James Varley, discoverer of the use of chloride of lime. At the age of twenty-five she married the poet and journalist George Linnaeus Banks, and it seems he must have encouraged her to write. Her first book appeared in 1865 and she went on to publish over twenty more. As well as *Through the Night,* Mrs. Banks wrote two other books of short stories—*The Watchmaker's Daughter* (1882) and *Sybilla* (1884)—which are almost perfectly representative of Victorian literature as it passed through its moral preaching stage.

A keen antiquarian, Isabella Banks amassed an extensive collection of shells and fossils, and garnered many odd tales for use in her stories. The bulk of her fiction seems to have appeared after her husband's death in 1881; she published at least two books the next year, and she continued writing until her death in 1897.

"The Pride of the Corbyns" comes from *Through the Night*, and is based on what has become a well known legend of the Caribbean (some works on the Devil's Triangle even drag the original legend in to their canon). Of this legend Mrs. Banks says the following: "A West Indian friend who described to me the mausoleum said to be the scene of midnight disturbance and consequent terror such as I have portrayed did so as a verity of which he had not the slightest doubt. The intrusion of alien dead is a motive, the potency of which can scarcely be understood at this time and in England. The two hurricanes which I attempt to describe are matters of Barbadian history; the family names are those of early settlers."

Mrs. Banks' potent motive, incidentally, is based on some racial prejudice which may seem odd in our more enlightened times. Please bear in mind that in Mrs. Banks' day, such things were taken far more seriously, and that the idiosyncrasy of our time was often the genuine concern of the 1880s.

The Pride of the Corbyns

I. The last of the Corbyns

Death stood knocking at Archibald Corbyn's door—not at the door of Corbyn Hall, but at the door of the Corbyn heart; and when that had ceased to beat, one of the oldest, wealthiest, proudest, and most aristocratic families in Barbados would be extinct.

It was a boast of Archibald that the highland district in the north-west, of which Mount Hillaby is the centre, owed its name of Scotland to the loyalty of the first Corbyn, who, settling beneath the shadow of those conical hills, first cleared away dense forests of the bearded fig for the better cultivation of cotton.

He was one of those nine British merchants who, in the reign of Charles I, landed and built Bridgetown as a commercial depot, each having a grant of a thousand acres. Tracing down the family history, Archibald would tell with a glow how another Corbyn had introduced the sugar-cane into the island, in spite of troublous times, and how he erected the first primitive wind-mill to crush out the sap, when he had only open-air boilers in which to crystallize that sap into golden sugar and golden coin.

Riding home from St. Andrew's church on one of these occasions, with his old friend and shipping agent, Matthias Walcot, he pointed to a mound, below which two streams, rushing right and left of Corbyn Hall from the mountains, there met at a sharp angle, and ran on to join Church River until that ended in a lakelet known as Long Pond, partially barred by sand and vegetable wash from the sea.

"There, Matthias," he said, "the first Corbyn roof-tree stood just where that group of courida-trees now casts a shadow over the grass. It was but a rude wooden shed with palm-leaf thatch but young colonists have to rough it, and if a man has pith in him, what matter?"

As they turned from the white mountain road into the long avenue of sandbox and cocoa-nut trees, and neared his handsome two-floored, square, stone mansion, with pillared piazzas and overhanging balconies on three sides, he told how he owed the substantial abode before them to the spirit of desolation which, riding on the wings of devastating hurricanes, had in two successive centuries swept homesteads and plantation into one indiscriminate wreck.

"That was in 1780, when Jamie Corbyn, my grandfather, was the owner. *He* was a man with pith in him, was Jamie; and when he saw his plank walls flying about like so many palm-leaves, he just made up his mind to build under a sheltering nook of the hills; and since stone came almost as handy as wood, he built a house that should stand during his lifetime and his son's after him."

"Well, Mr. Corbyn, it is an ill wind that blows no one good," Mr. Walcot put in. "It blew the Corbyns a house that will last."

Archibald's mood changed; he sighed heavily. "Ay, friend Matthias; it did blow the Corbyns a home to last—a home sacred from intrusion. Our dead were washed out of their graves, and my grandfather, horrified, planned and built yon solid half-sunken mausoleum at the extremity of the wood to receive the ancestors the hurricane had unearthed. And there he too lies, with his sons and daughters in niches by his side; and there I in time shall be laid, with no child nor relative to mourn or follow me. My dear brother Charles lies under the sea, and I am the last of the Corbyns," with another sigh. "He built a home for the living and a home for the dead, to serve for many generations to come; but I am the last of my uncontaminated race, and when the mausoleum doors close upon me they will close for ever."

Uncontaminated! Ah, there the full pride of the Corbyns spoke out. No drop of Indian or negro blood flowed in Corbyn veins. He was pure white as his first English ancestor; could draw his fingers through his hair without showing a tinge of blue in his oval nails, or the slightest "kink" in his flowing locks—a grand distinction this in Barbados, where so few even of the wealthy planters but had a taint of the creole in their composition, however infinitesimal. And no West Indian could more fully appreciate the value of the vaunt than Matthias Walcot.

But Death knocking at Archibald Corbyn's door was growing clamorous, and black blood or white would be all as one within the hour.

Dr. Hawley and Matthias Walcot stood by his bedside, and Dinah, his old negro nurse, readjusted his disordered pillow or wiped the heavy dew from his clammy forehead with gentle, sympathetic hands, and watched his wasted fingers pick the counterpane with sad forebodings.

With quick intelligence she caught the meaning of a glance from the doctor to Mr. Walcot, and escaping from the chamber by the open window, with her big black hands before her face, she leaned over the edge of the balcony to sob out of sight and hearing.

Yet her own ears were alert for any sound from the sick-room, and presently the faint voice of her dying master attracted her attention. True to negro instinct, curiosity arrested grief. She crept nearer to the open window.

He was saying, in feeble gasps, "Will in my desk—I've left you—sole executor, Matthias. I know I can trust you. Use my slaves well, and—no whipping, Matt!"

There was a pause. The doctor administered a stimulant; Archibald evidently revived.

"And, Matthias—I—charge you—leave no stone unturned—find a Corbyn to inherit—Charlie's dead body never found—may be after all—I—not—last of the Corbyns. Mausoleum close for ever—Corbyns extinct—pure race—"

The voice was lost in indistinct murmurs. There was silence.

"He's gone!" whispered Mr. Walcot; "hush!"

The doctor placed a finger on his lips, and with the other hand checked Dinah's impulsive return to the room.

"Matthias—England—advertise—I have—last Corb—"

Close the jalousies: exclude the light. The master of Corbyn Hall can neither see the sunshine nor hear the universal wail from every corner of that wide estate. Archibald Corbyn, too proud of birth to do aught unworthy his pure blood, has been a master without peer!

There was a small grating in the thick door of the mausoleum, which was reached by a descent of four or five steps. This entrance, which fronted a bye-road, was bricked up. The mausoleum itself was a solid stone structure, with little or no attempt at ornament; externally about fourteen yards square; with a domed roof rising not more than four feet above the level of the road; the ground on all four sides sloping downwards towards the building. It was consequently in a deep hollow, and was further sheltered from high winds by the hills which rose steeply above the road on the other side, and by the wood which had marched up to its three sides like a protecting army of giants.

It was mid-day. The ripe pendulous pods of the thorny sandbox tree burst one after another, and scattering their seed-rings to earth with sharp reports, as if a platoon of distant musketry proclaimed the fall of each. But another ripe seed was ready to be "sown in corruption," and a louder report proclaimed that.

It was the invariable gun fired through the unbricked grating, to dissipate noxious gases generated within, lest the opening of the vault for the dead should let out pestilence on the living.

A night had passed. The vault was purified; the door stood open. From all parts of Barbados planters and others had assembled to show their respect for the dead. Rising and falling with the undulations of the hills, a long procession of carriages and pedestrians marked the white road with a line of black for half a mile or more. Slaves and friends, bond and free, white, creole, quadroon, mulatto, and black, were there with sable suits and white head-gear; but of all those hundreds, not one relative to hold the pall or shed a tear over the silver-mounted black coffin as it was borne to its niche in the sepulchre with solemn funeral rites; and the door was closed on hospitable Archibald, the "last of the Corbyns."

"Brick it up close, Dan," said centenarian Cuffy to the labourer at work; "nebber be opened no more. Massa nebber rest in him grave if a drop of nigger blood be berried with him. An' I'm 'fraid, Dan, there be no real white massa to come after good ole massa."

"'Fraid not, Cuffy?" questioned Dan ruefully—for Cuffy was the oracle of the plantation—adding, "Ah, him proud gemp'lman, but him berry good to black man. Wonder who be massa now?"

A momentous question this to a slave!

Cuffy extended his withered arm to an opening between the distant foliage, where a glimpse of the shining Atlantic might be seen three miles away.

"Ib dat hungry sea swallow up young Massa Charles, I much 'fraid, Dan, Massa Walcot will be. *He* got a splash ob colour in *him,* but his heart no so warm as our poor massa's for all dat"; and old Cuffy turned away mournfully, shaking his head.

Corbyn Hall had got a new master. The will which made Matthias Walcot sole executor made him virtually proprietor.

All that stood between him and absolute ownership was the very improbable chance that Archibald's younger brother, Charles, had escaped when the *Mermaid,* in which he had sailed from Bristol seven years before, foundered off the Irish coast, and not a soul was known to be saved. There was also the remote possibility of his having left a legitimate heir on dry land; but as no echo of wedding-bells had ever wafted to the brother in Barbados, this was as improbable.

The brothers had parted in anger; and Archibald had never been his own man after the *Mermaid* went down. He was only forty-eight when he died; and his will was full of mournful regret. Matthias was enjoined to spare no cost, neglect no means to find a rightful heir; but if within ten years no claimant could be discovered, then—and not till then—Matthias Walcot and his heirs were to possess the Corbyn estate, with all its living brood, in perpetuity.

Matthias Walcot passed as an honourable man amongst men; had been esteemed and trusted by the dead; would have resented the charge of dishonesty. But the temptation was great, and *he* was *not.*

Prompt to take possession, he was not prompt in measures

which *might* eventually oust himself and his. He made languid official inquiries at first; sent occasional advertisements to an English newspaper; and persuaded himself, and tried to persuade Dr. Hawley, that he had been very active.

II. THE WALCOTS AT HOME

I said Corbyn Hall had a new master; I should have said a mistress and three masters, a younger lady being thrown in. There was Mrs. Walcot, dominant, of large dimensions and lofty pretensions; there was Miss Walcot, slight, languid, listless, and intensely fashionable; and there were two sons, William and Stephen, the most bumptious of all bumptious Barbadians.

What a revolution their advent created in that hospitable, free-and-easy bachelor household! The will interdicted unnecessary change until heirship was determined. But Mrs. Walcot was disposed to read its provisions liberally. She did not sell or destroy plain or old-fashioned fittings: they were simply huddled into a lumber-room out of her way, and replaced with the very brightest and newest importations from Europe, before even the dogs and horses had well learned to recognize the new mastership.

Matthias himself forgot he was only executor. He turned his shipping agency and his stifling office on the wharf over to his tall sons, and settled down comfortably at Corbyn Hall as proprietor and planter. But Mrs. Walcot was fond of society, and was not content to dwell for ever ten miles from town and two or three from their nearest neighbours; so their old house at the Folly was retained, ostensibly for the convenience of William and Stephen, and the lady rejoiced in a town-house and a country-house, and became a very grand personage indeed. She oscillated between the two houses, paid and received visits, went shopping, and ransacked the heterogeneous stores of every dealer in Broad-street, to the intense disgust of Scipio, her mulatto charioteer, whose lazy life was at an end.

Nor was Scipio the only grumbler on the estate. Flippant

lady's-maids invaded the sanctity of Chloe's kitchen and Cassy's laundry. Will and Steve in house or stable were as ready to use their riding-whips on the shoulders of valet or groom as on the flanks of their steeds. There were sharp overseers in the boiling-sheds, on the rocky slopes amongst the waving yellow canes and the changeful fields of Indian corn, and among the bursting cotton-pods. The change sank into the negro heart, and from Chloe in her kitchen to Cufly in his distant hut, there were sunken spirits and low-voiced murmurings. If a "boy" carried his dish of cuckoo to window or door sill, or squatted on mat or ground outside to eat his dinner at ease, he was sure to become the centre of a group no longer shaking their fat sides with laughter, but shaking their woolly heads mysteriously, and comparing the present *régime* with the past.

Dinah—or aunt Dinah, as she was called—who had nursed the infant, sick, and dying Corbyns for two generations, and ruled supreme in Archibald's home, had been deposed, and the poor old thing fretted much. It was none of Mr. Walcot's doing. Had he been consulted, he might have remembered her presence in the planter's death-chamber, and from motives of policy left her to govern her coloured blood as of yore.

Yet even he knew not what she had heard, nor how it had worked in her brain. As it was, she brooded over her dying master's words, and felt their import greater than reality.

Old Cuffy—still the nominal head-gardener—she made the depositary of her knowledge, and the pair held frequent and solemn conference. From these twain, no doubt, the first faint murmurings against Walcot rule went out like a breath, as soft and unsuspected. And now aunt Dinah was troubled with ominous dreams, and Cuffy grew portentously prophetic.

Meanwhile Mrs. Walcot, blessedly obtuse, prepared to give a grand ball before the rainy season should set in, with one matchmaking eye for Laura and another for William, who had set both his on a lovely orphan heiress, then the ward of the Rev. John Fulton.

Vainly Matthias, with due regard to appearances, urged that it was "too soon." Madam was wilful, and issued her invitations to the cream of Barbadian society, with a select few of her former Bridgetown friends, whom she hoped to overpower with her grandeur.

Mourning was all but discarded: a gauzy black scarf for herself, a black sash for Miss Walcot, were all that memory could spare for the late master of the mansion whose family diamonds they wore. The coloured attendants were arrayed in the gayest of tints: brilliant turbans, kerchiefs, and petticoats, flashing striped trousers and light jackets, fluttered everywhere, like swarms of black-bodied butterflies, to which every guest-bringing phaeton added its quota, either in driver or lackey.

Odour of fruits and flowers and wines, flash of glass and gilding, wax-lights and mirrors, sparkle of eyes and jewellery, flutter of satins, gauzes, and hearts, patter of feet and tongues, melody of piano, guitar and song within.

Banjo and beating feet, the rollicking song and the dance, a babel of laughter and gabble without; and Cuffy and Dinah sullenly aloof in the shadow of a manchineel-tree—the only two to whom Mrs. Walcot's magnificent ball had brought neither pleasure nor occupation. The hooting owls in the sandbox trees were scarcely such birds of ill-omen to the Walcots as were these two, brooding over that festival as being an indignity to the memory of their dead master.

Song, and dance, and rippling laughter, flushing cheeks and fluttering fans! A shrill scream, like that of the Shunammite's son—"My head, my head!"—and with one hand spasmodically raised to her brow, Laura Walcot fell back into the arms of her partner in the quadrille, speechless and gasping!

In vain ladies proffered scent bottles and vinaigrettes, and gentlemen darting through the open casements brought back clusters of soft sandbox leaves to bind on her throbbing forehead, as antidotes to pain. The dark green but served to show how deathly was her pallor; and Dr. Hawley, brushing in through the crowd from the card-room, could do little more than shake his head gravely, and say "No use, no use! Too much excitement!"

Mrs. Walcot shrieked in hysterics; Matthias sat with bowed head like one stupefied; the haughty brows of William and Stephen lowered in presence of the grim intruder—Death.

Startled visitors departed, or remained for the ceremonial of the morrow. An awful hush fell over and around the mansion. The negroes, strangely unlike themselves, indulged in no noisy demonstrations of grief. They were silent, save when whispers of "Doom" and "Judgement" passed from mouth to mouth in stifled undertones.

As the white coffin of the maiden was being carried into the house, Cuffy, standing under the piazza, heard William Walcot give Dan instructions for the opening of the Corbyn mausoleum. Uplifting his head and his bony hands in superstitious horror, he ejaculated: "There! Berry young Missy Walcot in Corbyn grabe! Nebber. Old massa's flesh creep in him shroud if dat blue-nailed missy laid inside there!"

The tall old man, venerable with the greyness of his hundred years, drew a long breath, then stalked unbidden into the presence of Matthias and Dr. Hawley, and stood before them erect, with fiery eyes, much as Elijah must have stood before usurping Ahab.

"Massa Walcot better not berry him dead with the Corbyn dead. Sure's you live, Massa Arch'bald nebber 'low it!"

"Not allow it, Cuffy! What do you mean?" said Mr. Walcot testily, looking up amazed and annoyed.

"Massa Corbyn leave him hall, leave him plantation, leave him money to him friend; but him keep de Corbyn maus'lum for de Corbyn *only*. IF"—and undaunted Cuffy laid special emphasis on the "if"—"If no heir, an Massa Arch'bald be last ob de Corbyns, den dat maus'lum be closed till Judgement-day!"

"Cuffy, you presume on your grey hairs. I shall lay my poor child where I think fit. I do not suffer my slaves to dictate to me. Your mind is wandering. Quit the room; this is no season for intrusion."

Dr. Hawley listened in silence. Cuffy still maintained his ground.

"Massa Walcot, de 'mighty God above send Cuffy to warn you. Dere am *doom* on dis house till Corbyn heir be found, and de first thun'erbolt fell last night. For own sake, Massa Walcot" (Cuffy never said "*massa*" only), "berry pretty missy in de churchyard!"

A similar scene was enacted upstairs.

Dinah, arranging the folds of the fine muslin shroud, and the fan-shaped face cover to stand stiffly up until the last moment, made way for the bereaved mother to kiss the pallid lips ere it was folded down. She ventured to ask the place of interment.

Being told, she bent her aged knees, and implored her mistress to change her plans, or evil would be sure to come of it.

Mr. and Mrs. Walcot were alike obdurate and indignant. Cuffy and Dinah were declared crazy and superstitious, and cautioned to make less free in future.

But though they laid their daughter's corpse in the Corbyn mausoleum, in spite of premonition, for some innate reason they did not place it in any one of the unfilled niches; it was left on the floor in the centre of the sepulchre.

And then the Corbyn vault closed for the first time on one of another name and another caste.

III. The Mystery of the Mausoleum

It is not customary for Barbadians to court the heavy noxious dews and the bloodthirsty mosquitoes by being abroad after nightfall; but the unwonted events of ball and burial on two consecutive days had brought to that lonely plantation a concourse of people, some of whom were detained by the claims of friendship, others of business, to a late hour.

It was close upon midnight when Dr. Hawley and another friend shook hands with Mr. Walcot under the portico of the Corbyn mansion; and stepping into his light cane phaeton, he bade his black Jehu "Tear away home."

Once clear of the sombre avenue, where accommodating fireflies hung out their tiny lamps, the white marly road shone like a streak of silver in the bright moonlight. They spun along rapidly, to the drowsy music of their own wheels, in concert with the droning trumpet of obsequious mosquitoes, and the thin metallic pipe of an occasional cicada, to which their pony's hoof beat time. Otherwise the stillness was unbroken, save by Sambo's involuntary ejaculations to the steed.

As they neared the point where the road branched off to the sea-coast, passing the mausoleum on its way through Corbyn Hall Wood, a shrill scream was borne up the bye-road on the clear midnight air.

The pony stopped involuntarily, quivering in every limb.

"Golla, massa! what am dat?" cried Sambo in a fright.

Before Dr. Hawley or his friend could reply, a second scream, louder and more piercing, smote upon the ear, and was followed by a succession of unearthly yells.

"Quick, Sambo! Turn to the left. There is some foul play going on down this road. Quick! or we may be too late to prevent a tragedy."

But Sambo's white teeth chattered, all the more because the pony obstinately refused to obey the rein—willing to bolt down the road home, but determined not to turn to the left for either man or master. As he snorted, reared, and plunged, threatening the slight vehicle with destruction, and the shrieks still continued, the doctor and his companion leapt out, and ran at full speed down the road, athwart which sparsely set palmetto, or cocoa-nut trees cast spectral shadows.

A faint sea-breeze met them, laden with the mingled perfumes of fruit and flower, but with it came more hideously the strange discordant noise. Then two or three wild dogs darted past them, howling as they went. Then with garments flying loose and eyeballs glaring, a negro woman, blind with terror, ran against the doctor. A man, little less excited, was close at her heels.

"Hallo! what is the meaning of this outcry?" demanded the doctor, grasping the man by the arm, under the impression the negress was escaping from ill-usage.

The man—who proved to be the undertaker's foreman—could only gasp between his chattering teeth, "Dre'ful! Dre'ful, doctor; dre'ful!"

The woman—a seamstress whom the foreman was gallantly escorting home—had continued her flight.

"You black scoundrel, what have you been doing?" cried the doctor, giving him a shake.

The man's protest was drowned by a fresh outbreak of the same appalling cries.

Dr. Hawley, exclaiming, "Again! What is that?" released his arm, convinced that he at least was not the peace breaker.

"O! doctor, dre'ful down dere! Dead man's fight."

"Pish!" "Rubbish!" from the doctor and his friend; and they rushed forward, drawing reluctant Cicero back with them.

But they too stood aghast as they approached the mausoleum. The noise—a demoniac compound of blows, groans, shrieks, and howls—evidently *issued from the bricked-up sepulchre!*

It seemed, indeed, as though a desperate combat raged within the closed-up tomb; and the blood of the spectators curdled as they listened.

They were not the only auditors. A neighbouring planter and a sturdy sea-captain, named Hudson, on their way inland, had been arrested on their journey likewise, and seemed rooted to the spot with a mysterious dread.

Could anyone imagine a scene more terrible! The mausoleum, worn with age and weather, overgrown with moss and lichens, sentinelled by sandbox trees and blighted cocoa palms, whose shroud-like drapery of creepers gave them the aspect of ghosts of dead trees keeping watch for ghosts of dead men; and scared by the unearthly din, owls and monkeys screeched and chattered, to make if possible a greater pandemonium.

"I have seen the ocean in its fury, heard the winds break loose, and the artillery of heaven rattle, but never did I hear anything so terrific as this. It makes my very flesh creep," said the captain, addressing Dr. Hawley. "Can you, sir, offer any solution of this mystery?"

What Dr. Hawley might have said was interrupted by a final burst of triumphant yells, followed by a peal of still more discordant laughter, which died away in feeble cachinnations, till silence scarcely less awful fell on all around.

A harmless snake then uncoiled itself on the mausoleum steps and dragged itself across the road, a pair of green lizards crawled over the dome of the mausoleum to bask in the moonlight; and the unaccountable noises having ceased entirely, the party drawn together so singularly moved away in a body.

As a natural sequence, conversation turned on the place they had just quitted, Archibald Corbyn's funeral, and that of Laura Walcot; and so much was Captain Hudson interested, that when they shook hands and separated at the fork of the roads, he had promised to call on Dr. Hawley at his house near Kissing Bridge before sailing for England.

Seven persons (including Sambo) went their several ways surcharged with the story of a horrible mystery.

What wonder that the succeeding midnight brought a crowd to the spot, to test, verify, or ridicule, as might be? Notwithstanding the previous shock to his nerves, Dr. Hawley made one. With him was Stephen Walcot, much concerned by this commotion over his sister's grave; and on the extreme verge of the assembly they saw a group of old Corbyn servants huddled together like a flock of timid sheep, with Cuffy and aunt Dinah at their head.

The doctor had lost no time in making Mr. Walcot acquainted with his nocturnal experience. Matthias had only curled his lip, shrugged his shoulders, and said, "Were I you, doctor, I would not repeat this nonsense. Your patients will not care to consult a medico who takes too much wine." He had spoken to the sons. William laughed outright. Steve, subdued by his sister's loss, gave their informant a more respectful hearing, and, in spite of his brother's banter, volunteered to watch the tomb that night with the doctor, little surmising how many would share that watch.

Twelve by Dr. Hawley's repeater! The silent expectant crowd shrank back with affright as, without one moment's premonition, the air was rent with a volley of shrieks and yells, which wakened the echoes of the hills, and a chorus from owls and monkeys drove the raccoon from his bed, the pigeons from their nests, and sent batwings from the shadows to flutter in the moonlight.

For one whole hour the noises were unceasing. If superstition drew the crowd together, fear dispersed it. Only the most daring of the auditors remained, and amongst these were Cuffy and Dinah, who stood apart with hands upraised, as if invoking unseen protection.

Bearing Cuffy's adjuration and previsions in mind, Dr. Hawley—well acquainted with negro subtlety, and anxious to find a natural solution for the phenomena—drew the centenarian apart, and, with Stephen by his side, subjected him to a fire of cross-questions.

"Know nuffink 'bout it, doctor; 'cept Massa Corbyn not rest. Him angry; all him dead family angry," was all they could elicit.

Yet, in spite of his genuine trepidation—for every nerve seemed to quiver—there appeared some reservation, of which the doctor took a mental note for question at a fitter time.

Mrs. Walcot was frantic. Sorrow for her daughter's loss was reduplicated by this scandal over her very grave. Mr. Walcot and William repudiated all notion of the supernatural, and ascribed the strange phenomena to a plot between Cuffy and his colleagues. Stringent orders were left with the overseers that no slave should quit the plantation after sundown, or approach within a given distance of the mausoleum, under penalty of a flogging.

But that did not quell the nocturnal riot. Matthias brought his own eyes and ears to the test, had the place examined by day, placed a cordon of military around, but all to no purpose.

For five nights the supernatural warfare continued. Trafalgar Square and the Bridgetown ice-houses were thronged with thirsty gossips, and Barbados throbbed with superstitious fear to its very finger-tips.

Then it ceased. The excitement gradually died out, business resumed its sway, the Walcots were condoled with, and the dead reposed in peace.

Still superstition held the haunted mausoleum in dread; and urgent must be the business and hardy must be the man that should travel that road by night.

Even over the Corbyn mansion crept a sort of eerie atmosphere. There was less laughter, and more whispering in secret corners. Every figure in mourning robes seemed to cast a shadow of death on the hearth. A cloud deeper than that of grief rested on the brows of Matthias and his wife; and the infection spread to the white tenantry on the estate.

IV. Obeah!

A fortnight later Dr. Hawley rode out to the Hall. It was purely a friendly visit, so he said; but ere he went away he asked his host how he was progressing in his search for a legitimate heir, adding that a friend of his, a Captain Hudson, of the barque *Adelaide,* would readily undertake any commission in further-ance of that end in the mother country.

Mrs. Walcot bridled up, and Matthias, reddening, answered stiffly, "Thank you, doctor, but I can manage my own business without the intervention of strangers. I need no reminder of my duty. A sea captain is scarcely the person to institute inquiries of this nature."

"Perhaps not," assented the doctor dryly, with a peculiar smile, as he took his departure, much like one who has but done half his errand.

Had their voices wafted to Cuffy through the open casement, that he should quit the jasmine he was pruning by the portico to hurry to the avenue? Whether or not, he stopped the pony under shadow of the large trees, and whispered earnestly and mysteriously:

"Dr. Hawley, you good man; you lub ole massa. Him spirit angry; all de Corbyn spirits angry. Last night Dinah dream—dream of Massa Charlie. He wet an' white upon the steps; he ask to come in, and Massa Walcot shut the door—an' Death come in instead! Doctor, dere be nudder Corbyn *somewhere,* an' Massa Walcot no try to find him; an' spirits *berry* angry. Cuffy work Obeah charm to-night, to keep de evil doom from de black boys and girls dat lub ole Massa Corbyn!"

"I would advise you to have nothing to do with Obeah, Cuffy. It may breed ill-feeling and do mischief," said the doctor, as Cuffy loosened his hold of the reins, and Sambo cracked his whip.

In Corbyn Hall Wood, remote from the Hall itself, close by a mountain streamlet which ran down to join the river, was a bub-bling boiling spring. The spot was lonely and sequestered, shad-owed by the palmetto and the machineel. Gourds and squashes trailed along the ground and hid the iguana, the green lizard, and the spotted toad. No pineapple or banana grew beside it; no seaside grape spread its branches low to the ground, hanging thick and ruddy clusters under every branch, glossy with leaves of green; but all that was dark or rank grew there.

It was a dismal spot. Yet hither dusky forms came stealthily in the middle of the night to watch and share with Cuffy in the dread rites of Obeah incantation. To his fellows he was known as a Mandingo priest, and the hold he had on their superstitious souls was strong and terrible. His hut was near at hand, and in this weird corner of the plantation had he been wont to concoct healing balms, philtres, and the yet more potent Obeah, whose spell, wrought in secret, was supposed to work in secret, and set human skill and precaution at defiance.

Dinah was there—a fitting priestess of these mysteries—and Dan and Scipio, and Chloe and Cassy, with others whose names are unrecorded.

There was a fissure in the ground close to the boiling spring. To this Cuffy applied a light, and instantly a jet of flame shot up, and the poor dupes bowed down to the fire-spirit. From a hollow tree was produced an iron pot. Half filling this from the boiling spring, it was suspended on a triangle of sticks over the natural naphtha flame, and the weird rites began.

There was a low monotonous chant in a strange tongue, a dance around the seething pot, which in the lurid light was half demoniac; and Cuffy, swaying to and fro, muttered words unknown even to his confederates, as one by one he threw into the pot snake-wood from the trumpet-tree, sap from the deadly manchineel, a snake cucumber, the poisonous sandbox leaves and rings, a living lizard and a toad, a turtle's egg, the root of the cat's-blood plant, a bat, a young owlet, a dead man's hair, pernicious scum from Long Pond, and other venomous ingredients with and without a name.

It was a horrible compound—a deadly poison; and as it bubbled in the pot, white teeth and eyes gleamed out from midnight faces, hideous from their own imaginings.

The charm wrought out, the mixture poured into a calabash bottle and closely stopped, the refuse buried in the ground, the pot restored to the hollow tree, the magic flame extinguished with wet sand, Cuffy dismissed his impish brood to their huts, and bore away his revolting decoction, to be buried the ensuing night under the threshold of the Hall. The doom hanging over Corbyn would then fall upon the fated mortals who should step across it first; and thus, Obeah satisfied, his followers would be protected.

Be sure there were early risers among the initiated, and sharp eyes to watch the threshold under ban, and warn off unwary footsteps.

Mr. William Walcot was the first to leave the house; but months went by and still he came and went healthily and haughtily, in spite of Obeah; and he was more frequently at the Hall than either his father or Stephen liked, the Folly being his home proper. The father considered that Will interfered too much on the plantation, to the neglect and detriment of his shipping agency; while Steve, aware of the comparative proximity of the Hall to the Parsonage, regarded him as a dangerous rival.

The fact was that the elder of the twain had determined most fraternally to "cut his brother out" of the favour of Miss Wolferstone, if the clergyman's rich and lovely ward had any leaning in that direction, and altogether comported himself as if he were his father's natural and certain successor on the estate.

But Mrs. Walcot sickened: an inexplicable disease, which caused her lower limbs to swell painfully, marred her enjoyment, and made her splendid mansion little better than a prison, although stately Augusta Wolferstone and lively Mary Fulton came like sunbeams now and again to brighten it up. Then Matthias grew aguish and shivery. Finally Steve, diverging from the wood-path on his way from the Parsonage one Sunday at the hour when sun and moon looked each other in the face, fell over a fern-covered boulder and broke his leg.

Cuffy and Scipio, out after dark on some occult errand, directed by his groans, found him lying amidst the rank vegetation, just over the spot where the Obeah refuse lay buried. "A coincidence," the old man observed to his companion; with the addendum, "Sorry Massa, Steve hurt: him best cane of bundle."

Cuffy moreover showed his sincerity by binding cooling herbs on the broken limb whilst Scipio ran for a litter, and by setting the said limb skilfully as a surgeon, long before Dr. Hawley could be found.

Superstition regarded these untoward circumstances as so many visitations of warning or admonition. Indeed, so freely did Barbadian society discuss the Walcot succession to the Corbyn property by the light of Walcot ill-luck, that Matthias found his bed of roses invaded by gnats stinging worse than mosquitoes, to say nothing of the private thorns planted by conscience under the rose leaves.

From the morning when Dr. Hawley entered his office like a spirit of evil, to tell how his dead child's rest was disturbed, his own rest had been disturbed by nightmare memories of Archibald's death-bed. The dying man had trusted him. He had ill-deserved that trust. He had not meant to defraud the heir, if there was one; he had only been lukewarm in his efforts to find him. But was there one? He thought not; and so advertising was only waste of good money. Besides, it might tempt some knave to worry him with fictitious claims. However, some day he would send Will or Steve to England to make inquiries; and there was time enough.

And so he tried to salve the conscience that would not be salved; especially as Dr. Hawley now and then gave it an unexpected prick, and Cuffy and Dinah looked unutterable thorns.

The rainy season had almost passed. Steve's leg was nearly well; he could move about by the help of crutches; and Scipio had more than once driven him, very gently, over to the Parsonage, to be especially petted, both by Miss Wolferstone and Mary Fulton, the English parson's English daughter.

It was Will's turn to be jealous. He "could not see why a broken leg and a pale face should be so devilish attractive to a woman. They didn't attract him!" It went to his heart to see Augusta Wolferstone place the easiest cane chair in the verandah ready for his brother, and adjust the softest cushions to his special need. He was exasperated, too, that business should keep him so much at the wharf, and an accident clear the way for Steve to woo the girl in his absence.

So persistent were his grumblings that Mr. Walcot, for the sake of peace, went back to his old office to lighten Will's labour and give him an occasional holiday. On one of these days, William, who slept chiefly at the Folly during the wet season, rode from Bridgetown to St. Andrew's, calling in to see his mother on his way. He there learned that Stephen, taking advantage of a fine day, had gone before him, and was then at St. Andrew's Parsonage.

This roused his domineering temper; and with scarcely a civil word to his ailing and querulous mother, and a very uncivil cut with his riding-whip to the creole groom who held his horse, he set off neck-or-nothing, resolved to try whether he or Steve had the best of it before the day was out. So vicious was he in his brotherly love that he cut at his horse as if it had been Stephen's self, and dismounted in front of the Parsonage, little improved by seeing Steve on a couch under the verandah holding a skein of purse-twist for Augusta, whilst Mary read aloud to both.

His first remark was a sneer at his disabled brother's womanish occupation, his next a rude retort to Augusta's defence of Stephen. A bad beginning this; and his consciousness that it was bad only paved the way for further discomfiture.

Later in the day, he demanded, rather than solicited, a *tête-à-tête* conversation with Miss Wolferstone, and with little delicacy and less tact urged his suit as one whose claims were imperial— urged it as Steve's elder brother, and heir to the Corbyn estate.

Whatever claim he might have had on the young lady's regard he lost in that interview. His rudeness and unbrotherly feeling were so palpable, she felt impelled to resent both.

"I have no desire, sir, to marry the heir to the Corbyn or any other estate; but I do choose to marry a gentleman. I must therefore decline the honour of your alliance"; and she swept from the library as she spoke, without giving him a chance for another syllable.

Without a word of adieu to the ladies he darted from the house, almost too impatient to wait for the saddling of his horse; certainly too much irritated to accept the genial invitation of Mr. Fulton to remain the night, even though the weather had changed, and the rain was the rain of the tropics.

A sane man would have remembered that previous rains had flooded lowlands, had swelled mountain runnels to rivers, and rivers to torrents, and, so remembering, have taken the safer high-road by which he came, however circuitous.

But he, blinded by passion, disappointment, and jealousy (had he not left his silken brother behind him?) dashed homewards the near way, across Church River and through the wood.

Over the bridge he went safely enough; but when he reached the Corbyn rivulet, fed from Haggart's spring, he found his way stopped by a formidable stream rushing tumultuously on towards Long Pond. In no mood to hesitate, he madly urged his reluctant animal to attempt the perilous crossing.

He must have either missed the ford, or the horse lost its footing, and been carried down by the force of the water. His body was found the following day at the entrance to Long Pond, blue, swollen, and swathed in a shroud of the poisonous green scum of the pond.

V. On the wings of the wind

Once more orders were given to open the Corbyn receptacle for the dead.

The preparatory gun was fired into the vault; the brickwork was removed, the door opened for ventilation then for preparation; and lo, the place was strewn with coffins and wrecks of coffins, skeletons and fragments of skeletons; and old Archibald's black coffin lay across Laura Walcot's white one, which was itself dinged and battered as if with heavy blows.

Scared out of his senses, Dan ran, as the crow flies, with his strange tale to the mourners at the Hall.

Incredulity faded before the fact. Matthias was staggered and terror-stricken. The air was sultry, even for sultry Barbados, and that left no time for fresh arrangements. The solemn ceremonial *must* proceed.

The hearse had reached the mausoleum before the disordered coffins could be replaced, or the *débris* collected and cleared into a vacant niche.

Then, with many misgivings and intensified anguish, Matthias saw the white coffin of the unmarried young man deposited by the side of his sister's, and the creaking door closed upon both.

And as he and Steve, now his only son, were driven back to the Hall, he saw how great a horror had fallen on the funeral guests one and all.

Nor did the horror end there.

Again scuffling, wild yells, and shrieks made darkness terrible for five successive midnights; and then the haunted mausoleum sank to silence like a common grave.

And now there was a lull. The calamitous storms of fate and the season seemed alike to have spent their fury. The earth was green, the sky was bright, and Matthias steadfastly put the past behind him, refusing to look back. Like Pharaoh of old, he hardened his heart, unwilling to "let go" his hold of Corbyn.

Not so Stephen. His bumptious front had lowered when his sister was striken down in the very midst of festivity. Old Cuffy's prophetic warnings had not fallen on deaf ears. He appealed to his father to remove the remains of sister and brother from the Corbyn mausoleum, and to take prompt steps to find a living heir, if such existed. Matthias was obstinate; so was he, and a *little* more conscientious.

He conferred with Dr. Hawley. Judge his surprise to find that the Captain Hudson, whose services his father had rejected with so much asperity, had eight years before picked up at sea a woman lashed to a spar, who supposed herself the sole survivor of the *Mermaid,* in which husband and son had both gone down. The *Mermaid's* destination had been Barbados, and the woman's name was *Corbyn.* Shortly after, happening to hail a passing schooner, the *Boyne* from Cork to Bristol, he transferred the rescued lady to that vessel, his own barque being outward bound.

"And, my young friend, as you appear anxious to see justice done," added the Doctor, "I may tell you I have already guaranteed Captain Hudson his expenses in the prosecution of a search for that lady."

A hearty hand-shake at parting sealed a cordial agreement between the twain, and Steve set off for the Parsonage with a lighter heart than had been his for many a day.

The season rounded, bringing with it a prospect of Steve's marriage with Miss Wolferstone when their term of mourning expired.

Long before that, fresh sables were called for.

Mrs. Walcot's unaccountable disease, aggravated by grief and her exclusion from society, had terminated fatally.

An altercation again arose between father and son respecting the place of sepulchre. It ended in orders for the opening of the mausoleum under Mr. Walcot's own eye.

The sight he beheld was enough to chill his blood; but it never turned him from his purpose. Scientific men discussing the phenomena had talked of gaseous forces; but he spoke only of conspiracy amongst his black slaves to bend his will to theirs.

Again the battered and broken coffins were replaced, and the fragments hid out of sight; again he laid his dead among the Corbyn dead.

Again the Corbyn dead arose at midnight to protest against intrusion; again the night was hideous with discordant cries; and, as if the free spirits of the air were leagued with the captives in that tomb, the rising wind howled and shrieked in unison.

Fiery Barbados could not remember more oppressive weather. The louring clouds, the stifling heat, the sultry heavy atmosphere had boded tempest, and at midnight came down the rain in sheets, driven by a breeze from the north-east which grew and strengthened to a tremendous gale. Then there was a treacherous calm, and then suddenly the winds ran riot; and from three to five o'clock mad hurricane swept the island from end to end, flashing lightnings forth to trace destruction by.

Daylight broke on August 11th, 1831, upon ruin and desolation. Houses and huts were blown down, fields laid waste, trees uprooted, valleys inundated. Wreck strewed the coast. The Government House was unroofed, the Custom House blown down, churches were damaged; the verdant paradise was a wilderness.

Amidst the general wreck, Corbyn had not escaped; yet the Hall itself stood firm, though the windmill sails and cap were torn to shivers. But the Walcot House at the Folly had disappeared, and with it much valuable property.

The coast had its black chronicles. A ship had been driven on the rocks in Long Bay, and only one of her crew was washed ashore. He was the second mate, a fine young man with light wavy hair, straight nose, ample forehead, and blue eyes. He had been borne on the crest of a wave, and cast on a rock with just strength left to scramble a few yards beyond the range of the swooping billows, and to thank God for his miraculous preservation.

He was bruised, ragged, and destitute; yet in the universal ruin his wants were all but disregarded. A compassionate negress gave him a draught of rum and a piece of corn-cake, but her own hut was dismantled, and shelter was far to seek.

On all sides he saw desolation and trouble. Dispirited, he turned to the highway, in hopes of gaining a shelter before nightfall. Some unseen hand led him in his helpless friendlessness to take the road William Walcot had traversed in his frenzy. Now, as then, the little stream was swollen to a great one; but the sailor was a good swimmer, and having daylight to his task crossed in safety where the other lost his life. The path through Corbyn Wood was blocked in places by fallen trees, which made his progress slow and perilous. There was no lack of scattered cocoa-nuts and other fruit to stay his hunger, but night fell as he slept the sleep of exhaustion on an uptorn tree-trunk.

He was awakened by loud shrieks. Following the sound, he emerged from the plantation on to the open road, and soon reached a low windowless building, across which a large sand-box tree had fallen. As he neared it the shrieks were overpowered by loud hurrahs, which somehow made his chilled blood tingle with a sensation akin to a shudder.

People like himself, cast adrift by the hurricane, were on the else-avoided road. In answer to his questions, he was told that the nearest habitation was Corbyn Hall, and that low-domed edifice, the haunted mausoleum of the Corbyns.

"Corbyn?" echoed the sailor; "did you say Corbyn? My name is Corbyn, and I have an uncle Corbyn living in Barbados!"

"Was your uncle's name Archibald?" asked a passing gentleman on horseback.

"Yes; and my name is Archibald. My father's name was Charles."

"Is not your father living?"

"Alas! no. He was drowned in the wreck of the *Mermaid,* on his way to Barbados, when I was only twelve years old."

"H'm! And where were you at the time, young man?"

"Shipwrecked too, sir, and my mother also. I clung to a hen-coop, and was picked up half-dead by the skipper of the *Boyne.*"

"And your mother?"

"She too was mercifully saved, as I have been this day; but as Providence willed it, the captain who had picked her up sent her aboard to us, his own vessel being bound on a long voyage; and we had reason to be thankful for it, or we might never have met again in this world. But"—impulsively—"are you my uncle, sir? You ask so many questions."

"No; Archibald Corbyn has lain for eighteen months in yonder tomb. But I knew him well. I see you are in a sad plight, and in no condition to walk a long distance; so I recommend you to present yourself at Corbyn Hall—no matter the hour at this awful crisis. I do not suppose you will be a very welcome visitor to Mr. Walcot. Executors seldom like to disgorge; and if you can prove your identity as old Archibald's nephew, you are heir to this estate, and my gentleman will have to turn out. In any case, should he treat you as an impostor—as is not unlikely—any of the old negroes will give you food and shelter, if they have it. Your name will ensure *that*."

"I thank you, sir," was all that Archie in his weakness and bewildering whirl of emotions could utter, as he bowed and turned as directed towards Corbyn Hall.

"Stay!" cried the stranger, wheeling his horse round. "I am a clergyman and a magistrate—the Rev. John Fulton, of St. Andrew's. There is my card. Show it. Should Mr. Walcot reject you, call upon me tomorrow; or upon Dr. Hawley, of Kissing Bridge, Bridgetown. We will see you are not wronged. My business is urgent, or I would accompany you now."

Bareheaded, barefooted, ragged, sea-stained, weary, footsore, and bleeding from sharp stones and sharper thorns, the famished, shipwrecked heir dragged himself slowly to Corbyn Hall, to sink exhausted on the very threshold.

There he was found by ever-wakeful Dinah, whose screams, "A ghost, a ghost!" roused the whole tribe of woolly heads from the mats on which they slept—and blown-down huts had filled house and piazza to overflowing.

"Massa Charlie's ghost!" from a chorus of tongues reached the chamber where Matthias lay shivering with ague. Watchful Stephen leaned over the balcony to seek the reason of the uproar.

Quick as thought he was in their midst, supporting the fainting youth in his strong arms. Little need to ask his name: the likeness to a picture in the house told it without voice.

Archie Corbyn was carried within; and while Scipio was despatched post-haste for Dr. Hawley, he was restored, refreshed, and tended with an assiduity no Walcot had ever been able to command. The previous day's hurricane had not created a greater commotion than the finding of the fainting sailor it had blown amongst them.

Matthias Walcot, however, was not disposed to receive Archie Corbyn on the strength of a likeness and his own *ipse dixit*. He put upon him the onus of proof, in the secret hope (hardly confessed to himself) that difficulties might arise and his own position continue intact. At all events he would remain master in the interim; and—but that he feared a rising amongst his slaves, headed by his own son—so much were his principles demoralized that, in the face of conviction, he would have compelled Archie Corbyn to seek other quarters until his rights were indisputably established.

Steve stood by the heir gallantly, though his coming did close the prospect of succession to a fine domain. So did Dr. Hawley and the Rev. John Fulton, his first adviser. Cuffy and Dinah worshipped him. But he had no warmer champions than Mary Fulton and Augusta Wolferstone, with whom, no doubt, it was more a matter of feeling than of legal right.

Dr. Hawley and Steve had opened their purses to him, and

once provided with means, he dressed, and looked the gentleman he was.

Archie's first care had been to write to his mother, begging her to leave England for Barbados without loss of time, armed with all necessary credentials.

Scarcely three weeks after the despatch of this letter, Dr. Hawley sought Stephen Walcot at the wharf.

In less than an hour Sambo was driving a party of four in the doctor's phaeton as fast as the unrepaired roads would permit.

They alighted at Corbyn Hall.

Archie Corbyn was at the Parsonage.

Steve was glad of an excuse for a visit there. Resuming his seat, he was whirled thither, carried off Archie without a word of explanation, and left the young ladies excited and curious.

In the drawing-room of Corbyn Hall Archie found, to his joy and amazement, his mother. With her was Captain Hudson, to whom he was indebted for her appearance on the scene before his own missive was half-way over the ocean. The sea-captain had proved too good a seeker for Matthias Walcot, who sat there nervous and fidgety, with one arm resting on a side table, on which he kept up a spasmodic tattoo with his long finger-nails.

What further credentials were wanted than certificates of birth and marriage, and magisterial attestations, and Captain Hudson's testimony?

Corbyn Hall was once more in the hands of a Corbyn, and from Cuffy the news spread like an electric flame.

Archie Corbyn was magnanimous. Setting Stephen's heartiness against his father's tardiness (he called it by no worse name), he offered both a home until their own house at the Folly could be rebuilt; and he did not call on his executor to refund the moneys so lavishly expended out of the Corbyn coffers.

Yet Matthias had another bitter draught to swallow before he returned to his shipping agency and to the Folly.

The midnight outcry at the mausoleum had never ceased since Mrs. Walcot was laid therein. The hurricane had torn away the newly-plastered brickwork, and now it sounded as if heavy hands were beating down the door.

Dinah took care that Mrs. Corbyn should not remain uninformed; and ancient Cuffy gave to Archie his version of the mystery with fervid impressiveness.

"It Cuffy's 'pinion, massa, dat Massa Arch'bald nebber rest till dem Walcots be cleared out. Him berry proud ob him pure white blood, an' dem Walcots hab got berry mixed blood under dere white skins."

Archie took counsel with his friends, Steve among the rest. The result was the removal of the Walcot coffins to a vault in St. Andrew's churchyard. They were found, strange to relate, wedged together close to the door by the coffins of Archibald and Jamie Corbyn.

Quiet fell on the mausoleum after that—a quiet in nowise disturbed when, after the lapse of some three or four years, the elder Mrs. Corbyn was placed there reverently by her son.

In saying the elder Mrs. Corbyn, it must be understood that when, proud of her generous lover, Augusta Wolferstone gave herself and her money to Steve Walcot, Archie Corbyn took to wife without a fortune the fair English girl, Mary Fulton, whose heart he had won as a poor shipwrecked sailor before it was proved that old Archibald was not the last of the Corbyns.

Cuffy and Dinah lived to see slavery abolished in the West Indies, and to watch the toddling feet of more than one young Corbyn, into whose undeveloped minds they did their best to infuse the old Corbyn pride of race and pure blood.

Charles J. Mansford

Charles J. Mansford was a mystery author. He seems to be
highly regarded by macabre fiction enthusiasts for his contribu-
tions to Victorian magazines (many of which went to make up
the book from which this tale is taken). He wrote one or two
other weird novels. But Mansford himself seems an enigma. His
short story volume *Shafts from an Eastern Quiver* was a sump-
tuously produced volume, published in 1894 by Newnes and
extensively illustrated by Arthur Pearse. *The Spectator* said at
the time: "Mr. Mansford has the gift of a story teller and he
uniformly writes like a scholar." The twelve stories in *Shafts
from an Eastern Quiver* (all of which first appeared in *Strand
Magazine*) concern the adventures of the author and his friend,
Frank Denviers, in Africa, Asia, India and Russia. In *Maw-
Sayah* we find the two travellers in Burma, where they help rid
a terrorised village of a rather nasty and unwelcome visitor.

Maw-Sayah

I

"The fine points of an elephant, sahib," said our guide Hassan, "are a colour approaching to white, the nails perfectly black, and an intact tail."

"I am glad to hear that an elephant has some qualities which recommend it," said Denviers, good-humouredly. "I should think that the one upon which we are riding is about as lazy as it is possible to be. I suppose slowness is an unusually good point, isn't it, Hassan?"

The Arab who was sitting before us on the elephant, gave it a stir with the sharply-pointed spear which he held in his hand to urge it on, and then glancing back at us, as we reclined lazily in the cushioned howdah, he said, inquiringly:—

"Are the sahibs tired already of travelling thus? Yet we have fully two hours' journey before us."

"Hassan," I interposed, "this is a good opportunity for you to tell us exactly what you heard about the Maw-Sayah when we were at Bhamo. It is in consequence of that, indeed, that we are going to try to get among these strange Kachyens; but as we are not quite sure of the details, you may as well repeat them."

"The sahib shall be obeyed," responded our guide, and although careful to keep a good watch in front, he turned his body slightly towards us as he prepared to begin the narrative.

On reaching Burmah we stayed for several days in Rangoon, the Queen of the East, as it is called nowadays, although only remarkable formerly for its famous monasteries of Talapoins and as a halting-place for the bands of pilgrims on their way to the mighty Shway Dagohn pagoda. Thence we journeyed up the Irawaddy, and having duly paid reverence to some of the nine thousand nine hundred and ninety-nine pagodas of Pagan—the outcast slaves of which city seemed a strange contrast to its otherwise absolute desertion—we continued our journey by steamer as far as Mandalay. Having endured the doubtful pleasure of a jaunt in a seatless, jolting bullock-carriage—the bruises from which were not easily forgotten—we eventually reached Bhamo, where Hassan entered into conversation with a hillman. From the latter he learnt a strange story, which was later on told to us and the truth of which we hoped before long to fully test, for soon afterwards we set out on an elephant, our faithful guide in this new adventure again proving himself of the greatest service.

"Now, Hassan," said Denviers, "we are quite ready to hear this story fully, but don't add any imaginary details of your own."

"By the Koran, sahib," began the Arab, "these are the words which were those of him to whom I spoke under the shade of the log stockade."

"Which are, of course, unimpeachable," responded Denviers. "Anyone could tell that from his shifty eyes, which failed to rest upon us fixed even for a minute when we spoke to him afterwards."

The Arab seemed a little disconcerted at this, but soon continued:—

"The great Spirits, or Nats, who guard the prosperity of Burmah, have become greatly incensed with the Kachyens, not because they failed to resist stoutly when the monarch was deposed a few years ago—"

"Then we are to have a modern story this time, Hassan?" interrupted Denviers. "I quite expected that you would commence with some long worn-out tradition."

"The sahibs shall hear," the Arab went on. "No one who offends the Nats of Burmah need expect anything but evil to follow. There are the Nats of the sky, the Nats of the earth, the Nats of the Irawaddy, the Nats of the five hundred little rivers, and the thousand Nats which guarded the sacred person of the monarch—"

"Yes, Hassan," said Denviers, impatiently, "you mentioned them all before. We haven't time to hear the list enumerated now; go on about this one particular Nat which you say is causing such havoc among the hill-tribes."

"Patience, sahib. The Nats were justly roused to anger because the deposed monarch was not afterwards taken to the water's edge riding upon an elephant instead of in a bullock-carriage."

"Well, Hassan," said Denviers, "judging from our own experience the Nats seem to be pretty sensible, I must say—but how do they affect the peace of mind of the Kachyens?"

"Listen, sahib. High among the hills which may be seen stretching before us lies a village in which many of the Kachyens dwell, their occupation being sometimes that of tillers of the land, but more often consisting in planning and carrying out raids upon other hill-men, or of descending at times to the plains, and there looting the towns wherein dwell more peaceable tribes. In all their forays they had been successful, for whenever their trusty dahs or swords were drawn, those who opposed them invariably obtained the worst of the encounter. So powerful did they become that at last those dwelling in the plains—Shans, Karenns, and Talaings, too—made no resistance against their attacks; and when they saw the produce of their fields carried away, thought themselves happy not to have been slain. The reason why the Kachyens became so successful in all they undertook was that a powerful forest Nat placed them under its protection, and hence they could not be harmed by their foes.

"Now it chanced that the King was in great danger through following the advice of his impetuous Ministers, whereupon he summoned the Kachyens to his assistance—for their fame as warriors had reached his ears long before. But they, confident in securing their own safety whatever happened to the monarch, refused to obey his command to march against the Burman foes. The consequence was that when the indignity which I have mentioned was offered to the deposed monarch, the Nats throughout Burmah were furious with that one who ruled the village in which the Kachyens dwelt, and they sent some of their number to destroy it. The latter, however, appeased them by making a grim promise, which has been only too faithfully kept.

"A few days afterwards a hill-man, who was clearing a part of the land on the woody slope of the height, *saw the Nat,* which had never before been visible, and, terrified at the strange form which it had assumed, he ran hastily to the rest of the tribe, and, gathering them together, held a consultation as to what should be done to appease it. Some suggested that upon every tree trunk should be scratched appealing messages, which the Nat might read; others were in favour of placing a huge heap of spears and swords near the spot where the embodied Nat had been seen, in order that it might be tempted to destroy all those who urged it to injure them. The messages and weapons, however, when placed for the Nat to observe did no good, for one dreadful night a rattling was heard of the bamboos which lay before one of the Kachyens' huts, and the man, going hastily to see what caused it, was swiftly carried away in the darkness without apparently uttering a single cry! For many nights in succession a similar scene was enacted, for he at whose door the dire summons came dared not refuse to answer it lest the whole household might perish.

"Nothing more was ever seen on those thus strangely carried off, and the Kachyens, each of whom feared that his own end might come next, determined to consult some famous Buddhist priests who dwelt not far from them, and who held charge over the famous marble slabs which the great War Prince of Burmah had caused to be engraved concerning their illustrious traditions. The man whom ye saw me conversing with by the stockade was the one whom the tribe entrusted with the task; but the priests, after much consideration among themselves of the object of his visit, refused to have anything to do with such a tragic affair, and thereupon dismissed their suppliant.

"This Kachyen, when sorrowfully returning towards the hills, fearing that the tribe would destroy him because of his nonsuccess, chanced to meet on his way a Mogul, to whom he repeated the story. The latter, laying his hand on his red-dyed and fierce-looking beard, advised the Kachyen to enter a hole in

the mountain side and to consult a famous Maw-Sayah, or juggler, who dwelt there. This juggler promised assistance if the
tribe would pay him a great reward in the event of his success,
and when they agreed to this he entered the village and waited
for dusk to arrive. Again the dreadful rattling was heard, and
another Kachyen stepped out to meet his fate. None of the tribe
dared to look at what transpired, except the juggler, and he too
disappeared! The next morning, however, he came into the village and called its inhabitants together. When they had solemnly agreed to his conditions, he stated that the Nat was bent
upon destroying them all, and that to attempt to escape by
means of flight would only lead to quicker death. Then he told
them what the result of his intercession for them had been.

"The Nat had been persuaded to destroy only one victim on
each seventh evening at dusk, and had appointed him to see that
certain conditions were not broken. He was to have a hut at his
disposal, and into this the men were to go by lot, and thus the
Nat would obtain a victim when the time came round. They
were forbidden to wander about after sunset, and whatever
noises were made not to hearken to them, since the Maw-Sayah
would see that the others were unharmed. So long had this
dreadful destruction lasted that more than one-half of the men
in the Kachyen village, or town, as it might well be called from
the large number who inhabited it, had perished, and yet the
Nat still demanded a victim, and the Maw-Sayah is there to see
that the compact is fulfilled.

"The man who told this story, sahibs, declares that the keeper
of the Nat has by this means obtained sway over the Kachyens
to such an extent that they have become his abject slaves, for the
custom of drawing lots has been abolished, and he selects whom
he will to sacrifice to the Nat. By some means this Kachyen
offended the Maw-Sayah, who thereupon condemned him, but
he, in terror of the sudden and silent death in store for him, fled
to Bhamo, where he lives in momentary fear of destruction.
Such, then, sahibs, is the story, and it is to see this Maw-Sayah
and the Nat at their fell work to-night that even now our faces
are turned to the high land before us, up which we must climb,
for there is but one narrow pathway leading to the village."

Hassan ceased, and then Denviers turned to me as he said:—

"I think that this Maw-Sayah, as Hassan calls him, has about as much faith in Nats as we have. It suits his purpose to league himself with something mysterious; whatever it is we will try to find out," and he glanced at the weapons which we carried.

II

"The sahibs must dismount here," said Hassan shortly afterwards, and, following to the ground our guide, we began to climb the mountain path which stretched before us.

The ascent was exceedingly steep and several times we stopped to rest after pushing our way through the tangled masses which almost hid the path, which was itself cut here and there, apparently through the rocky strata. When we had reached about three-fourths of our journey, Hassan stopped and pointed out to us one of the thatched roofs of a hut, which seemed in the distance scarcely noticeable until his keen eyesight discovered it. The village, we found, lay a little to the left of the mountain path, for on nearing the summit we found ourselves passing through a peculiar avenue of trees interspersed with long bamboo poles. From the tops of the latter there were stretched across the approach strong, rough-looking cords, which supported various uncouth emblems, and among which were large triangles, circles, and stars, cut apparently out of the stems of huge bamboos. After traversing this avenue for nearly three hundred yards we saw the tree trunks which Hassan had mentioned, and which were deeply scarred with cabalistic messages to the fierce Nat, which we could not of course understand. Affixed to some of the trees farther on we saw a number of spears and dahs mingled with shorter weapons, the latter being made of some species of hard wood, and close to them we observed the skulls of several large animals, one of which we judged was that of an elephant.

In spite of the fact that the village was a large one, the buildings were of a very primitive construction, being made of bamboos with thatched coverings, reaching almost to the piles on which the huts were placed. We did not observe any openings made to serve as windows, the only ones noticeable being those by which the Kachyens entered, placed above a bamboo ladder, which seemed to serve instead of steps. Although the sun had scarcely set, the village was wrapped in a strange silence, the sound of our footsteps alone being heard. The smoke that seemed to be forcing its way through stray holes in the thatch amply convinced us, however, that the inhabitants were within doors, and, turning to our Arab guide, I asked him if he could distinguish among the many huts the one in which we expected to find the Maw-Sayah. He seemed a little uncertain at first, but after wandering through the village together we returned, and then Hassan, who had been very observant the whole time, pointed to one of the rudely-constructed huts and said:—

"I think that is the one into which we seek to enter; it is situated according to the position in which the Kachyen said it was, and, besides, it bears a strange proof of the story which ye have listened to with such ill-concealed disbelief."

"Why do you think that is the hut, Hassan?" I asked, for, to my eyes, no difference between that and the others close to it was distinguishable.

"If the sahib will look at the bamboo ladder and observe it carefully, he will see that it is unlike the others round," said the Arah.

"I suppose you refer to these deep scratches upon it, don't you, Hassan?" asked Denviers, as he pointed to some marks, a few of which were apparently fairly recent.

"The sahib guesses rightly," answered our guide. "You will remember that the Kachyen stated to me that the Nat is accustomed to obtain its victim now from the abode of the Maw-Sayah; those marks, then, have been made by it when it dragged its human prey out of the hut."

We gazed curiously at the marks for a few minutes, then Denviers broke the silence by asking the Arab why it was that the Nat made marks at all.

"I should have thought that such a powerful spirit could prevent such evidences of its presence becoming observed," he continued. "My respect for it is certainly not increased by seeing those deep scars; they seem to be made by something which has sharp claws."

"That is because of the shape which it has assumed, sahib," said the Arah, "for the Nats have wondrous powers—"

"Very likely, Hassan," interposed Denviers; "I suppose they can do exactly what they like, can they not?"

I was much surprised at the limit which was, however, placed upon their powers by our guide, for he responded, quickly:—

"Not altogether, sahib. There is one thing that a Nat cannot do, according to the reports of the Kachyens, and that is, they are unable to move in a direction which is not straight, and hence they are careful to avoid rough ground, where tangled masses and boulders bar their progress, so they usually frequent the open avenues, such as the one which we have just passed through. The symbols above it and the writings and weapons are all for the Nat's benefit."

"And the elephant's skull?" asked Denviers, irreverently. "What is that put up for?"

The Arab, however, had an explanation ready, for he promptly replied:—

"That indicates where the supplies of food are to be found when the Nat requires any."

Denviers turned to me for a moment as he said:—

"I should have thought it a good plan, then, to have put it upon the hut of this Maw-Sayah whom we are about to interview. See that your weapons are in good order, Harold, we may soon need them."

Giving a cautious look at my belt and the weapons thrust into it, I followed Denviers, who had mounted the short bamboo ladder, and ws endeavouring to obtain admission to the hut. We heard a harsh sound within, then the cry of someone apparently terror-stricken, and a moment afterwards we had pushed past the Maw-Sayah, who by no means was willing to allow us to enter the rude dwelling.

The single room, which seemed to constitute the hut, was extremely low and bare of furniture entirely. A few bamboos were spread in one part of it, while at the far end was a fire, the light from which was partly obscured by the smoke, which almost suffocated us, so thickly did it roll up and then spread through the hut. Near the door stood a man scarcely clothed, upon whose face we saw a look of the most abject terror, for, as we surmised, the noise of our entry was mistaken by him for the approach of the fell thing to which he was condemned by the Maw-Sayah. We moved towards the latter as he threw himself down by the fire, which he had only left to see who it was that came unbidden to the hut where to enter was the preceding event to death. He was clothed in a long blue strip of linen, which wound round his waist and covered his body, partly leaving his dark chest uncovered. His features were stamped with an appearance of supreme cunning, his oblique eyes reminding us of a Chinaman, while the fierce look in them as they glared at us from either side of an aquiline nose, which betrayed his Burmese descent, did not increase our confidence in the man as he stretched out his bony hands over the fire as if for warmth, although outside the hut we had found the heat almost insupportable.

"What do ye seek?" he demanded, as he looked into our faces in turn and seemed astonished at our strange features.

"We are travellers who wished to see a Kachyen village," responded Denviers, "and we further desired to see some of its inhabitants; but as none were visible we entered this hut, even against your will. Where are the people who dwell here?"

The man whom my companion addressed pointed to the Kachyen near the doorway, as he responded:—

"There is one of them, and in a short time even he will never be seen again."

"Can you give us food?" hazarded Hassan, in order to get the man to continue his conversation, for the Arab evidently was expecting that the Nat would soon arrive upon the scene. The Maw-Sayah rose and pointed to the entrance as he cried:—

"That way ye came, that way shall ye depart. Food for ye I have not, nor would I give it if I had."

I turned to Denviers and said, in a low tone:—

"What shall we do, Frank? I don't think our opportunity of seeing what may transpire will be as good within the hut as without it. Whatever the solution is to this affair, if we are outside we shall see this Kachyen dragged away, and may further watch the approach of whatever caused those strange marks which we observed."

"One thing is clear," said my companion; "we will attempt to save this intended victim, at all events. I expect that if we tried we could get him away easily enough, but that plan would not be of much service. We must attack this being, whatever it is, with which this Maw-Sayah is leagued. How I should like to hand him over as a victim instead of that trembling captive by the door. It shows to what extent this juggler has acquired power over this tribe, for I notice that his captive is unbound, and is certainly a much finer built man than the other."

"It wants less than an hour to dusk, sahibs," said Hassan, who had listened carefully to our remarks; "if we were to station ourselves a little away from the hut we could see what took place, and if the Nat were mortal we might attack it."

Denviers shrugged his shoulders at the Arab's supposition as he responded:—

"There is little doubt, Hassan, that the Nat would smart if that keen blade of yours went a little too near it; but I think your plan is a good one, and we will adopt it, as it falls in with what has already been said."

We gave a final look at the crafty face of the man who was still seated by the fire, and then brushing past the captive we made for the open village again.

"I feel sorry for this Kachyen," said Denviers. "He will have a dreadful five minutes of it, I expect; but it is our only way of preventing, if possible, such an affair from occurring again."

On leaving the hut we stationed ourselves almost opposite to it, and then began to keep watch. What we should see pass up the avenue we could only surmise, but our suppositions certainly did not lead us to imagine in the faintest degree the sight which before long was destined to completely startle us.

III

The grey dusk was becoming night when among the dark stems of the trees we saw some black form move over the ground. We could scarcely distinguish it as it crawled over the bamboo logs and made a rasping noise as it clung to the ladder. The door of the hut yielded to it, and a minute after it again emerged and bore with it the terrified Kachyen. We crept after it as it dragged its captive down the avenue, striving our utmost to make out its shape. One thing we could tell, which was that the creature was not upright; but our movement behind it was apparently known, for it struggled to move quicker over the ground with its human burden.

"Shall I shoot it?" I whispered to Denviers, as my nerves seemed to be almost unstrung at the unknowableness of the creeping thing.

"You would more likely kill the man," he responded. "Follow as noiselessly as you can—it will not let its prey escape, be sure of that. Once we track it to its haunt we will soon dispatch it, big and fierce as it seems."

We drew nearer and nearer to it, until it had passed half-way down the avenue, then it seemed to become lost to our view, although we were, as we knew, close to it. I felt Denviers' hand upon my shoulder, and then he whispered:—

"The Kachyen is being dragged up a tree just in front—look!"

I could just distinguish something moving up the trunk, when suddenly the captive, who had hitherto been apparently paralyzed with terror, uttered a cry and then must have succeeded in disengaging himself from the dreadful thing that had held him, for the noise of someone falling to the ground was heard, and a minute after we distinguished the form of a man rushing headlong back to the village for safety.

We did not anticipate such an event, and were contemplating a search for the captor of the Kachyen, when a cold sweat broke out upon me, for the clammy claws of the man-hunter had touched me! The sensation which seized me was only of short duration, for I felt myself released just as Denviers said:—

"Harold, the Kachyen has fled, and his captor, determined to secure its prey, has betaken its crawling body after him. If only we had a light! I saw something like a black shadow moving onwards; get your pistol ready and follow."

I just distinguished Denviers as he passed on in front of me, Hassan coming last. When we reached the hut of the Maw-Sayah we stopped at once, for, from the cry which came from it, we rightly surmised that the terrible seeker for human prey had made for this place, thinking in its dull intelligence, that its captive had returned. We thrust ourselves into the hut, and saw by the red firelight a sanguinary contest between the Maw-Sayah and the black object which we had endeavoured to track. Thinking that the Kachyen was being destroyed, the juggler had not fastened his door, and the enraged man-eater had seized him as he rested on the ground, quite at its mercy!

The Maw-Sayah was struggling with his bony hands to extricate himself from the clutches of a monstrous tree-spider! We had seen, on an island in the South Seas, several cocoa-nut crabs, and this reptile somewhat resembled them, but was even larger. Grasping the juggler with several of its long, furry-looking claws, it fixed its glaring red eyes in mad anger upon him as he grasped in each hand one of its front pair of legs, which were armed with strong, heavy-looking pincers. He besought us wildly to shoot, even if we killed him, held as he was by his relentless foe.

"Harold," cried my companion, "keep clear, and look out for yourself when I fire at this reptile; most likely it will make for one of us."

He drew right close to it, and thrusting the barrel of his pistol between its eyes touched the trigger. The explosion shook the hut, its effect upon the spider being to cause it to rush frantically about the floor, dragging the Maw-Sayah as if he were some slight burden scarcely observable.

"You missed it!" I cried. "Look out, Hassan, guard the door-way!"

The Arab stood, sword in hand, waiting for it to make for the entrance, while Denviers exclaimed:—

"I shot it through the head!" and a minute afterwards the

trueness of his aim was manifest, for the claws released, and the Maw-Sayah, wounded badly, but saved, stood free from the muscular twitchings of the dead spider.

"You scoundrel!" said Denviers to him, "I have a good mind to serve you the same. You deserve to die as so many of these simple-minded, credulous Kachyens have done."

I thought for one brief second that my companion was about to kill the juggler, for through all our adventures I had never seen him so thoroughly roused. I stood between them; then, when Denviers quickly recovered his self-command, I turned to the Maw-Sayah and asked:—

"If we spare your life, will you promise to leave this village and never to return?"

He turned his evil-looking but scared face towards us eagerly as he replied:—

"I will do whatever you wish."

Denviers motioned to him to rest upon the ground, which he did, then turning to me, said:—

"It is pretty apparent what this juggler has done. The man who first reported the discovery of this Nat, as the foolish Kachyens call it, simply disturbed a monstrous spider which had lived in the trees which he felled—that accounts for his seeing it. Finding animal food scarce, the reptile ventured into this village and tried to get into one of the huts. Its exertions were rewarded by the Kachyen coming to the door, whom it accordingly seized. To continue its plan, which proved so successful, needed very little reasoning power on the part of such a cunning creature. No doubt this Maw-Sayah purposely left the door of his hut unfastened each seventh night, and the spider thus became accustomed to seek for its victim there. I daresay it came the other nights, but the juggler was then careful enough to keep his hut well fastened."

"What do the sahibs propose to do?" interrupted Hassan.

Denviers turned to him, as he responded:—

"We will wait for daybreak; then having dragged the dead spider out where the Kachyens may see that it is no longer able to harm them, we will take this Maw-Sayah down the mountain path away from the village as poor as he came."

"A good plan," I assented, and we followed it out, eventually leaving the juggler, and climbing once more into the howdah upon the elephant, which we found close to the spot where we had left it, secured from wandering far away by the rope which Hassan had used to hinder its movements.

We entered Bhamo, and while we took a much-needed rest our guide—as we afterwards learnt—searched for and found the fugitive Kachyen, who, on hearing that his safety was secured, hastily departed to the village to rejoice with the rest of his tribe that the so-called Nat would not do them any more injury.

Mrs. L.T. Meade
and Robert Eustace

Now for two mystery writers who left behind a real-life mystery all their own. It seems there are two candidates for the role of the pen-name Robert Eustace—it is by no means certain which is the right one.

Elizabeth Thomasina Meade (1844–1914)—who was incorrectly called Mrs. Meade, when she should have been named Mrs. Toulmin Smith—was born in Ireland, the daughter of a Cork rector.

She became a prolific and well respected writer, both of children's books (over 150!) and detective stories, which she wrote in collaboration with two writers, Clifford Halifax (six books) and Robert Eustace (five books).

Space prevents me setting out the full story here, but I recommend interested readers to consult Trevor Hall's valuable book *Dorothy L. Sayers: Nine Literary Studies* (1980), where he sets out his argument in a chapter on Eustace and Sayers. He finds two likely candidates for the role of Robert Eustace: Dr. Eustace Robert Barton or Eustace Rawlins, both of whom have good credentials. Both wrote under other names than their own.

Hall favours Dr. Barton, but whichever one it was, they made a good job of their collaboration with Mrs. Meade. One book which resulted from the Meade/Eustace partnership was *A Master of Mysteries* (1898), the adventures of a detective called

Mr. John Bell, clearly modelled—as many were in those days—on Sherlock Holmes.

Bell investigated haunted houses as his speciality, and called himself a "a professional exposer of ghosts." Note the word "exposer"—that was indeed the fate of many of Bell's cases. As he put it, his cases were "enveloped at first in mystery, and apparently dark with portent, but, nevertheless, when grappled with in the true spirit of science, capable of explanation."

"The Mystery of the Felwyn Tunnel" was one of John Bell's better cases, here returned to print after an absence of over 100 years. It bears an interesting resemblance to Charles Dickens' famous story "The Signalman," and I do not think it over-fanciful to see in the line on page 64 starting "What the . . ." an affectionate nod at the famous author.

The Mystery of the Felwyn Tunnel

I was making experiments of some interest in South Kensington, and hoped that I had perfected a small but not unimportant discovery, when, on returning home one evening in late October in the year 1893, I found a visiting card on my table. On it were inscribed the words, "Mr. Geoffrey Bainbridge." This name was quite unknown to me, so I rang the bell and inquired of my servant who the visitor had been. He described him as a gentleman who wished to see me on most urgent business, and said further that Mr. Bainbridge intended to call again later in the evening. It was with both curiosity and vexation that I awaited the return of the stranger. Urgent business with me generally meant a hurried rush to one part of the country or the other. I did not want to leave London just then; and when at half-past nine Mr. Geoffrey Bainbridge was ushered into my room, I received him with a certain coldness which he could not fail to perceive. He was a tall, well-dressed, elderly man. He immediately plunged into the object of his visit.

"I hope you do not consider my unexpected presence an intrusion, Mr. Bell," he said. "But I have heard of you from our mutual friends, the Greys of Uplands. You may remember once doing that family a great service."

"I remember perfectly well," I answered more cordially. "Pray tell me what you want; I shall listen with attention."

"I believe you are the one man in London who can help me," he continued. "I refer to a matter especially relating to your own particular study. I need hardly say that whatever you do will not be unrewarded."

"That is neither here nor there," I said; "but before you go any further, allow me to ask one question. Do you want me to leave London at present?"

He raised his eyebrows in dismay.

"I certainly do," he answered.

"Very well; pray proceed with your story."

He looked at me with anxiety.

"In the first place," he began, "I must tell you that I am chairman of the Lytton Vale Railway Company in Wales, and that it is on an important matter connected with our line that I have come to consult you. When I explain to you the nature of the mystery, you will not wonder, I think, at my soliciting your aid."

"I will give you my closest attention," I answered; and then I added, impelled to say the latter words by a certain expression on his face, "if I can see my way to assisting you I shall be ready to do so."

"Pray accept my cordial thanks," he replied. "I have come up from my place at Felwyn today on purpose to consult you. It is in that neighbourhood that the affair has occurred. As it is essential that you should be in possession of the facts of the whole matter, I will go over things just as they happened."

I bent forward and listened attentively.

"This day fortnight," continued Mr. Bainbridge, "our quiet little village was horrified by the news that the signalman on duty at the mouth of the Felwyn Tunnel had been found dead under the most mysterious circumstances. The tunnel is at the end of a long cutting between Llanlys and Felwyn stations. It is about a mile long, and the signal-box is on the Felwyn side. The place is extremely lonely, being six miles from the village across the mountains. The name of the poor fellow who met his death in this mysterious fashion was David Pritchard. I have known him from a boy, and he was quite one of the steadiest and most trustworthy men on the line. On Tuesday evening he went on duty at six o'clock; on Wednesday morning the day-man who had come to relieve him was surprised not to find him in the box. It was just getting daylight, and the 6:30 local was coming down, so he pulled the signals and let her through. Then he

went out, and looking up the line towards the tunnel, saw
Pritchard lying beside the line close to the mouth of the tunnel.
Roberts, the day-man, ran up to him and found, to his horror,
that he was quite dead. At first Roberts naturally supposed that
he had been cut down by a train, as there was a wound at the
back of his head; but he was not lying on the metals. Roberts ran
back to the box and telegraphed through the Felwyn Station.
The message was sent on to the village, and at half-past seven
o'clock the police inspector came up to my house with the news.
He and I, with the local doctor, went off at once to the tunnel.
We found the dead man laying beside the metals a few yards
away from the mouth of the tunnel, and the doctor immediately
gave him a careful examination. There was a depressed fracture
at the back of the skull, which must have caused his death; but
how he came by it was not so clear. On examining the whole
place most carefully, we saw, further, that there were marks on
the rocks at the steep side of the embankment as if someone had
tried to scramble up them. Why the poor fellow had attempted
such a climb, God only knows. In doing so he must have slipped
and fallen back on to the line, thus causing the fracture of the
skull. In no case could he have gone up more than eight or ten
feet, as the banks of the cutting run sheer up, almost perpen-
dicularly, beyond that point for more than a hundred and fifty
feet. There are some sharp boulders beside the line, and it was
possible that he might have fallen on one of these and so sus-
tained the injury. The affair must have occurred some time
between 11:45 P.M. and 6 A.M., as the engine-driver of the
express at 11:45 P.M. states that the line was signalled clear, and
he also caught sight of Pritchard in his box as he passed."

"This is deeply interesting," I said; "pray proceed."

Bainbridge looked at me earnestly; he then continued:—

"The whole thing is shrouded in mystery. Why should
Pritchard have left his box and gone down to the tunnel? Why,
having done so, should he have made a wild attempt to scale the
side of the cutting, an impossible feat at any time? Had danger
threatened, the ordinary course of things would have been to
run up the line towards the signal-box. These points are quite
unexplained. Another curious fact is that death appears to have

taken place just before the day-man came on duty, as the light at the mouth of the tunnel had been put out, and it was one of the night signalman's duties to do this as soon as daylight appeared; it is possible, therefore, that Pritchard went down to the tunnel for that purpose. Against this theory, however, and an objection that seems to nullify it, is the evidence of Dr. Williams, who states that when he examined the body his opinion was that death had taken place some hours before. An inquest was held on the following day, but before it took place there was a new and most important development. I now come to what I consider the crucial point in the whole story.

"For a long time there had been a feud between Pritchard and another man of the name of Wynne, a platelayer on the line. The object of their quarrel was the blacksmith's daughter in the neighbouring village—a remarkably pretty girl and an arrant flirt. Both men were madly in love with her, and she played them off one against the other. The night but one before his death Pritchard and Wynne had met at the village inn, had quarrelled in the bar—Lucy, of course, being the subject of their difference. Wynne was heard to say (he was a man of powerful build and subject to fits of ungovernable rage) that he would have Pritchard's life. Pritchard swore a great oath that he would get Lucy on the following day to promise to marry him. This oath, it appears, he kept, and on his way to the signal-box on Tuesday evening met Wynne, and triumphantly told him that Lucy had promised to be his wife. The men had a hand-to-hand fight on the spot, several people from the village being witnesses of it. They were separated with difficulty, each vowing vengeance on the other. Pritchard went off to his duty at the signal-box and Wynne returned to the village to drown his sorrows at the public-house.

"Very late that same night Wynne was seen by a villager going in the direction of the tunnel. The man stopped him and questioned him. He explained that he had left some of his tools on the line, and was on his way to fetch them. The villager noticed that he looked queer and excited, but not wishing to pick a quarrel thought it best not to question him further. It has been proved that Wynne never returned home that night, but came back at an early hour on the following morning, looking dazed and stupid. He was arrested on suspicion, and at the inquest the verdict was against him."

"Has he given any explanation of his own movements?" I asked.

"Yes; but nothing that can clear him. As a matter of fact, his tools were nowhere to be seen on the line, nor did he bring them home with him. His own story is that being considerably the worse for drink, he had fallen down in one of the fields and slept there till morning."

"Things look black against him," I said.

"They do; but listen, I have something more to add. Here comes a very queer feature in the affair. Lucy Ray, the girl who had caused the feud between Pritchard and Wynne, after hearing the news of Pritchard's death, completely lost her head, and ran frantically about the village declaring that Wynne was the man she really loved, and that she had only accepted Pritchard in a fit of rage with Wynne for not himself bringing matters to the point. The case looks very bad against Wynne, and yesterday the magistrate committed him for trial at the coming assizes. The unhappy Lucy Ray and the young man's parents are in a state bordering on distraction."

"What is your own opinion with regard to Wynn's guilt?" I asked.

"Before God, Mr. Bell, I believe the poor fellow is innocent, but the evidence against him is very strong. One of the favourite theories is that he went down to the tunnel and extinguished the light, knowing that this would bring Pritchard out of his box to see what was the matter, and that he then attacked him, striking the blow which fractured the skull."

"Has any weapon been found about, with which he could have given such a blow?"

"No; nor has anything of the kind been discovered on Wynne's person; that fact is decidedly in his favour."

"But what about the marks on the rocks?" I asked.

"It is possible that Wynne may have made them in order to divert suspicion by making people think that Pritchard must have fallen, and so killed himself. The holders of this theory base their belief on the absolute want of cause for Pritchard's trying to scale the rock. The whole thing is the most absolute enigma. Some of the country folk have declared that the tunnel is haunted (and there certainly has been such a rumour current among them for years). That Pritchard saw some apparition, and in wild terror sought to escape from it by climbing the rocks, is another theory, but only the most imaginative hold it."

"Well, it is a most extraordinary case," I replied.

"Yes, Mr. Bell, and I should like to get your opinion of it. Do you see your way to elucidate the mystery?"

"Not at present; but I shall be happy to investigate the matter to my utmost ability."

"But you do not wish to leave London at present?"

"That is so; but a matter of such importance cannot be set aside. It appears, from what you say, that Wynne's life hangs more or less on my being able to clear away the mystery?"

"That is indeed the case. There ought not to be a single stone left unturned to get at the truth, for the sake of Wynne. Well, Mr. Bell, what do you propose to do?"

"To see the place without delay," I answered.

"That is right; when can you come?"

"Whenever you please."

"Will you come down to Felwyn with me tomorrow? I shall leave Paddington by the 7.10, and if you will be my guest I shall be only too pleased to put you up."

"That arrangement will suit me admirably," I replied. "I will meet you by the train you mention, and the affair shall have my best attention."

"Thank you," he said, rising. He shook hands with me and took his leave.

The next day I met Bainbridge at Paddington Station, and we were soon flying westward in the luxurious private compartment that had been reserved for him. I could see by his abstracted manner and his long lapses of silence that the mysterious affair at Felwyn Tunnel was occupying all his thoughts.

It was two o'clock in the afternoon when the train slowed down at the little station of Felwyn. The station-master was at the door in an instant to receive us.

"I have some terribly bad news for you, sir," he said, turning to Bainbridge as we alighted; "and yet in one sense it is a relief, for it seems to clear Wynne."

"What do you mean?" cried Bainbridge. "Bad news? Speak out at once!"

"Well, sir, it is this: there has been another death at Felwyn signal-box. John Davidson, who was on duty last night, was found dead at an early hour this morning in the very same place where we found poor Pritchard."

"Good God!" cried Bainbridge, starting back, "what an awful thing! What, in the name of Heaven, does it mean. Mr. Bell? This is too fearful. Thank goodness you have come down with us."

"It is as black a business as I ever heard of, sir," echoed the station-master; "and what we are to do I don't know. Poor Davidson was found dead this morning, and there was neither mark nor sign of what killed him—that is the extraordinary part of it. There's a perfect panic abroad, and not a signalman on the line will take duty to-night. I was quite in despair, and was afraid at one time that the line would have to be closed, but at last it occurred to me to wire to Lytton Vale, and they are sending down an inspector. I expect him by a special every moment. I believe this is he coming now," added the station-master, looking up the line.

There was the sound of a whistle down the valley, and in a few moments a single engine shot into the station, and an official in uniform stepped on to the platform.

"Good-evening, sir," he said, touching his cap to Bainbridge; "I have just been sent down to inquire into this affair at the Felwyn Tunnel, and though it seems more of a matter for a Scotland Yard detective than one of ourselves, there was nothing for it but to come. All the same, Mr. Bainbridge, I cannot say that I look forward to spending tonight alone at the place."

"You wish for the services of a detective, but you shall have some one better," said Bainbridge, turning towards me. "This gentleman, Mr. John Bell, is the man of all others for our business. I have just brought him down from London for the purpose."

An expression of relief flitted across the inspector's face.

"I am very glad to see you, sir," he said to me, "and I hope you will be able to spend the night with me in the signal-box. I must say I don't much relish the idea of tackling the thing single-handed; but with your help, sir, I think we ought to get to the bottom of it somehow. I am afraid there is not a man on the line who will take duty until we do. So it is most important that the thing should be cleared, and without delay."

I readily assented to the inspector's proposition, and Bainbridge and I arranged that we should call for him at four o'clock at the village inn and drive him to the tunnel.

We then stepped into the wagonette which was waiting for us, and drove to Bainbridge's house.

Mrs. Bainbridge came out to meet us, and was full of the tragedy. Two pretty girls also ran to greet their father, and to glance inquisitively to me. I could see that the entire family was in a state of much excitement.

"Lucy Ray has just left, father," said the elder of the girls. "We had much trouble to soothe her; she is in a frantic state."

"You have heard, Mr. Bell, all about this dreadful mystery?" said Mrs. Bainbridge as she led me towards the dining-room.

"Yes," I answered; "your husband has been good enough to give me every particular."

"And you have really come here to help us?"

"I hope I may be able to discover the cause," I answered.

"It certainly seems most extraordinary," continued Mrs. Bainbridge. "My dear," she continued, turning to her husband, "you can easily imagine the state we were all in this morning when the news of the second death was brought to us."

"For my part," said Ella Bainbridge, "I am sure that Felwyn Tunnel is haunted. The villagers have thought so for a long time, and this second death seems to prove it, does it not?" Here she looked anxiously at me.

"I can offer no opinion," I replied, "until I have sifted the matter thoroughly."

"Come, Ella, don't worry Mr. Bell,' said her father; "if he is as hungry as I am, he must want his lunch."

We then seated ourselves at the table and commenced the

meal. Bainbridge, although he professed to be hungry, was in such a state of excitement that he could scarcely eat. Immediately after lunch he left me to the care of his family and went into the village.

"It is just like him," said Mrs. Bainbridge; "he takes these sort of things to heart dreadfully. He is terribly upset about Lucy Ray, and also about the poor fellow Wynne. It is certainly a fearful tragedy from first to last."

"Well, at any rate," I said, "this fresh death will upset the evidence against Wynne."

"I hope so, and there is some satisfaction in the fact. Well, Mr. Bell, I see you have finished lunch; will you come into the drawing-room?"

I followed her into a pleasant room overlooking the valley of the Lytton.

By and by Bainbridge returned, and soon afterwards the dog-cart came to the door. My host and I mounted, Bainbridge took the reins, and we started off at a brisk pace.

"Matters get worse and worse," he said the moment we were alone. "If you don't clear things up to-night, Bell, I say frankly that I cannot imagine what will happen."

We entered the village, and as we rattled down the ill-paved streets I was greeted with curious glances on all sides. The people were standing about in groups, evidently talking about the tragedy and nothing else. Suddenly as our trap bumped noisily over the paving-stones, a girl darted out of one of the houses and made frantic motions to Bainbridge to stop the horse. He pulled the mare nearly up on her haunches, and the girl came up to the side of the dog-cart.

"You have heard it?" she said, speaking eagerly and in a gasping voice. "The death which occurred this morning will clear Stephen Wynne, won't it, Mr. Bainbridge? It will, you are sure, are you not?"

"It looks like it, Lucy, my poor girl," he answered. "But there, the whole thing is so terrible that I scarcely know what to think."

She was a pretty girl with dark eyes, and under ordinary circumstances must have had the vivacious expression of face and the brilliant complexion which so many of her countrywomen possess. But now her eyes were swollen with weeping and her complexion more or less disfigured by the agony she had gone through. She looked piteously at Bainbridge, her lips trembling. The next moment she burst into tears.

"Come away, Lucy," said a woman who had followed her out of the cottage; "Fie—for shame! don't trouble the gentlemen; come back and stay quiet."

"I can't, mother, I can't," said the unfortunate girl. "If they hang him, I'll go clean off my head. Oh, Mr. Bainbridge, do say that the second death has cleared him!"

"I have every hope that it will do so, Lucy," said Bainbridge, "but now don't keep us, there's a good girl; go back into the house. This gentleman has come down from London on purpose to look into the whole matter. I may have good news for you in the morning."

The girl raised her eyes to my face with a look of intense pleading. "Oh, I have been cruel and a fool, and I deserve everything," she gasped; "but, sir, for the love of Heaven, try to clear him."

I promised to do my best.

Bainbridge touched up the mare, she bounded forward, and Lucy disappeared into the cottage with her mother.

The next moment we drew up at the inn where the Inspector was waiting, and soon afterwards were bowling along between the high banks of the country lanes to the tunnel. It was a cold, still afternoon; the air was wonderfully keen, for a sharp frost had held the countryside in its grip for the last two days. The sun was just tipping the hills to westward when the trap pulled up at the top of the cutting. We hastily alighted, and the Inspector and I bade Bainbridge goodbye. He said that he only wished that he could stay with us for the night, assured us that little sleep would visit him, and that he would be back at the cutting at an early hour on the following morning; then the noise of his horse's feet was heard fainter and fainter as he drove back over the frost-bound roads. The Inspector and I ran along the little path to the wicket-gate in the fence, stamping our feet on the hard ground to restore circulation after our cold drive. The next moment we were looking down upon the scene of the mysterious deaths, and a weird and lonely place it looked. The tunnel was at one end of the rock cutting, the sides of which ran sheer down to the line for over a hundred and fifty feet. Above the tunnel's mouth the hills rose one upon the other. A more dreary place it would have been difficult to imagine. From a little clump of pines a delicate film of blue smoke rose straight up on the still air. This came from the chimney of the signal-box.

As we started to descend the precipitous path the Inspector sang out a cheery "Hullo!" The man on duty in the box immediately answered. His voice echoed and reverberated down the cutting, and the next moment he appeared at the door of the box. He told us that he would be with us immediately; but we called back to him to stay where he was, and the next instant the Inspector and I entered the box.

"The first thing to do," said Henderson the Inspector, "is to send a message down the line to announce our arrival."

This he did, and in a few moments a crawling goods train came panting up the cutting. After signalling her through we descended the wooden flight of steps which led from the box down to the line and walked along the metals towards the tunnel till we stood on the spot where poor Davidson had been found dead that morning. I examined the ground and all around it most carefully. Everything tallied exactly with the description I had received. There could be no possible way of approaching the spot except by going along the line, as the rocky sides of the cutting were inaccessible.

"It is a most extraordinary thing, sir," said the signalman whom we had come to relieve. "Davidson had neither mark nor sign on him—there he lay stone dead and cold, and not a bruise nowhere; but Pritchard had an awful wound at the back of the head. They said he got it by climbing the rocks—here, you can see the marks for yourself, sir. But now, is it likely that Pritchard would try to climb rocks like these, so steep as they are?"

"Certainly not," I replied.

"Then how do you account for the wound, sir?" asked the man with an anxious face.

"I cannot tell you at present," I answered.

"And you and Inspector Henderson are going to spend the night in the signal-box?"

"Yes."

A horrified expression crept over the signalman's face.

"God preserve you both," he said; "I wouldn't do it—not for fifty pounds. It's not the first time I have heard tell that Felwyn Tunnel is haunted. But, there, I won't say any more about that. It's a black business, and has given trouble enough. There's poor Wynne, the same thing as convicted of the murder of Pritchard; but now they say that Davidson's death will clear him. Davidson was as good a fellow as you would come across this side of the country; but for the matter of that, so was Pritchard. The whole thing is terrible—it upsets one, that it do, sir."

"I don't wonder at your feelings," I answered; "but now, see here, I want to make a most careful examination of everything. One of the theories is that Wynne crept down this rocky side and fractured Pritchard's skull. I believe such a feat to be impossible. On examining these rocks I see that a man might climb up the side of the tunnel as far as from eight to ten feet, utilizing the sharp projections of rock for the purpose; but it would be out of the question for any man to come down the cutting. No; the only way Wynne could have approached Pritchard was by the line itself. But, after all, the real thing to discover is this," I continued, "what killed Davidson? Whatever caused his death is, beyond doubt, equally responsible for Pritchard's. I am now going into the tunnel."

Inspector Henderson went in with me. The place struck damp and chill. The walls were covered with green, evil-smelling fungi, and through the brickwork the moisture was oozing and had trickled down in long lines to the ground. Before us was nothing but dense darkness.

When we re-appeared the signalman was lighting the red lamp on the post, which stood about five feet from the ground just above the entrance to the tunnel.

"Is there plenty of oil?" asked the Inspector.

"Yes, sir, plenty," replied the man. "Is there anything more I can do for either of you gentlemen?" he asked, pausing, and evidently dying to be off.

"Nothing," answered Henderson; "I will wish you good-evening."

"Good-evening to you both," said the man. He made his way quickly up the path and was soon lost to sight.

Henderson and I then returned to the signal-box.

By this time it was nearly dark.

"How many trains pass in the night?" I asked of the Inspector.

"There's the 10.20 down express," he said, "it will pass here at about 10.40; then there's the 11.45 up, and then not another train till the 6.30 local tomorrow morning. We shan't have a very lively time," he added.

I approached the fire and bent over it, holding out my hands to try and get some warmth into them.

"It will take a good deal to persuade me to go down to the tunnel, whatever I may see there," said the man. "I don't think, Mr. Bell, I am a coward in any sense of the word, but there's something very uncanny about this place, right away from the rest of the world. I don't wonder one often hears of signalmen going mad in some of these lonely boxes. Have you any theory to account for these deaths, sir?"

"None at present," I replied.

"This second death puts the idea of Pritchard being murdered quite out of court," he continued.

"I am sure of it," I answered.

"And so am I, and that's one comfort," continued Henderson. "That poor girl, Lucy Ray, although she was to be blamed for her conduct, is much to be pitied now; and as to poor Wynne himself, he protests his innocence through thick and thin. He was a wild fellow, but not the sort to take the life of a fellow-creature. I saw the doctor this afternoon while I was waiting for you at the inn, Mr. Bell, and also the police sergeant. They both say they do not know what Davidson died of. There was not the least sign of violence on the body."

"Well, I am as puzzled as the rest of you," I said. "I have one or two theories in my mind, but none of them will quite fit the situation."

The night was piercingly cold, and, although there was not a breath of wind, the keen and frosty air penetrated into the lonely signal-box. We spoke little, and both of us were doubtless absorbed by our own thoughts and speculations. As to Henderson, he looked distinctly uncomfortable, and I cannot say that my own feelings were too pleasant. Never had I been given a tougher problem to solve, and never had I been so utterly at my wits' end for a solution.

Now and then the Inspector got up and went to the telegraph instrument, which intermittently clicked away in its box. As he did so he made some casual remark and then sat down again. After the 10.40 had gone through, there followed a period of silence which seemed almost oppressive. All at once the stillness was broken by the whirr of the electric bell, which sounded so sharply in our ears that we both started. Henderson rose.

"That's the 11.45 coming," he said, and, going over to the three long levers, he pulled two of them down with a loud clang. The next moment, with a rush and a scream, the express tore down the cutting, the carriage lights streamed past in a rapid flash, the ground trembled, a few sparks from the engine whirled up into the darkness, and the train plunged into the tunnel.

"And now," said Henderson, as he pushed back the levers, "not another train till daylight. My word, it is cold!"

It was intensely so. I piled some more wood on the fire and, turning up the collar of my heavy ulster, sat down at one end of the bench and leant my back against the wall. Henderson did likewise; we were neither of us inclined to speak. As a rule, whenever I have any night work to do, I am never troubled with sleepiness, but on this occasion I felt unaccountably drowsy. I soon perceived that Henderson was in the same condition.

"Are you sleepy?" I asked of him.

"Dead with it, sir," was his answer; "but there's no fear, I won't drop off."

I got up and went to the window of the box. I felt certain that if I sat still any longer I should be in a sound sleep. This would never do. Already it was becoming a matter of torture to keep my eyes open. I began to pace up and down; I opened the door of the box and went out on the little platform.

"What's the matter, sir?" inquired Henderson, jumping up with a start.

"I cannot keep awake," I said.

"Nor can I," he answered, "and yet I have spent nights and nights of my life in signal-boxes and never was the least bit drowsy; perhaps it's the cold."

"Perhaps it is," I said; "but I have been out on as freezing nights before, and . . ."

The man did not reply; he had sat down again; his head was nodding.

I was just about to go up to him and shake him, when it suddenly occurred to me that I might as well let him have his sleep out. I soon heard him snoring, and he presently fell forward in a heap on the floor. By dint of walking up and down, I managed to keep from dropping off myself, and in torture which I shall never be able to describe, the night wore itself away. At last, towards morning, I awoke Henderson.

"You have had a good nap," I said; "but never mind, I have been on guard and nothing has occurred."

"Good God! have I been asleep?" cried the man.

"Sound," I answered.

"Well, I never felt anything like it," he replied. "Don't you find the air very close, sir?"

"No," I said; "it is as fresh as possible; it must be the cold."

"I'll just go and have a look at the light at the tunnel," said the man; "it will rouse me."

He went on to the little platform, whilst I bent over the fire and began to build it up. Presently he returned with a scared look on his face. I could see by the light of the oil lamp which hung on the wall that he was trembling.

"Mr. Bell," he said, "I believe there is somebody or something down at the mouth of the tunnel now." As he spoke he clutched me by the arm. "Go and look," he said; "whoever it is, it has put out the light."

"Put out the light?" I cried. "Why, what's the time?"

Henderson pulled out his watch.

"Thank goodness, most of the night is gone," he said; "I didn't know it was so late, it is half past five."

"Then the local is not due for an hour yet?" I said.

"No; but who should put out the light?" cried Henderson.

I went to the door, flung it open, and looked out. The dim outline of the tunnel was just visible looming through the darkness, but the red light was out.

"What the dickens does it mean, sir?" gasped the Inspector. "I know the lamp had plenty of oil in it. Can there be anyone standing in front of it, do you think?"

We waited and watched for a few moments, but nothing stirred.

"Come along," I said, "let us go down together and see what it is."

"I don't believe I can do it, sir; I really don't!"

"Nonsense!" I cried. "I shall go down alone if you won't accompany me. Just hand me my stick, will you?"

"For God's sake, be careful, Mr. Bell. Don't go down, whatever you do. I expect this is what happened before, and the poor fellows went down to see what it was and died there. There's some devilry at work, that's my belief."

"That is as it may be," I answered shortly; "but we certainly shall not find out by stopping here. My business is to get to the bottom of this, and I am going to do it. That there is danger of some sort, I have very little doubt; but danger or not, I am going down."

"If you'll be warned by me, sir, you'll just stay quietly here."

"I must go down and see the matter out," was my answer. "Now listen to me, Henderson. I see that you are alarmed, and I don't wonder. Just stay quietly where you are and watch, but if I call come at once. Don't delay a single instant. Remember I am putting my life into your hands. If I call 'Come,' just come to me as quick as you can, for I may want help. Give me that lantern."

He unhitched it from the wall, and taking it from him. I walked cautiously down the steps on to the line. I still felt curiously, unaccountably drowsy and heavy. I wondered at this, for the moment was such a critical one as to make almost any man wide awake. Holding the lamp high above my head, I walked rapidly along the line. I hardly knew what I expected to find.

Cautiously along the metals I made my way, peering right and left until I was close to the fatal spot where the bodies had been found. An uncontrollable shudder passed over me. The next moment, to my horror, without the slightest warning, the light I was carrying went out, leaving me in total darkness. I started back, and stumbling against one of the loose boulders reeled against the wall and nearly fell. What was the matter with me? I could hardly stand. I felt giddy and faint, and a horrible sensation of great tightness seized me across the chest. A loud ringing noise sounded in my ears. Struggling madly for breath, and with the fear of impending death upon me, I turned and tried to run from a danger I could neither understand nor grapple with. But before I had taken two steps my legs gave way from under me, and uttering a loud cry I fell insensible to the ground.

Out of an oblivion which, for all I knew, might have lasted for moments or centuries, a dawning consciousness came to me. I knew that I was lying on hard ground; that I was absolutely incapable of realizing, nor had I the slightest inclination to discover, where I was. All I wanted was to lie quite still and undisturbed. Presently I opened my eyes.

Some one was bending over me and looking into my face.

"Thank God, he is not dead," I heard in whispered tones. Then, with a flash, memory returned to me.

"What has happened?" I asked.

"You may well ask that, sir," said the Inspector gravely. "It has been touch and go with you for the last quarter of an hour, and a near thing for me too."

I sat up and looked around me. Daylight was just beginning to break, and I saw that we were at the bottom of the steps that led up to the signal-box. My teeth were chattering with the cold and I was shivering like a man with ague.

"I am better now," I said; "just give me your hand."

I took his arm, and holding the rail with the other hand staggered up into the box and sat down on the bench.

"Yes, it has been a near shave," I said; "and a big price to pay for solving a mystery."

"Do you mean to say you know what it is?" asked Henderson eagerly.

"Yes," I answered, "I think I know now; but first tell me how long was I unconscious?"

"A good bit over half an hour, sir, I should think. As soon as I heard you call out I ran down as you told me, but before I got to you I nearly fainted. I never had such a horrible sensation in my life. I felt as weak as a baby, but I just managed to seize you by the arms and drag you along the line to the steps, and that was about all I could do."

"Well, I owe you my life," I said; "just hand me that brandy flask, I shall be the better for some of its contents."

I took a long pull. Just as I was laying the flask down Henderson started from my side.

"There," he cried, "the 6.30 is coming." The electric bell at the instrument suddenly began to ring. "Ought I to let her go through, sir?" he inquired.

"Certainly," I answered. "That is exactly what we want. Oh, she will be all right."

"No danger to her, sir?"

"None, none; let her go through."

He pulled the lever and the next moment the train tore through the cutting.

"Now I think it will be safe to go down again," I said. "I believe I shall be able to get to the bottom of this business."

Henderson stared at me aghast.

"Do you mean that you are going down again to the tunnel?" he gasped.

"Yes," I said; "give me those matches. You had better come too. I don't think there will be much danger now; and there is daylight, so we can see what we are about."

The man was very loth to obey me, but at last I managed to persuade him. We went down the line, walking slowly, and at this moment we both felt our courage revived by a broad and cheerful ray of sunshine.

"We must advance cautiously," I said, "and be ready to run back at a moment's notice."

"God knows, sir, I think we are running a great risk," panted poor Henderson; "and if that devil or whatever else it is should happen to be about—why, daylight or no daylight—"

"Nonsense, man!" I interrupted; "if we are careful, no harm will happen to us now. Ah! and here we are!" We had reached the spot where I had fallen. "Just give me a match, Henderson."

He did so, and I immediately lit the lamp. Opening the glass of the lamp, I held it close to the ground and passed it to and fro. Suddenly the flame went out.

"Don't you understand now?" I said, looking up at the Inspector.

"No, I don't, sir," he replied with a bewildered expression.

Suddenly, before I could make an explanation, we both heard shouts from the top of the cutting, and looking up I saw Bainbridge hurrying down the path. He had come in the dog-cart to fetch us.

"Here's the mystery," I cried as he rushed up to us, "and a deadlier scheme of Dame Nature's to frighten and murder poor humanity I have never seen."

As I spoke I lit the lamp again and held it just above a tiny fissure in the rock. It was at once extinguished.

"What is it?" said Bainbridge, panting with excitement.

"Something that nearly finished *me*," I replied. "Why, this is a natural escape of choke damp. Carbonic acid gas—the deadliest gas imaginable, because it gives no warning of its presence, and it has no smell. It must have collected here during the hours of the night when no train was passing, and gradually rising put out the signal light. The constant rushing of the trains through the cutting all day would temporarily disperse it."

As I made this explanation Bainbridge stood like one electrified, while a curious expression of mingled relief and horror swept over Henderson's face.

"An escape of carbonic acid gas is not an uncommon phenomenon in volcanic districts," I continued, "as I take this to be; but it is odd what should have started it. It has sometimes been known to follow earthquake shocks, when there is a profound disturbance of the deep strata."

"It is strange that you should have said that," said Bainbridge, when he could find his voice.

"What do you mean?"

"Why, that about the earthquake. Don't you remember, Henderson," he added, turning to the Inspector, "we had felt a slight shock all over South Wales about three weeks back?"

"Then that, I think, explains it," I said. "It is evident that Pritchard really did climb the rocks in a frantic attempt to escape from the gas and fell back on to these boulders. The other man was cut down at once, before he had time to fly."

"But what is to happen now?" asked Bainbridge. "Will it go on for ever? How are we to stop it?"

"The fissure ought to be drenched with lime water, and then filled up; but all really depends on what is the size of the supply and also the depth. It is an extremely heavy gas, and would lie at the bottom of a cutting like water. I think there is more here just now than is good for us," I added.

"But how," continued Bainbridge, as we moved a few steps from the fatal spot, "do you account for the interval between the first death and the second?"

"The escape must have been intermittent. If wind blew down the cutting, as probably was the case before this frost set in, it would keep the gas so diluted that its effects would not be noticed. There was enough down here this morning, before that train came through, to poison an army. Indeed, if it had not been for Henderson's promptitude, there would have been another inquest—on myself."

I then related my own experience.

"Well, this clears Wynne, without doubt," said Bainbridge; "but alas! for the two poor fellows who were victims. Bell, the Lytton Vale Railway Company owe you unlimited thanks; you have doubtless saved many lives, and also the Company, for the line must have been closed if you had not made your valuable discovery. But now come home with me to breakfast. We can discuss all those matters later on."

Bernard Capes

Bernard Capes wrote five collections of strange stories in the late 1890s and early 1900s and was ignored by anthologists from then on. If you think it may have been because of the quality of his work, read on and be amazed.

Capes, who was born in London in 1854, died in 1918 of heart failure compounding influenza. His writing career, as far as books were concerned, spanned only twenty years, yet he was one of the era's most prolific authors. He contributed stories to at least twenty-one of the magazines then prevalent, very often with a dozen appearances in the same journal over the years. His most popular work was probably the novel *The Lake of Wine* (1898) and all told he produced over thirty-five books, the last being the posthumous *The Skeleton Key* (1919).

Bernard Capes was undoubtedly one of the Victorian age's great fantasists and I think it hard that he has not been given the recognition due him. I hope this story will help. Not the least strange thing about Capes' work is the startling similarity it bears to later writers' plots. His tale "The Moon Stricken" is almost identical to a later work from M. P. Shiel, "The Place of Pain." I think it likely Shiel was influenced by Capes, but what of the strange likeness between Capes' "The Black Reaper" (which appeared in his *At a Winter's Fire* in 1899) and Ray Bradbury's classic story "The Scythe"? See for yourself when you read this forgotten classic from Bernard Capes.

The Black Reaper

Taken from the Q— Register of Local
Events, as Compiled from Authentic Narratives

I

Now I am to tell you of a thing that befell in the year 1665 of the Great Plague, when the hearts of certain amongst men, grown callous in wickedness upon that rebound from an inhuman austerity, were opened to the vision of a terror that moved and spoke not in the silent places of the fields. Forasmuch as, however, in the recovery from delirium a patient may marvel over the incredulity of neighbours who refuse to give credence to the presentiments that have been *ipso facto* to him, so, the nation being sound again, and its constitution hale, I expect little but a laugh for my piety in relating of the following incident; which, nevertheless, is as essential true as that he who shall look through the knot-hole in the plank of a coffin shall acquire the evil eye.

For, indeed, in those days of a wild fear and confusion, when every condition that maketh for reason was set wandering by a devious path, and all men sitting as in a theatre of death looked to see the curtain rise upon God knows what horrors, it was vouchsafed to many to witness sights and sounds beyond the compass of Nature, and that as if the devil and his minions had profited by the anarchy to slip unobserved into the world. And I know that this is so, for all the insolence of a recovered scepticism; and, as to the unseen, we are like one that traverseth the dark with a lanthorn, himself the skipper of a little moving blot of light, but a positive mark for any secret foe without the circumference of its radiance.

Be that as it may, and whether it was our particular ill-fortune, or, as some asserted, our particular wickedness, that made of our village an inviting back-door of entrance to the Prince of Darkness, I know not; but so it is that disease and contagion are ever inclined to penetrate by way of flaws or humours where the veil of the flesh is already perforated, as a kite circleth round its quarry, looking for the weak place to strike: and, without doubt, in that land of corruption we were a very foul blot indeed.

How this came about it were idle to speculate; yet no man shall have the hardihood to affirm that it was otherwise. Nor do I seek to extenuate myself, who was in truth no better than my neighbours in most that made us a community of drunkards and forswearers both lewd and abominable. For in that village a depravity that was like madness had come to possess the heads of the people, and no man durst take his stand on honesty or even common decency, for fear he should be set upon by his comrades and drummed out of his government on a pint pot. Yet for myself I will say was one only redeeming quality, and that was the pure love I bore to my solitary orphaned child, the little Margery.

Now, our Vicar—a patient and God-fearing man, for all his predial tithes were impropriated by his lord, that was an absentee and a sheriff in London—did little to stem that current of lewdness that had set in strong with the Restoration. And this was from no lack of virtue in himself, but rather from a natural invertebracy, as one may say, and an order of mind that, yet being no order, is made the sport of any sophister with a wit for paragram. Thus it always is that mere example is of little avail without precept—of which, however, it is an important condition—and that the successful directors of men be not those who go to the van and lead, unconscious of the gibes and mockery in their rear, but such rather as drive the mob before them with a smiting hand and no infirmity of purpose. So, if a certain affection for our pastor dwelt in our hearts, no tittle of respect was there to leaven it and justify his high office before Him that consigned the trust; and ever deeper and deeper we sank in the slough of corruption, until was brought about this pass—that naught but some scourging despotism of the Church should acquit us of the fate of Sodom. That such, at the eleventh hour, was vouchsafed us of God's mercy, it is my purpose to show; and, doubtless, this offering of a loop-hole was to account by reason of the devil's having debarked his reserves, as it were, in our port; and so quartering upon us a soldiery that we were, at no invitation of our own, to maintain, stood us a certain extenuation.

It was late in the order of things before in our village so much as a rumour of the plague reached us. Newspapers were not in those days, and reports, being by word of mouth, travelled slowly, and were often spent bullets by the time they fell amongst us. Yet, by May, some gossip there was of the distemper having gotten a hold in certain quarters of London and increasing, and this alarmed our people, though it made no abatement of their profligacy. But presently the reports coming thicker, with confirmation of the terror and panic that was enlarging on all sides, we must take measures for our safety; though into June and July, when the pestilence was raging, none infected had come our way, and that from our remote and isolated position. Yet it needs but fear for the crown to that wickedness that is self-indulgence; and forasmuch as this fear fattens like a toadstool on the decomposition it springs from, it grew with us to the proportions that we were set to kill or destroy any that should approach us from the stricken districts.

And then suddenly there appeared in our midst *he* that was appointed to be our scourge and our cautery.

Whence he came, or how, no man of us could say. Only one day we were a community of roysterers and scoffers, impious and abominable, and the next he was amongst us smiting and thundering.

Some would have it that he was an old collegiate of our Vicar's, but at last one of those wandering Dissenters that found never as now the times opportune to their teachings—a theory to which our minister's treatment of the stranger gave colour. For from the moment of his appearance he took the reins of government, as it were, appropriating the pulpit and launching his bolts therefrom, with the full consent and encouragement of the other. There were those, again, who were resolved that his commission was from a high place, whither news of our infamy had reached, and that we had best give him a respectful hearing, lest we should run a chance of having our hearing stopped altogether. A few were convinced he was no man at all, but rather a fiend sent to thresh us with the scourge of our own contriving, that we might be tender, like steak, for the cooking; and yet other few regarded him with terror, as an actual figure or embodiment of the distemper.

But, generally, after the first surprise, the feeling of resentment at his intrusion woke and gained ground, and we were much put about that he should have thus assumed the pastorship without invitation, quartering with our Vicar, who kept himself aloof and was little seen, and seeking to drive us by terror, and amazement, and a great menace of retribution. For, in truth, this was not the method to which we were wont, and it both angered and disturbed us.

This feeling would have enlarged the sooner, perhaps, were it not for a certain restraining influence possessed of the newcomer, which neighboured him with darkness and mystery. For he was above the common tall, and ever appeared in public with a slouched hat, that concealed all the upper part of his face and showed little otherwise but the dense black beard that dropped upon his breast like a shadow.

Now with August came a fresh burst of panic, how the desolation increased and the land was overrun with swarms of infected persons seeking an asylum from the city; and our anger rose high against the stranger, who yet dwelt with us and encouraged the distemper of our minds by furious denunciations of our guilt.

Thus far, for all the corruption of our hearts, we had maintained the practice of church-going, thinking, maybe, poor fools! to hoodwink the Almighty with a show of reverence; but now, as by a common consent, we neglected the observances and loitered of a Sabbath in the fields, and thither at the last the strange man pursued us and ended the matter.

For so it fell that at the time of the harvest's ripening a goodish body of us males was gathered one Sunday for coolness about the neighbourhood of the dripping well, whose waters were a tradition, for they had long gone dry. This well was situated in a sort of cave or deep scoop at the foot of a cliff of limestone, to which the cultivated ground that led up to it fell somewhat. High above, the cliff broke away into a wide stretch of pasture land, but the face of the rock itself was all patched with bramble and little starved birch-trees clutching for foothold; and in like manner the excavation beneath was half-stifled and gloomed over with undergrowth, so that it looked a place very dismal and uninviting, save in the ardour of the dog-days.

Within, where had been the basin, was a great shattered hole going down to unknown depths; and this no man had thought to explore, for a mystery held about the spot that was doubtless the foster-child of ignorance.

But to the front of the well and of the cliff stretched a noble field of corn, and this field was of an uncommon shape, being, roughly, a vast circle and a little one joined by a neck and in suggestion not unlike an hour-glass; and into the crop thereof, which was of goodly weight and condition, were the first sickles to be put on the morrow.

Now as we stood or lay around, idly discussing of the news, and congratulating ourselves that we were for once quit of our incubus, to us along the meadow path, his shadow jumping on the corn, came the very subject of our gossip.

He strode up, looking neither to right nor left, and with the first word that fell, low and damnatory, from his lips, we knew that the moment had come when, whether for good or evil, he intended to cast us from him and acquit himself of further responsibility in our direction.

"Behold!" he cried, pausing over against us, "I go from among ye! Behold, ye that have not obeyed nor inclined your ear, but have walked every one in the imagination of his evil heart! Saith the Lord, 'I will bring evil upon them, which they shall not be able to escape; and though they shall cry unto Me, I will not hearken unto them.'"

His voice rang out, and a dark silence fell among us. It was pregnant, but with little of humility. We had had enough of this interloper and his abuse. Then, like Jeremiah, he went to prophesy:—

"I read ye, men of Anathoth, and the murder in your hearts. Ye that have worshipped the shameful thing and burned incense to Baal—shall I cringe that ye devise against me, or not rather pray to the Lord of Hosts, 'Let me see Thy vengeance on them'? And He answereth, 'I will bring evil upon the men of Anathoth, even the year of their visitation.'"

Now, though I was no participator in that direful thing that followed, I stood by, nor interfered, and so must share the blame. For there were men risen all about, and their faces lowering, and it seemed that it would go hard with the stranger were he not more particular.

But he moved forward, with a stately and commanding gesture, and stood with his back to the well-scoop and threatened us and spoke.

"Lo!" he shrieked, "your hour is upon you! Ye shall be mowed down like ripe corn, and the shadow of your name shall be swept from the earth! The glass of your iniquity is turned, and when its sand is run through, not a man of ye shall be!"

He raised his arm aloft, and in a moment he was overborne. Even then, as all say, none got sight of his face; but he fought with lowered head, and his black beard flapped like a wounded crow. But suddenly a boy-child ran forward of the bystanders, crying and screaming,—

"Hurt him not! They are hurting him—oh, me! oh, me!"

And from the sweat and struggle came his voice, gasping, "I spare the little children!"

Then only I know of the surge and the crash towards the well-mouth, of an instant cessation of motion, and immediately of men toiling hither and thither with boulders and huge blocks, which they piled over the rent, and so sealed it with a cromlech of stone.

II

That, in the heat of rage and of terror, we had gone further than we had at first designed, our gloom and our silence on the morrow attested. True we were quit of our incubus, but on such

terms as not even the severity of the times could excuse. For the
man had but chastised us to our improvement; and to destroy
the scourge is not to condone the offence. For myself, as I bore
up the little Margery to my shoulder on my way to the reaping,
I felt the burden of guilt so great as that I found myself muttering of an apology to the Lord that I durst put myself into touch
with innocence. "But the walk would fatigue her otherwise," I
murmured; and, when we were come to the field, I took and
carried her into the upper or little meadow, out of reach of the
scythes, and placed her to sleep amongst the corn, and so left
her with a groan.

But when I was come anew to my comrades, who stood at the
lower extremity of the field—and this was the bottom of the
hour-glass, so to speak—I was aware of a stir amongst them,
and, advancing closer, that they were all intent upon the neighbourhood of the field I had left, staring like distraught creatures,
and holding well together, as if in a panic. Therefore, following
the direction of their eyes, and of one that pointed with rigid
finger, I turned me about, and looked whence I had come; and
my heart went with a somersault, and in a moment I was all sick
and dazed.

For I saw, at the upper curve of the meadow, where the well
lay in gloom, that a man had sprung out of the earth, as it
seemed, and was started reaping; and the face of this man was
all in shadow, from which his beard ran out and down like a
stream of gall.

He reaped swiftly and steadily, swinging like a pendulum;
but, though the sheaves fell to him right and left, no swish of the
scythe came to us, nor any sound but the beating of our own
hearts.

Now, from the first moment of my looking, no doubt was in
my lost soul but that this was him we had destroyed come back
to verify his prophecy in ministering to the vengeance of the
Lord of Hosts; and at the thought a deep groan rent my bosom,
and was echoed by those about me. But scarcely was it issued
when a second terror smote me as that I near reeled. Margery—
my babe! put to sleep there in the path of the Black Reaper!

At that, though they called to me, I sprang forward like a

madman, and running along the meadow, through the neck of the glass, reached the little thing, and stooped and snatched her into my arms. She was sound and unfrighted, as I felt with a burst of thankfulness; but, looking about me, as I turned again to fly, I had near dropped in my tracks for the sickness and horror I experienced in the nearer neighbourhood of the apparition. For, though it never raised its head, or changed the steady swing of its shoulders, I knew that it was aware of and was *reaping at me*. Now, I tell you, it was ten yards away, yet the point of the scythe came gliding upon me silently, like a snake, through the stalks, and at that I screamed out and ran for my life.

I escaped, sweating with terror; but when I was sped back to the men, there was all the village collected, and our Vicar to the front, praying from a throat that rattled like a dead leaf in a draught. I know not what he said, for the low cries of the women filled the air; but his face was white as a smock, and his fingers writhed in one another like a knot of worms.

"The plague is upon us!" they wailed. "We shall be mowed down like ripe corn!"

And even as they shrieked the Black Reaper paused, and, putting away his scythe, stooped and gathered up a sheaf in his arms and stood it on end. And, with the very act, a man—one that had been forward in yesterday's business—fell down amongst us yelling and foaming; and he rent his breast in his frenzy, revealing the purple blot thereon, and he passed blaspheming. And the reaper stooped and stooped again, and with every sheaf he gathered together one of us fell stricken and rolled in his agony, while the rest stood by palsied.

But, when at length all that was cut was accounted for, and a dozen of us were gone each to his judgment, and he had taken up his scythe to reap anew, a wild fury woke in the breasts of some of the more abandoned and reckless amongst us.

"It is not to be tolerated!" they cried. "Fire the corn and burn this sorcerer!"

And with that, some five or six of them, emboldened by despair, ran up into the little field, and, separating, had out each his flint and fired the crop in his own place, and retreated to the narrow part for safety.

Now the reaper rested on his scythe, as if unexpectedly acquitted of a part of his labour; but the corn flamed up in these five or six directions, and was consumed in each to the compass of a single sheaf: whereat the fire died away. And with its dying the faces of those that had ventured went black as coal; and they flung up their arms, screaming, and fell prone where they stood, and were hidden from our view.

Then, indeed, despair seized upon all of us that survived, and we made no doubt but that we were to be exterminated and wiped from the earth for our sins, as were the men of Anathoth. And for an hour the Black Reaper mowed and trussed, till he had cut all from the little upper field and was approached to the neck of juncture with the lower and larger. And before us that remained, and who were drawn back amongst the trees, weeping and praying, a fifth of our comrades lay foul, and dead, and sweltering, and all blotched over with the dreadful mark of the pestilence.

Now, as I say, the reaper was nearing the neck of juncture; and so we knew that if he should once pass into the great field towards us and continue his mowing, not one of us should be left to give earnest of our repentance.

Then, as it seemed, our Vicar came to a resolution, moving forward with a face all wrapt and entranced; and he strode up the meadow path and approached the apparition, and stretched out his arms to it entreating. And we saw the other pause, awaiting him; and, as he came near, put forth his hand, and so, gently, on the good old head. But as we looked, catching at our breaths with a little pathos of hope, the priestly face was thrown back radiant, and the figure of him that would give his life for us sank amongst the yet standing corn and disappeared from our sight.

So at last we yielded ourselves fully to our despair; for if our pastor should find no mercy, what possibility of it could be for us!

It was in this moment of an uttermost grief and horror, when each stood apart from his neighbour, fearing the contamination of his presence, that there was vouchsafed to me, of God's pity, a wild and sudden inspiration. Still to my neck fastened the little Margery—not frighted, it seemed, but mazed—and other babes there were in plenty, that clung to their mothers' skirts and peeped out, wondering at the strange show.

I ran to the front and shrieked: "The children! the children! He will not touch the little children! Bring them and set them in his path!" And so crying I sped to the neck of meadow and loosened the soft arms from my throat, and put the little one down within the corn.

Now at once the women saw what I would be at, and full a score of them snatched up their babes and followed me. And here we were reckless for ourselves; but we knelt the innocents in one close line across the neck of land, so that the Black Reaper should not find space between any of them to swing his scythe. And having done this, we fell back with our hearts bubbling in our breasts, and we stood panting and watched.

He had paused over that one full sheaf of his reaping; but now, with the sound of the women's running, he seized his weapon again and set to upon the narrow belt of corn that yet separated him from the children. But presently, coming out upon the tender array, his scythe stopped and trailed in his hand, and for a full minute he stood like a figure of stone. Then thrice he walked slowly backwards and forwards along the line, seeking for an interval whereby he might pass; and the children laughed at him like silver bells, showing no fear, and perchance meeting that of love in his eyes that was hidden from us.

Then of a sudden he came to before the midmost of the line, and, while we drew our breath like dying souls, stooped and snapped his blade across his knee, and, holding the two parts in his hand, turned and strode back into the shadow of the dripping well. There arrived, he paused once more, and, twisting him about, waved his hand once to us and vanished into the blackness. But there were those who affirmed that in that instant of his turning, his face was revealed, and that it was a face radiant and beautiful as an angel's.

Such is the history of the wild judgment that befell us, and by grace of the little children was foregone; and such was the stranger whose name no man ever heard tell, but whom many have since sought to identify with that spirit of the pestilence that entered into men's hearts and confounded them, so that they saw visions and were afterwards confused in their memories.

But this I may say, that when at last our courage would fetch us to that little field of death, we found it to be all blackened and blasted, so as nothing would take root there then or ever since; and it was as if, after all the golden sand of the hour-glass was run away and the lives of the most impious with it, the destroyer saw fit to stay his hand for sake of the babes that he had pronounced innocent, and for such as were spared to witness to His judgment. And this I do here, with a heart as contrite as if it were the morrow of the visitation, the which with me it ever has remained.

S. Levett-Yeats

Here's a story to gladden the heart of any publisher: the definitive method of finding a sure-fire best seller. Whether all publishers would welcome the cost is another matter.

It comes from a book of short stories by a now-forgotten writer of the turn of the century, Sidney Kilner Levett-Yeats. Levett-Yeats served in the cavalry in India for some years, and then went into government service. He was mentioned in the Birthday Honours in 1912 as Accountant-General, Posts and Telegraphs in the Indian civil service but seems to have sunk into obscurity thereafter.

He published nine books between 1893 and 1904, starting with an interesting book of short stories, *The Romance of Guard Mulligan* (1893). His last listed work is the novel *Orrain* (1904).

"The Devil's Manuscript" comes from his second book of short stories, *The Heart of Denise* (1899). Why it has escaped reprinting for over 100 years is a mystery.

The Devil's Manuscript

I. The black packet

"**M.** De Bac? De Bac? I do not know the name."
"Gentleman says he knows you, sir, and has called on urgent business."

There was no answer, and John Brown, the ruined publisher, looked about him in a dazed manner. He knew he was ruined; tomorrow the world would know it also, and then—beggary stared him in the face, and infamy too. For this the world would not care. Brown was not a great man in "the trade," and his name in the *Gazette* would not attract notice; but his name, as he stood in the felon's dock, and the ugly history a cross-examination might disclose would probably arouse a fleeting interest, and then the world would go on with a pitiless shrug of its shoulders. What does it matter to the moving wave of humanity if one little drop of spray from its crest is blown into nothing by the wind? Not a jot. But it was a terrible business for the drop of spray, otherwise John Brown, publisher. He was at his best not a good-looking man, rather mean-looking than otherwise, with a thin, angular face, eyes as shifty as a jackal's and shoulders shaped like a champagne-bottle. As the shadow of coming ruin darkened over him, he seemed to shrink and look meaner than ever. He had almost forgotten the presence of his clerk. He could think of nothing but the morrow, when Simmonds' voice again broke the stillness.

"Shall I say you will see him, sir?"

The question cut sharply into the silence, and brought Brown to himself. He had half a mind to say "No." In the face of the

coming tomorrow, business, urgent or otherwise, was nothing to
him. Yet, after all, there could be no harm done in receiving the
man. It would, at any rate, be a distraction, and, lifting his head,
Brown answered:

"Yes, I will see him, Simmonds."

Simmonds went out, closing the green baize door behind
him. There was a delay of a moment, and M. De Bac entered—
a tall, thin figure, bearing an oblong parcel, packed in shiny,
black paper, and sealed with flame-coloured wax.

"Good-day, Mr. Brown"; and M. De Bac, who, for all his for-
eign name, spoke perfect English, extended his hand.

Brown rose, put his own cold fingers into the warm grasp of
his visitor, and offered him a seat.

"With your permission, Mr. Brown, I will take this other
chair. It is nearer the fire. I am accustomed to warm climates,
as you doubtless perceive"; and De Bac, suiting his action to his
words, placed his packet on the table, and began to slowly rub
his long, lean fingers together. The publisher glanced at him
with some curiosity. M. De Bac was as dark as an Italian, with
clear, resolute features, and a moustache, curled at the ends,
thick enough to hide the sarcastic curve of his thin lips. He was
strongly if sparely built, and his fiery black eyes met Brown's
gaze with a look that ran through him like a needle.

"You do not appear to recognize me, Mr. Brown?"—De Bac's
voice was very quiet and deep-toned.

"I have not the honour—" began the publisher; but his visitor
interrupted him.

"You mistake. We are quite old friends; and in time will
always be very near each other. I have a minute or two to
spare"—he glanced at a repeater—"and will prove to you that I
know you. You are John Brown, that very religious young man
of Battersea, who, twelve years ago, behaved like a blackguard
to a girl at Homerton, and sent her to—but no matter. You
attracted my attention then; but, unfortunately, I had no time to
devote to you. Subsequently, you effected a pretty little swin-
dle—don't be angry, Mr. Brown—it *was* very clever. Then you
started in business on your own account, and married. Things
went well with you; you know the art of getting at a low price,

and selling at a high one. You are a born "sweater." Pardon the word. You know how to keep men down like beasts, and go up yourself. In doing this, you did me yeoman's service, although you are even now not aware of this. You had one fault, you have it still, and had you not been a gambler you might have been a rich man. Speculation is a bad thing, Brown—I mean gambling speculation."

Brown was an Englishman, and it goes without saying that he had courage. But there was something in De Bac's manner, some strange power in the steady stare of those black eyes, that held him to his seat as if pinned there.

As De Bac stopped, however, Brown's anger gave him strength. Every word that was said was true, and stung like the lash of a whip. He rose white with anger.

"Sir!" he began with quivering lips, and made a step forward. Then he stopped. It was as if the sombre fire in De Bac's gaze withered his strength. An invisible hand seemed to drag him back into his seat and hold him there.

"You are hasty, Mr. Brown"; and De Bac's even voice continued: "you are really very rash. I was about to tell you a little more of your history, to tell you you are ruined, and tomorrow every one in London—it is the world for you, Brown—will know you are a beggar, and many will know you are a cheat."

The publisher swore bitterly under his breath.

"You see, Mr. Brown," continued his strange visitor, "I know all about you, and you will be surprised, perhaps, to hear that you deserve help from me. You are too useful to let drift. I have therefore come to save you."

"Save me?"

"Yes. By means of this manuscript here," he pointed to the packet, "which you are going to publish."

Brown now realized that he was dealing with a lunatic. He tried to stretch out his arm to touch the bell on the table; but found that he had no power to do so. He made an attempt to shout to Simmonds; but his tongue moved inaudibly in his mouth. He seemed only to have the faculty of following De Bac's words, and of answering them. He gasped out:

"It is impossible!"

"My friend"—and De Bac smiled mirthlessly—"you will publish that manuscript. I will pay. The profits will be yours. It will make your name, and you will be rich. You will even be able to build a church."

"Rich!" Brown's voice was very bitter. "M. De Bac, you said rightly. I am a ruined man. Even if you were to pay for the publication of that manuscript I could not do it now. It is too late. There are other houses. Go to them."

"But not other John Browns. You are peculiarly adapted for my purpose. Enough of this! I know what business is, and I have many things to attend to. You are a small man, Mr. Brown, and it will take little to remove your difficulties. See! Here are a thousand pounds. They will free you from your present troubles," and De Bac tossed a pocket-book on the table before Brown. "I do not want a receipt," he went on. "I will call tomorrow for your final answer, and to settle details. If you need it I will give you more money. This hour—twelve—will suit me. *Adieu!*" He was gone like a flash, and Brown looked around in blank amazement. He was as if suddenly aroused from a dream. He could hardly believe the evidence of his senses, although he could see the black packet, and the neat leather pocket-book with the initials "L. De B." let in in silver on the outside. He rang his bell violently, and Simmonds appeared.

"Has M. De Bac gone?"

"I don't know, sir. He didn't pass out through the door."

"There is no other way. You must have been asleep."

"Indeed I was not, sir."

Brown felt a chill as of cold fingers running down his backbone, but pulled himself together with an effort. "It does not matter, Simmonds. You may go."

Simmonds went out scratching his head. "How the demon did he get out?" he asked himself. "Must have been sleeping after all. The guv'nor seems a bit dotty to-day. It's the smash coming—sure."

He wrote a letter or two, and then taking his hat, sallied forth to an aërated bread-shop for his cheap and wholesome lunch, for Simmonds was a saving young man, engaged to a young lady living out Camden Town way. Simmonds perfectly understood the state of affairs, and was not a little anxious about matters, for the mother of his fiancée, a widow who let lodgings, had only agreed to his engagement after much persuasion; and if he had to announce the fact that, instead of "thirty bob a week," as he put it, his income was nothing at all, there would be an end of everything.

"M'ria's all right," he said to his friend Wilkes, in trustful confidence as they sat over their lunch; "but that old torpedo"—by which name he designated his mother-in-law-elect—"she'll raise Cain if there's a smash-up."

In the meantime, John Brown tore open the pocket-book with shaking hands, and, with a crisp rustling, a number of new bank-notes fell out, and lay in a heap before him. He counted them one by one. They totalled to a thousand pounds exactly. He was a small man. M. De Bac had said so truly, if a little rudely, and the money was more than enough to stave off ruin. De Bac had said, too, if needed he would give him more, and then Brown fell to trembling all over. He was like a man snatched from the very jaws of death. At Battersea he wore a blue ribbon; but now he went to a cabinet, filled a glass with raw brandy, and drained it at a gulp. In a minute or so the generous cordial warmed his chilled blood, and picking up the notes, he counted them again, and thrust them into his breast-pocket. After this he paced the room up and down in a feverish manner, longing for the morrow when he could settle up the most urgent demands against him. Then, on a sudden, a thought struck him. It was almost as if it had been whispered in his ear. Why trouble at all about matters? He had a clear thousand with him, and in an hour he could be out of the country! He hesitated, but prudence prevailed. Extradition laws stretched everywhere; and there was another thing—that extraordinary madman, De Bac, had promised more money on the morrow. After all, it was better to stay.

As he made this resolve his eyes fell on the black packet on the table. The peculiar colour of the seals attracted his attention. He bent over them, and saw that the wax bore an impress of a V-shaped shield, within which was set a trident. He noticed also that the packet was tied with a silver thread. His curiosity was excited. He sat down, snipped the threads with a penknife, tore off the black paper covering, flung it into the fire, and saw before him a bulky manuscript exquisitely written on very fine paper. A closer examination showed that they were a number of short stories. Now Brown was in no mood to read; but the title of the first tale caught his eye, and the writing was so legible that he had glanced over half a dozen lines before he was aware of the fact. Those first half-dozen lines were sufficient to make him read the page, and when he had read the page the publisher felt he was before the work of a genius.

He was unable to stop now; and, with his head resting between his hands, he read on tirelessly. Simmonds came in once or twice and left papers on the table, but his master took no notice of him. Brown forgot all about his lunch, and turning over page after page read as if spellbound. He was a business-man, and was certain the book would sell in thousands. He read as one inspired to look into the author's thoughts and see his design. Short as the stories were, they were Titanic fragments, and everyone of them taught a hideous lesson of corruption. Some of them cloaked in a religious garb, breathed a spirit of pitiless ferocity; others were rich with the sensuous odours of an Eastern garden; others, again, were as the tender green of moss hiding the treacherous deeps of a quicksand; and all of them bore the hall-mark of genius. They moved the man sitting there to tears, they shook him with laughter, they seemed to rock his very soul asleep; but through it all he saw, as the mariner views the beacon fire on a rocky coast, the deadly plan of the writer. There was money in them—thousands—and all was to be his. Brown's sluggish blood was running to flame, a strange strength glowed in his face, and an uncontrollable admiration for De Bac's evil power filled him. The book, when published, might corrupt generations yet unborn; but that was nothing to Brown. It meant thousands for him, and an eternal fame to De Bac. He did not grudge the writer the fame as long as he kept the thousands.

"By Heaven!" and he brought his fist down on the table with a crash, "the man may be a lunatic; but he is the greatest genius the world ever saw—or he is the devil incarnate."

And somebody laughed softly in the room.

The publisher looked up with a start, and saw Simmonds standing before him:

"Did you laugh, Simmonds?"

"No, sir!" replied the clerk with a surprised look.

"Who laughed then?"

"There is no one here but ourselves, sir—and I didn't laugh."

"Did you hear nothing?"

"Nothing, sir."

"Strange!" and Brown began to feel chill again.

"What time is it?" he asked with an effort.

"It is half-past six, sir."

"So late as that? You may go, Simmonds. Leave me the keys. I will be here for some time. Good evening."

"Mad as a coot," muttered Simmonds to himself; "must break the news to M'ria to-night. Oh, Lor'!" and his eyes were very wet as he went out into the Strand, and got into a blue omnibus.

When he was gone, Brown turned to the fire, poker in hand. To his surprise he saw that the black paper was still there, burning red hot, and the wax of the seals was still intact—the seals themselves shining like orange glow-lights. He beat at the paper with the poker; but instead of crumbling to ashes it yielded passively to the stroke, and came back to its original shape. Then a fury came on Brown. He raked at the fire, threw more coals over the paper, and blew at the flames with his bellows until they roared up the chimney; but still the coppery glare of the packet-cover never turned to the grey of ashes. Finally, he could endure it no longer, and, putting the manuscript into the safe, turned off the electric light, and stole out of his office like a thief.

II. THE RED TRIDENT

When Beggarman, Bowles & Co., of Providence Passage, Lombard Street, called at eleven o'clock on the morning following De Bac's visit, their representative was not a little surprised to find the firm's bills met in hard cash, and Simmonds paid him with a radiant face. When the affair was settled, the clerk leaned back in his chair, saying half-aloud to himself, "By George! I am glad after all M'ria did not keep our appointment in the Camden Road last night." Then his face began to darken, "Wonder where she could have been, though?" his thoughts ran on; "half sorry I introduced her to Wilkes last Sunday at Victoria Park. Wilkes ain't half the man I am though," and he tried to look at himself in the window-pane, "but he has two pound ten a week—Lord! There's the guv'nor ringing." He hurried into Brown's room, received a brief order, and was about to go back when the publisher spoke again.

"Simmonds!"

"Sir."

"If M. De Bac calls, show him in at once."

"Sir," and the clerk went out.

Left to himself, Brown tried to go on with the manuscript; but was not able to do so. He was impatient for the coming of De Bac, and kept watching the hands of the clock as they slowly travelled towards twelve. When he came to the office in the morning Brown had looked with a nervous fear in the fireplace, half expecting to find the black paper still there; and it was a considerable relief to his mind to find it was not. He could do nothing, not even open the envelopes of the letters that lay on his table. He made an effort to find occupation in the morning's paper. It was full of some absurd correspondence on a trivial subject, and he wondered at the thousands of fools who could waste time in writing and in reading yards of print on the theme of "Whether women should wear neckties." The ticking of the clock irritated him. He flung the paper aside, just as the door opened and Simmonds came in. For a moment Brown thought he had come to announce De Bac's arrival; but no— Simmonds simply placed a square envelope on the table before Brown.

"Pass-book from Bransom's, sir, just come in"; and he went out.

Brown took it up mechanically, and opened the envelope. A type-written letter fell out with the pass-book. He ran his eyes over it with astonishment. It was briefly to inform him that M. De Bac had paid into Brown's account yesterday afternoon the sum of five thousand pounds, and that, adjusting overdrafts, the balance at his credit was four thousand seven hundred and twenty pounds thirteen shillings and three pence. Brown rubbed his eyes. Then he hurriedly glanced at the pass-book. The figures tallied—there was no error, no mistake. He pricked himself with his penknife to see if he was awake, and finally shouted to Simmonds:

"Read this letter aloud to me, Simmonds," he said.

Simmonds' eyes opened, but he did as he was bidden, and there was no mistake about the account.

"Anything else, sir?" asked Simmonds when he had finished.

"No—nothing," and Brown was once more alone. He sat staring at the figures before him in silence, almost mesmerizing himself with the intentness of his gaze.

"My God!" he burst out at last, in absolute wonder.

"Who is your God, Brown?" answered a deep voice.

"I—I—M. De Bac! How did you come?"

"I did not drop down the chimney," said De Bac with a grin; "your clerk announced me in the ordinary way, but you were so absorbed you did not hear. So I took the liberty of sitting in this chair, and awaiting your return to earthly matters. You were dreaming, Brown—by the way, who *is* your God?" he repeated with a low laugh.

"I—I do not understand, sir."

"Possibly not, possibly not. I wouldn't bother about the matter. Ah! I see Bransom's have sent you your pass-book! Sit down, Brown. I hate to see a man fidgeting about—I paid in that amount yesterday on a second thought. It is enough—eh?"

Brown's jackal eyes contracted. Perhaps he could get more out of De Bac? But a look at the strong impassive face before him frightened him.

"More than enough, sir," he stammered; and then, with a rush, "I am grateful—anything I can do for you?"

"Oh! I know, I know, Brown—by the way, you do not object to smoke?"

"Certainly not. I do not smoke myself."

"In Battersea, eh?" And De Bac, pulling out a silver cheroot case, held it out to Brown. But the publisher declined.

"Money wouldn't buy a smoke like that in England," remarked De Bac, "but as you will. I wouldn't smoke if I were you. Such abstinence looks respectable and means nothing." He put a cigar between his lips, and pointed his forefinger at the end. To Brown's amazement an orange-flame licked out from under the fingernail, and vanished like a flash of lightning; but the cigar was alight, and its fragrant odour filled the room. It reached even Simmonds, who sniffed at it like a buck scenting the morning air. "By George!" he exclaimed in wonder, "what baccy!"

M. De Bac settled himself comfortably in his chair, and spoke with the cigar between his teeth. "Now you have recovered a little from your surprise, Brown, I may as well tell you that I never carry matches. This little scientific discovery I have made is very convenient, is it not?"

"I have never seen anything like it."

"There are a good many things you have not seen, Brown—but to work. Take a pencil and paper and note down what I say. You can tell me when I have done if you agree or not."

Brown did as he was told, and De Bac spoke slowly and carefully.

"The money I have given you is absolutely your own on the following terms. You will publish the manuscript I left you, enlarge your business, and work as you have hitherto worked—as a 'sweater.' You may speculate as much as you like. You will not lose. You need not avoid the publication of religious books, but you must never give in charity secretly. I do not object to a big cheque for a public object, and your name in all the papers. It will be well for you to hound down the vicious. Never give them a chance to recover themselves. You will be a legislator. Strongly uphold all those measures which, under a moral cloak, will do harm to mankind. I do not mention them. I do not seek to hamper you with detailed instructions. Work on these general lines, and you will do what I want. A word more. It will be advisable whenever you have a chance to call public attention to a great evil which is also a vice. Thousands who have never heard of it before will hear of it then—and human nature is very frail. You have noted all this down?"

"I have. You are a strange man, M. De Bac."

M. De Bac frowned, and Brown began to tremble.

"I do not permit you to make observations about me, Mr. Brown."

"I beg your pardon, sir."

"Do not do so again. Will you agree to all this? I promise you unexampled prosperity for ten years. At the end of that time I shall want you elsewhere. And you must agree to take a journey with me."

"A long one, sir?" Brown's voice was just a shade satirical.

M. De Bac smiled oddly. "No—in your case I promise a quick passage. These are all the conditions I attach to my gift of six thousand pounds to you."

Brown's amazement did not blind him to the fact of the advantage he had, as he thought, over his visitor. The six thousand pounds were already his, and he had given no promise. With a sudden boldness he spoke out.

"And if I decline?"

"You will return me my money, and my book, and I will go elsewhere."

"The manuscript, yes—but if I refuse to give back the money?"

"Ha! ha! ha!" M. De Bac's mirthless laugh chilled Brown to the bone. "Very good, Brown—but you won't refuse. Sign that like a good fellow," and he flung a piece of paper towards Brown, who saw that it was a promissory note, drawn up in his name, agreeing to pay M. De Bac the sum of six thousand pounds on demand.

"I shall do no such thing," said Brown stoutly.

M. De Bac made no answer, but calmly touched the bell. In a half-minute Simmonds appeared.

"Be good enough to witness Mr. Brown's signature to that document," said De Bac to him, and then fixed his gaze on Brown. There was a moment of hesitation and then—the publisher signed his name, and Simmonds did likewise as a witness.

When the latter had gone, De Bac carefully put the paper by in a letter-case he drew from his vest pocket.

"Your scientific people would call this an exhibition of odic force, Brown—eh?"

Brown made no answer. He was shaking in every limb, and great pearls of sweat rolled down his forehead.

"You see, Brown," continued De Bac, "after all you are a free agent. Either agree to my terms and keep the money, or say you will not, pay me back, receive your note-of-hand, and I go elsewhere with my book. Come—time is precious."

And from Brown's lips there hissed a low "I agree."

"Then that is settled," and De Bac rose from his chair. "There is a little thing more—stretch out your arm like a good fellow— the right arm."

Brown did so; and De Bac placed his forefinger on his wrist, just between what palmists call "the lines of life." The touch was as that of a red-hot iron, and with a quick cry Brown drew back his hand and looked at it. On his wrist was a small red trident, as cleanly marked as if it had been tattooed into the skin. The pain was but momentary; and, as he looked at the mark, he heard De Bac say, "Adieu once more, Brown. I will find my way out—don't trouble to rise." Brown heard him wish Simmonds an affable "Good-day," and he was gone.

III. THE MARK OF THE BEAST

It was early in the spring that Brown published *The Yellow Dragon*—as the collection of tales left with him by De Bac was called—and the success of the book surpassed his wildest expectations. It became the rage. There were the strangest rumours afloat as to its authorship, for no one knew De Bac, and the name of the writer was supposed to be an assumed one. It was written by a clergyman; it was penned by a schoolgirl; it had employed the leisure of a distinguished statesman during his retirement; it was the work of an ex-crowned head. These, and such-like statements, were poured forth one day to be contradicted the next. Wherever the book was noticed it was either with the most extravagant praise or the bitterest rancour. But friend and foe were alike united on one thing—that of ascribing to its unknown author a princely genius. The greatest of the reviews, after pouring on *The Yellow Dragon* the vials of its wrath, concluded with these words of unwilling praise: "There is not a sentence of this book which should ever have been written, still less published; but we do not hesitate to say that, having been written and given to the world, there is hardly a line of this terrible work which will not become immortal—to the misery of mankind."

Be this as it may, the book sold in tens of thousands, and Brown's fortune was assured. In ten years a man may do many things; but during the ten years that followed the publication of *The Yellow Dragon,* Brown did so many things that he astonished "the City," and it takes not a little to do that. It was not alone the marvellous growth of his business—although that advanced by leaps and bounds until it overshadowed all others—it was his wonderful luck on the Stock Exchange. Whatever he touched turned to gold. He was looked upon as the Napoleon of finance. His connection with *The Yellow Dragon* was forgotten when his connection with the yellow sovereign was remembered. He had a palace in Berkshire; another huge pile owned by him overlooked Hyde Park. He was a county member and a cabinet-minister. He had refused a peerage and built a church. Could ambition want more? He had clean forgotten De Bac. From him he had heard no word, received no sign, and he looked upon him as dead. At first, when his eyes fell on the red trident on his wrist, he was wont to shudder all over; but as years went on he became accustomed to the mark, and thought no more of it than if it had been a mole. In personal appearance he was but little changed, except that his hair was thin and grey, and there was a bald patch on the top of his head. His wife had died four years ago, and he was now contemplating another marriage—a marriage that would ally him with a family dating from the Confessor.

Such was John Brown, when we meet him again ten years after De Bac's visit, seated at a large writing-table in his luxurious office. A clerk standing beside him was cutting open the envelopes of the morning's post, and placing the letters one by one before his master. It is our friend Simmonds—still a young man, but bent and old beyond his years, and still on "thirty bob" a week. And the history of Simmonds will show how Brown carried out De Bac's instructions.

When *The Yellow Dragon* came out and business began to expand, Simmonds, having increased work, was ambitious enough to expect a rise in his salary, and addressed his chief on the subject. He was put off with a promise, and on the strength of that promise Simmonds, being no wiser than many of his fellows, married M'ria; and husband and wife managed to exist somehow with the help of the mother-in-law. Then the mother-in-law died, and there was only the bare thirty shillings a week on which to live, to dress, to pay Simmonds' way daily to the City and back, and to feed more than two mouths—for Simmonds was amongst the blessed who have their quivers full. Still the expected increase of pay did not come. Other men came into the business and passed over Simmonds. Brown said they had special qualifications. They had; and John Brown knew Simmonds better than he knew himself. The other men were paid for doing things Simmonds could not have done to save his life; but he was more than useful in his way. A hundred times it was in the mind of the wretched clerk to resign his post and seek to better himself elsewhere. But he had given hostages to fortune. There was M'ria and her children, and M'ria set her face resolutely against risk. They had no reserve upon which to fall back, and it was an option between partial and total starvation. So "Sim," as M'ria called him, held on and battled with the wolf at the door, the wolf gaining inch by inch. Then illness came, and debt, and then—temptation. "Sim" fell, as many a better man than he has fallen.

Brown found it out, and saw his opportunity to behave generously, and make his generosity pay. He got a written confession of his guilt from Simmonds, and retained him in his service forever on thirty shillings a week. And Simmonds' life became such as made him envy the lot of a Russian serf, of a Siberian exile, of a negro in the old days of the sugar plantations. He became a slave, a living machine who ground out his daily hours of work;

he became mean and sordid in soul, as one does become when hope is extinct. Such was Simmonds as he cut open the envelopes of Brown's letters, and the great man, reading them quickly, endorsed them with terse remarks in blue pencil, for subsequent disposal by his secretary. A sudden exclamation from the clerk, and Brown looked up.

"What is it?" he asked sharply.

"Only this, sir," and Simmonds held before Brown's eyes a jet black envelope; and as he gazed at it, his mind travelled back ten years, to that day when he stood on the brink of public infamy and ruin, and De Bac saved him. For a moment everything faded before Brown's eyes, and he saw himself in a dingy room, with the gaunt figure of the author of *The Yellow Dragon,* and the maker of his fortune, before him.

"Shall I open it, sir?" Simmonds' voice reached him as from a far distance, and Brown roused himself with an effort.

"No," he said, "give it to me, and go for the present."

When the bent figure of the clerk had passed out of the room, Brown looked at the envelope carefully. It bore a penny stamp and the impress of the postmark was not legible. The superscription was in white ink and it was addressed to Mr. John Brown. The "Mr." on the letter irritated Brown, for he was now The Right Hon'ble John Brown, and was punctilious on that score. He was so annoyed that at first he thought of casting the letter unopened into the waste-paper basket beside him, but changed his mind, and tore open the cover. A note-card discovered itself. The contents were brief and to the point:

"Get ready to start. I will call for you at the close of the day. L. De B."

For a moment Brown was puzzled, then the remembrance of his old compact with De Bac came to him. He fairly laughed. To think that he, The Right Hon'ble John Brown, the richest man in England, and one of the most powerful, should be written to like that! Ordered to go somewhere he did not even know! Addressed like a servant! The cool insolence of the note amused Brown first, and then he became enraged. He tore the note into fragments and cast it from him. "Curse the madman," he said aloud, "I'll give him in charge if he annoys me." A sudden twinge in his right wrist made him hurriedly look at the spot. There was a broad pink circle, as large as a florin, around the mark of the trident, and it smarted and burned as the sting of a wasp. He ran to a basin of water and dipped his arm in to the elbow; but the pain became intolerable, and, finally, ordering his carriage, he drove home. That evening there was a great civic banquet in the city, and amongst the guests was The Right Hon'ble John Brown.

All through the afternoon he had been in agony with his wrist, but towards evening the pain ceased as suddenly as it had come on, and Brown attended the banquet, a little pale and shaken, but still himself. On Brown's right hand sat the Bishop of Browboro', on his left a most distinguished scientist, and amongst the crowd of waiters was Simmonds, who had hired himself out for the evening to earn an extra shilling or so to eke out his miserable subsistence. The man of science had just returned from Mount Atlas, whither he had gone to observe the transit of Mercury, and had come back full of stories of witchcraft. He led the conversation in that direction, and very soon the Bishop, Brown, and himself were engaged in the discussion of *diablerie*. The Bishop was a learned and a saintly man, and was a "believer"; the scientist was puzzled by what he had seen, and Brown openly scoffed.

"Look here!" and pulling back his cuff, he showed the red mark on his wrist to his companions, "if I were to tell you how that came here, you would say the devil himself marked me."

"I confess I am curious," said the scientist; and the Bishop fixed an inquiring gaze upon Brown. Simmonds was standing behind, and unconsciously drew near. Then the man, omitting many things, told the history of the mark on his wrist. He left out much, but he told enough to make the scientist edge his chair a little further from him, and a look of grave compassion, not untinged with scorn, to come into the eyes of the Bishop. As Brown came to the end of his story he became unnaturally excited, he raised his voice, and, with a sudden gesture, held his wrist close to the Bishop's face, "There!" he said, "I suppose you would say the devil did that?"

And as the Bishop looked, a voice seemed to breathe in his ear: "*And he caused all . . . to receive a mark in their right hand, or in their foreheads.*" It was as if his soul was speaking to him and urging him to say the words aloud. He did not; but with a pale face gently put aside Brown's hand. "I do not know, Mr. Brown—but I think you are called upon for a speech."

It was so; and, after a moment's hesitation, Brown rose. He was a fluent speaker, and the occasion was one with which he was peculiarly qualified to deal. He began well; but as he went on those who looked upon him saw that he was ghastly pale, and that the veins stood out on his high forehead in blue cords. As he spoke he made some allusion to those men who have risen to eminence from an obscure position. He spoke of himself as one of these, and then began to tell the story of "The Devil's Manuscript," as he called it, with a mocking look at the Bishop. As he went on he completely lost command over himself, and the story of the manuscript became the story of his life. He concealed nothing, he passed over nothing. He laid all his sordid past before his hearers with a vivid force. His listeners were astonished into silence; perhaps curiosity kept them still. But, as the long tale of infamy went on, some, in pity for the man, and believing him struck mad, tried to stop him, but in vain. He came at last to the incident of the letter, and told how De Bac was to call for him tonight. "The Bishop of Brownboro'," he said with a jarring laugh, "thought De Bac was the fiend himself," but he (Brown) knew better; he—he stopped, and, with a half-inarticulate cry, began to back slowly from the table, his eyes fixed on the entrance to the room. And now a strange thing happened. There was not a man in the room who had the power to move or to speak; they were as if frozen to their seats; as if struck into stone. Some were able to follow Brown's glance, but could see nothing. All were able to see that in Brown's face was an awful fear, and that he was trying to escape from a horrible presence which was moving slowly towards him, and which was visible to himself alone. Inch by inch Brown gave way, until he at last reached the wall, and stood with his back to it, with his arms spread out, in the position of one crucified. His face was marble white, and a dreadful terror and a pitiful appeal shone in his eyes. His blue lips were parted as of one in the dolors of death.

The silence was profound.

There were strong men there; men who had faced and over-come dangers, who had held their lives in their hands, who had struggled against desperate odds and won; but there was not a man who did not now feel weak, powerless, helpless as a child before that invisible, advancing terror that Brown alone could see. They could move no hand to aid, lift no voice to pray. All they could do was to wait in that dreadful silence and to watch. Time itself seemed to stop. It was as if the stillness had lasted for hours.

Suddenly Brown's face, so white before, flushed a crimson purple, and with a terrible cry he fell forwards on the polished woodwork of the floor.

As he fell it seemed as if the weight which held all still was on the moment removed, and they were free. With scared faces they gathered around the fallen man and raised him. He was quite dead; but on his forehead, where there was no mark before, was the impress of a red trident.

A man, evidently one of the waiters, who had forced his way into the group, laid his finger on the mark and looked up at the Bishop. There was an unholy exultation in his face as he met the priest's eyes, and said:

"He's marked twice—*curse him!*"

Dick Donovan

Subtitled "A Weird Story of Brazil" this florid piece comes from *Tales of Terror* (1899), probably the best macabre work of Dick Donovan and certainly the most widely sought by ghost story enthusiasts. Donovan was the *nom-de-plume* of Joyce E. Preston-Muddock (1842–1934), one of the era's most prolific authors. In the space of just over thirty years, he published seventy books under his own name, and another seventy under the Dick Donovan alias.

Muddock started his career in Government service in India then travelled extensively all over Asia, America, Canada, Russia and Europe. He contributed articles to various publications, and spent five years as Swiss correspondent of the *Daily News*. He edited and published *Muddock's Guide to Switzerland* and *Muddock's Guide to Davos Platz,* and also edited a volume of the Savage Club papers.

His phenomenal output was made up largely of thrillers and spy stories, but when he did turn to macabre fiction he did so with a master's hand. Despite one or two very obvious cribs from older stories, *Tales of Terror* is a masterful collection. See for yourself from "The Mystic Spell" which takes a lengthy tour of some enchanting South American countryside and sets out a tale of supernatural terror.

The Mystic Spell

A Weird Story of Brazil

TOLD BY SIGNOR DON ALONZO RODERICK,
SPANISH CONSUL AT RIO DE JANEIRO

R io and its neighbourhood is perhaps one of the most beautiful spots on the face of the globe. Indeed, I am not sure but
what it may claim to be absolutely without a rival, for it has features that are unique. Nature would almost seem to have
exhausted her efforts to build up a scene which lacks no single
detail necessary for imposing pictorial effect, though, as most
people know, hidden beneath all this entrancing beauty death
lurks in a hundred forms; and he who is not wary and ever on
his guard is liable to be struck down with appalling suddenness.

My predecessor had suffered much in his health, and suc-
cumbed at last to the scourge of yellow fever. When I arrived to
take up his work I found everything in such confusion that I had
to labour very hard to reduce chaos to order and put the con-
sular business shipshape. It thus came about that for many
months I was unable to leave my post in Rio, and as a consequence my health began to suffer. Soon after my arrival I made
the acquaintance of a Portuguese gentleman named Azevedo
Souza, a merchant of high standing in Rio. His business was of
a very mixed character, and amongst other things he was an
orchid exporter. In this branch of his trading he had been exceptionally successful. Through his instrumentality collectors had
had brought under their notice some wonderful and hitherto
unknown specimens of these marvels of nature. His collecting

105

station was far up north in the interior. He spoke of it enthusiastically as an earthly paradise, and gave me many pressing invitations to be his guest, when he paid his periodical visits to look after his affairs in that region.

Senhor Souza was an estimable gentleman, and very highly respected. He had a charming family, amongst them being a daughter, Juliette by name, and one of the sweetest young ladies I have ever had the pleasure of associating with. At this period Juliette was about seven-and-twenty, and as the apple of his eye to her father. She was invaluable to him in his business, at any rate to the orchid branch of it; for not only had she an all-round cleverness, but probably she knew more about orchids than any living woman. She herself was the means of introducing to the scientific world an entirely new orchid, the flower of which was of such transcendent beauty that the Brazilians, used as they are to floral glories, said that this particular bloom must have been "specially cultivated in God's own garden." Juliette made a most arduous and hazardous journey into the depths of virgin forests in search of this plant, and narrowly escaped losing her life.

Perhaps, when I say that I was a bachelor the reader will readily guess that my acquaintance with Juliette aroused in me an admiration which I devoutly hoped would find its consummation in a happy union, for she was by no means indifferent to my attentions. Not only was she highly cultivated, but had astonishing linguistic powers, and spoke many languages fluently. She was perfectly acquainted with Spanish, and had read the beautiful literature of Spain extensively. Senhor Souza encouraged my suit, and at last the time came when I was emboldened to tell Juliette she was the one woman in the world who could make me happy. Ah, I shall never forget that night until the grave closes over me. We were seated in the veranda of Senhor Souza's splendid villa, situated just on the outskirts of the town, and commanding an enchanting view of the bay of Rio, with its remarkable Sugar Loaf Mountain and the marvellous range beyond it. And what a night it was! The glory of the stars, shining as they can only shine in the tropics; the sparkling moonlit sea; the soft, flower-perfumed breeze that stirred the foliage to a languorous *susurrus;* the fireflies that like living jewels filled the air, begot in one a feeling of reverence, and strengthened one's faith in the Great God who created such a world of beauty. Those who have never experienced such a night under a tropical sky know nothing of what the true poetry of nature means. It stirs one with a ravishing, ecstatic feeling of delight which is a foretaste of the joys of heaven.

I had been sitting for some time with Juliette's hand in mine. We were silent, being deeply impressed with the magical beauty of the night, for we both had poetical instincts; indeed, Juliette's was a highly strung romantic temperament, and she was able to express her thoughts in language that could stir the pulses and move to tears.

But this night of all nights was a night for love, and as I pressed her hand I asked her to crown my happiness by becoming my wife. To my astonishment she shuddered, sighed deeply, and then in a tone of the most touching pathos exclaimed:

"Oh, why—oh, why have you asked me that?"

"Juliette," I answered in amazement, "is it not a natural question for a man to ask a woman sooner or later, when every beat of his heart tells him that he loves her?"

"Yes, yes," she replied in distressful tones, and shuddering again violently, "but—"

"But what?" I asked as she paused.

"I pray you press me not for an answer."

"This is extraordinary!" I remarked, feeling distressed beyond the power of words to express; and yet, distressed as I was, she was infinitely more troubled; she sobbed like one whose heart was rent. "You know that I love you, Juliette," I went on. "You have encouraged me. You have tacitly bidden me to hope; and now—"

"Oh, yes, yes," she cried with a catching of her breath, and a spasmodic closing of her fingers round mine. "And I love you, I love you. But I have been living in a fool's paradise. I have been dreaming dreams. I thought that the sweet delicious time would go on indefinitely. You waken me now abruptly, and I no longer dream. I must not, cannot be your wife."

"Juliette, what is this mystery?" I exclaimed, growing excited, for I was sure some extraordinary influence was at work, and that she was under a spell.

She laughed, though it wasn't the light laugh of joy peculiar to her, but a little forced spasmodic laugh of bitterness and despair.

"I will tell you," she answered, trying to master her emotions by a mighty effort of will. "It is better that you should know, otherwise you may deem me fickle, and think that I have trifled with your feelings. Years ago, when I was a little girl, I had a nurse, a strange old Brazilian crone who had been in the family service for many years. She was very fond of all my brothers and sisters, but for some reason I could never understand took a strong dislike to me. I think this dislike was mutual, for I remember that she used to make me shudder at times, and fill me with a nameless dread. This, perhaps, was hardly to be wondered at, for she treated me roughly and unkindly, and many a time I complained to my father. He, however, shared my mother's belief in the old woman's fidelity and gentleness, and would chide me for what he termed my unfounded, childish fears. Consequently I ceased to complain, and kept my little sorrows to myself.

"The name of this old nurse was Joanna Maria. One day she and I and an elder sister who was about two years my senior had been down to the bay, and wandering about the sea-shore in search of the beautiful shells which are often thrown up after a storm. Old Joanna was peculiarly irritable and fretful that morning. Once, when I stumbled over a rock and fell into a pool of sea-water, she snatched me up fiercely, and shook me until nearly all the life was frightened out of me. Then she sat down, made me sit beside her, and, looking at me fixedly with her bleared eyes, said:

"'I am going to tell you your future. It grows dark, very dark; a foreigner will come from over the sea and will talk love to you, but if you listen to him and become his wife, a sudden and awful death will overtake you; you will leave him a widow while yet he is a bridegroom. Love and wifedom are not for you. I put a curse upon you.'"

In spite of the fact that dear Juliette told me this with moving solemnity and gravity, I burst into laughter, and taking her in my arms said:

"Juliette, my beloved, what nonsense all this is! Surely you with your high intelligence and great learning, do not attach the slightest importance to the malicious and spiteful utterances of an ignorant old crone. No, no, I am sure you don't. You are too sensible. Put these phantom fears away, darling, and trust to my great love to shield you from all harm. Say you love me; say you will be my bride. Do not send me from you on this wonderful night of beauty with a great load of sorrow at my heart. Speak, Juliette, my love, my life—comfort me. Tell me you will link your fate with mine."

She sighed in response to my appeal. Then pressing her soft, fair cheek against mine, she tightened her arms around my neck and murmured low and sweetly:

"Yes, beloved, you are right. I will put the foolish, superstitious fear behind me. Old Joanna has long been dead, and I ought never to have allowed her empty, spiteful words to have influenced me. Take me, dear, when you will. I am yours only. I will be your wife! I will be faithful unto death!"

Scarcely had she uttered the words when she broke from me, and uttering a shrill scream of terror, sank into her chair, and, pointing to the far end of the veranda like one distraught, cried:

"There she is, there she is! Take her away, take her away, for I am horrified!"

Naturally my eyes turned to where she pointed, and though I was neither a nervous nor a superstitious man, I started with a feeling of horror, for I beheld the shadowy form of an old negress. The moonlight fell full upon her repulsive face, which was filled with a look of hatred, while her eyes, glowing like a wild cat's, glared at me with a spite that would be difficult to describe. In a few moments her lips parted, revealing the white teeth that glistened in the pale light, and distinctly and unmistakably I heard these words: "Shun her, the curse is on her! She will die as I foretold."

Juliette heard this too, and with a pitiable scream of fright she fell in a swoon on the floor. The scream brought the servants and her father rushing from the house, and as they raised the prostrate lady up, they directed angry glances at me, as though they thought that I had done some wrong.

I was confused and trembling. I glanced towards the end of the veranda to where I had seen the vision, but there was nothing in sight, and I was recalled to my senses by the voice of Senhor Souza, who somewhat peremptorily demanded to know what had caused his daughter's illness.

"Senhor Souza," I answered, thinking it was better to be perfectly frank with him, "as you know, Juliette and I love each other. To-night I have asked her to be my wife. She consented. Immediately afterwards we heard a sigh, and turning beheld a vision which so alarmed your daughter that she screamed and fainted."

"This is a strange story, very strange," he muttered; "and it is ominous. Tell me more about it?" The Brazilians are all more or less superstitious, and Senhor Souza was no exception. Having seen his daughter borne into the house and attended to by her maid and the female servants, he returned to me and made me relate minutely all that had passed.

As I felt that I ought not to conceal anything I gave him a plain, straightforward statement of the facts. He was much impressed and evidently uneasy. Again and again he asked me if I had seen the vision. Of course I had no alternative but to assure him that I could not have been mistaken, although I had no explanation to offer. I told him I was not given to seeing visions, that up to that night I had always been very sceptical; but now I was either a victim of a trick of the brain or I had seen what I had described. Moreover, I was certain, I said, that Juliette had seen it too. Otherwise, why did she scream and faint?

Senhor Souza showed decided reluctance to discuss the subject further that night, for he was evidently deeply affected, and much concerned about his daughter. So when I had been assured that Juliette was recovering, and would probably be all right in the morning, I returned to the town. As I drove along in the moonlight, I recalled all that had transpired, and I confess to a feeling of decided uneasiness. The fact is, I was unnerved a little. I had received a shock and its effects were not easily shaken off.

I did not sleep very well that night, but with the coming day my fears dispelled, and I quite recovered my wonted buoyancy when a special messenger brought me a little note from my Juliette to say that she was much better. That cheered me, and I was inclined to rate myself for having been so weak. But, of course, we are always brave in the day. Darkness makes cowards of us.

As soon as my duties permitted I rode out to Senhor Souza's villa and was pleased at being met on the threshold by Juliette. She looked pale and anxious, and a trace of fear still lingered in her beautiful eyes. We wandered into the garden together, and when the psychological moment had arrived, as I thought, I renewed my love-vows, and again urged her to consent to become my wife. Something of the previous night's agitation affected her, and as she clung to my arm as though she was afraid an unseen force might attempt to pluck her from my side, she said:

"Are we justified, think you, in defying fate, and in linking our lives together in spite of the curse?"

"Yes, undoubtedly," I answered. "The curse is nonsense. We can afford to laugh at the curse of a human being."

"You saw the vision last night?" she asked.

"Yes."

"And heard it speak?"

"I did."

"You know then that I am not the victim of a delusion. At least, if I am so are you."

"Beloved," I cried, "we are both victims of a delusion. It is well that we should think so. Curses avail not, neither can the dead harm us. Our happiness is in each other's keeping. Why should we throw it away? Surely we are strong-minded enough to be indifferent to the meaningless croakings of a spiteful and imbecile old woman. Hesitate, therefore, no longer; say you will be my wife."

Although my argument evidently told with her, she could not

quite make up her mind, and she murmured like one who was still under the influence of a great fear:

"I should like to, I should like to, dear one; but supposing that dreadful prophecy *should* come true?"

"It won't, my own love," I answered. "We have nothing to fear from the living, and the dead—well, the dead are done with."

"Ah, you don't know. Perhaps, perhaps not. Who knows, who can tell? It may be that those who have passed away may still have power to injure us. The old nurse hated me, and I fear that she has carried her hate beyond the grave."

I used every argument I could to comfort and calm her. I urged her again and again to speak the word that would make my happiness complete. I told her that I was then suffering in health as a result of the climate, and weakened as I was, her refusal to comply with my request would probably have a fatal effect.

This latter argument appealed so forcibly to her that even her superstitious fears were overcome, and she said at last that if her father offered no objection she would not. Speaking for myself, although the night previous I had been much impressed, I was no longer so; nor was I inclined to attach any importance to the supernatural incident which had so alarmed us, consequently I felt perfectly justified in leaving nothing undone to overcome Juliette's scruples and fears. And now, as I had gained her consent, I suggested that we should go at once to her father and get his sanction, for the time had come when the state of my health demanded imperatively that I should seek a change; that I should go away into the highlands to recoup. But I was resolved not to go alone.

By this time I had completely won her, and so we went to Senhor Souza and told him of our wishes and desires. I noticed that his olive cheeks blanched a little, and a look of ineffable love and tenderness filled his eyes as he gazed on his child, whose beauty at that moment seemed to me the beauty of heaven, not of earth. The Senhor appealed to her to speak her mind freely and candidly, holding nothing in reserve. So she turned to me, and laid both her soft white hands in mine, saying:

"Father, this man has my heart. My body, therefore, belongs to him. Give me to him with your blessing, for I love him."

The Senhor was deeply affected, and his voice was broken by emotion as he spoke. He stepped towards us and placed one hand on my head and the other on hers, and looking at me with misty eyes, said:

"I give her to you; take her. Guard her, watch over her, for she is my life; she is the core of my heart, the apple of my eye. Be good to each other, be true, loyal, and upright; and may God in His infinite mercy and wisdom bless and prosper you, and give you long years of peace, joy, and contentment. God bless you, God bless you," he repeated with great fervency.

The old man ceased. He could say no more, emotion choked him. Juliette and I muttered a fervent "Amen, amen!" and then we were alone; the Senhor had hurried from the room. I took my affianced wife in my arms, and kissing her passionately, told her that every dark cloud had gone. She sighed a sigh of joy, and nestled to me; but instantly the joy was turned to a cry of horror and alarm, for a mocking, bitter, fiendish laugh broke on our ears, and turning from whence the sound came, we saw a nebulous form defined against a background of velvet curtain that hung as a portière before a door. It was impossible to recognise the figure, and it faded in a few moments like a passing shadow. The laugh, however, was unmistakable. We both heard it. It struck against our hearts; it beat in on our brains.

"My love, my love!" I whispered in Juliette's ear, as she seemed as if she would swoon in my arms; "be strong, be brave. God will smile upon us. The saints will watch over us."

"Ah, dear one," she exclaimed; "let me go from you for ever, for it is destined I shall bring you woe and lifelong sorrow."

"Juliette, not all the fiends in the nether world shall part me from you," I answered firmly. "We are pledged to each other, and your father has blessed us. We will have no fear, but go on our way with light hearts, and put our trust in God."

She seemed comforted, and I remained there until late. The morrow was to see the commencement of the preparation for our nuptials.

During the ensuing weeks Juliette quite recovered her spirits.

Or, at any rate, whatever her feelings and thoughts were, she was at pains to conceal them. It was arranged that our honeymoon was to be spent in the highlands, at the Senhor's orchid station. I was looking forward to the time of my departure from Rio with intense joy, as I was terribly enervated, and yearned to breathe the pure and bracing air of the mountain lands.

At length our marriage morning came, as bright and brilliant a day as ever broke on the fair earth. A few fleecy clouds flecked the deep blue sky, and a fresh wind blowing in from the sea tempered the great heat of the sun. Surely no woman ever looked more divinely beautiful than did my sweet wife on that her bridal morn. It seemed to me that she was touched with a spiritual beauty that was not of the earth. The pure white lilies that lay upon her heaving bosom were not more wondrous fair than she. When the ceremony had ended, she expressed a wish to retire with me to a little chapel. There for a brief space we might offer up silent prayer, and commune with our hearts. Devoutly did she cross herself, and fervently did she pray that she might make me happy.

Ah, sweet Juliette, as I think, even at this far-off time, of that morning, my heart turns to lead, and my brain would give way, were it not that your sweet and gentle spirit is ever near me, and bids me be of good cheer.

When we had done justice to the sumptuous repast provided for us by my father-in-law at the principal Rio hotel, we left by the railway known as the *Estrada de Ferro Dom Pedro,* and travelled for many hours to the extreme northern limit of the line, a place called Carandahy. My father-in-law was to follow us in a few days. He would have started with us, but was compelled to remain behind to settle up certain business matters. My love and I remained that night at Carandahy, at the house of Senhor Oliveira, a great friend of my wife's father, who had kindly placed his house at our disposal.

We spent three days in that bracing mountain station, where every breath I drew seemed to put new life into my enervated frame. And my dear wife had now quite recovered her spirits, and was as blithe and happy as a lark. Every one was so kind; the scenery was so wonderful; the air so invigorating, and we twain were so perfectly happy that we felt a thankfulnes which could find no expression in mere words. But there is a dumb eloquence which is greater than speech; and there are moments of ecstasy when one can only express one's feelings by silence. Such moments were those we passed at the mountain station of Carandahy. The joy was great; alas! too great to last, as was soon to be proved.

As our destination was Paraúna, on the banks of the river of the same name, we left Carandahy on horseback, with a number of servants and attendants, while our baggage was to be brought on by ox waggon.

At Paraúna Senhor Souza had one of his orchid collecting stations, and in due course we arrived at the place, which is magnificently situated, while the dense forests in the neighbourhood are the homes of some of the most beautiful orchids in the world. It is a small town, but of no small importance, as in the neighbouring mountains there are some mines of precious stones which, though worked in a very desultory and halfhearted way, produce considerable wealth.

The Senhor's station was situated a little distance from the town, in a rather lonely spot on the banks of the river. It was in charge of a foreman named Chrispiniano Soares, and he had under him five or six Brazilian packers, and many orchid hunters, mostly Indians, who were intimately acquainted with the country round about for leagues and leagues. .

My dear Juliette knew the place well also, as she had been there before; and now she displayed the greatest interest in the work that was being carried on, while her knowledge of the various species of plants brought in was wonderful. She could classify and name every plant.

Those were long delightful happy days. I was her willing, loving, devoted student, and she was my worshipped teacher. It made her so happy to explain to me the names and habits of the plants; and it filled me with happiness to see her happy. Neither of us ever reverted to the strange visitation in Rio, nor to the prophecy of the old nurse. Indeed, I don't think we thought of it—at least I didn't—our happiness was too great. No shadow fell upon it, and yet an awful, damnable shadow was creeping up. Oh, if I had only had some faint warning! Why was there no angel in heaven to give me some sign so that I might have saved my darling? But no sound came. No sign arose. It seemed as if all the people worshipped my sweet wife. She was so beautiful, so kind, so gentle, so womanly. But no one was possessed with prescience to utter a word of alarm to put me on my guard, so that I might have striven to avert the awful doom.

One day it chanced that a mule I was riding stumbled over a piece of timber and threw me, somewhat injuring my right leg, so that I had to lay up for a little while. I urged my dear one not to let my enforced imprisonment—which I was assured would only be of a few days' duration—prevent her from taking her accustomed exercise. She said that she should remain by my side; but, oh, poor blind being that I was, the fiend prompted me to insist that she should go out and enjoy herself. It was not the custom of the country for ladies to go out alone, but in Juliette's case the circumstances were somewhat different. Firstly, her father, who had travelled a good deal, had brought her up more in the English fashion, and she was accorded vastly more liberty than is generally accorded to Brazilian girls. And secondly, she had proved herself so useful in the orchid branch of her father's business that he had allowed her to do much as she liked; and she had on more than one occasion gone out with some of the hunters into the very depths of the virgin forests, braving all the terrible dangers incidental to the pursuit of the blooms, and braving the hardships inseparable from it. In many ways Juliette was a wonderful woman. She was as clever as she was beautiful, and I who pen these lines declare solemnly that she was without a fault. Of course you will say I speak with a lover's enthusiasm. Very well, let it be so. But I think of her, and I see her, as an angel of God, with the golden light of heaven upon her wings. In the first hours of my awful sorrow, when my heart was rent in twain and my poor brain was bursting, I think I cursed God, and called impiously upon Heaven to justify the act which plunged me suddenly from the happiest man on earth to the depths of a blank, maddening, damnable despair. But Heaven was silent, and God in His infinite wisdom let me suffer until the awful revelation was made to me which I shall presently record. Then I bowed my head and prayed to Him to smite me. But I lived. And it is only now, when long years have passed, and I draw nearer and nearer to the hour when I shall take my departure to my love, who waits for me with outstretched arms on Heaven's frontiers, that I am able to write calmly and think calmly.

In this necessarily brief record I have shown no disposition to moralise; but I would venture to observe here that some lives are mysteries from their beginning to their end. The majority of people perhaps lead common, humdrum, vulgar, unemotional lives. And they die, never having known what it is to live; but few I fancy could be found who will venture to deny that in the words of the great English poet, "There are more things in Heaven and earth than are dreamt of in our philosophy." We are after all but poor weak things, with but a limited vision, and to few only is it given to pierce the veil that screens us from Sheol. But to return to the thread of my story.

Juliette yielded to my persuasions, and one morning she said, if I could spare her, she was going with an old and faithful attendant, one Jocelino who all his life had been in her father's employ, to a fazenda (farm), about a two leagues' ride, to see a negro who, according to a report, had secured a specimen of an orchid not at that time classified. In my sweet love's interest, as I thought then, I bade her go. And so her dear lips pressed mine, and promising that before the sun was below the horizon she would be at my side again, she went from me, and I looked upon her living face for the last time.

The sun gradually declined, and sank in gold and blood-red glory, but my love came not. One by one the great stars defined themselves in the deep blue heavens, but my love came not. The moon climbed up and flooded the earth with a mystic silver sheen, and yet she who was my heart and soul was still absent. A deadly fear stole upon me, and a strange foreboding turned me cold. I summoned Chrispiniano to my side and commanded him to get as many of his men together as he could, and, dividing them into parties, send them out to search for my missing love. He tried to reassure me that all was well. She had been benighted he said, and had found refuge at some fazenda. Old

Jocelino, he declared, knew every inch of the country for scores of leagues, and was so devotedly attached to the young mistress that he would gladly yield up his life for her.

"Yes, Senhor," continued Chrispiniano, "take my word for it. Your dear lady is safe with old Jocelino, and the morrow will be but young when your eyes will again be gladdened with the sight of your wife."

I admit that the foreman's words did afford me some comfort. Juliette, I thought, had allowed her enthusiasm to make her forgetful of the flight of time; and as night travelling in that country is out of the question, owing to the hundred and one dangers that beset the traveller who ventures to go forth in the darkness, she had sought the shelter of some hospitable roof, and so I countermanded the order for the search parties. But I passed an awful, restless night. No sleep came to me, and when the morning dawned I uttered a fervent "Thank God!" But that day was to prove worse than the preceding night—a day of awful, brain-corroding suspense. Instead of my love coming to me with the golden morn, no tidings of her were obtainable when the day was darkening to its close. Crippled as I was, I insisted on a horse being saddled, as I was determined to go and seek her; but when I attempted to mount into the saddle I found it to be physically impossible. So I had myself lifted up, but was unable to grip with my legs, and fell off again. I was therefore perforce compelled to desist in my attempt, but I sent into the town of Paraúna and offered a big reward to any one who would go in search of my dear one, and bring me tidings. In less than an hour a party of two dozen mounted men was formed, and, dividing into sixes, each set off in a different direction.

I will make no attempt to describe the horrible suspense of that night. When the sun began to glow again in the heavens it found me feverish and wellnigh distraught. The people at the station did their best to comfort me. They tried to cheer me; they spoke hopefully; they expressed themselves as certain that all would be well. But all their good-intentioned efforts were fruitless; some strange foreboding possessed me. If I looked up to the heavens it seemed to me as if I were looking through smoked glass; and during those heavy hours I fancied I heard a weird and hollow voice repeating in my ears these words:

"At last it is fulfilled! At last it is fulfilled!"

I had had myself placed on a couch in the veranda which commanded a view of the wood, and there I sat, and endured and suffered—not from the physical pain of my injured limb, for I felt nothing of it, but from mental torture.

As the afternoon waned I suddenly saw an Indian rushing down the road in an excited state. My heart leapt into my mouth, for I was sure he was the bearer of tidings. He tore up the steps of the veranda without any ceremony, and falling at my feet began to smite his breast, as is the custom of these people when they are the bearers of bad news. Then he wailed out his message:

"They have been found, and are being brought here; but they are both dead."

The words beat in upon my tortured brain like the blows from a sledge-hammer. I have only a vague, dream-like knowledge of what followed. In my frenzy I rose like a giant in wrath, and I hurled the poor Indian from me with such terrific force that concussion of the brain, as I understand, ensued, and for days his life was despaired of. But I knew naught of all this. A merciful Providence stunned me, and day after day went by and I lay like one entranced. During this blank, my sweet wife and old Jocelino were hidden from the sight of men for ever and ever, for quick burial in that climate is imperatively necessary.

Senhor Souza, my father-in-law, arrived in time to attend the funeral of his child, but the poor old man's heart was broken. They aver that when he turned from the graveside he looked twenty years older. All the light had gone out of his eyes, his back was bent, and he tottered and reeled and staggered like one who had the palsy. But a strong will-power upheld him for a time, because he had a duty to fulfil, which was to endeavour to bring the murderer or murderers to justice, for my dear one and Jocelino were both barbarously done to death.

You who have never suffered a great wrong at the hands of your fellow man may preach against vengeance; but as it is no virtue for a man to be honest when he has well-filled coffers, so

he who decries vengeance when he has not been wronged is but
an idle preacher. Let someone rob you of your most precious
inheritance, and see then if you can sit calmly and exclaim
"Kismet!"

Now listen to the story as it was gradually revealed to me
when, after lying stunned and dazed for nearly three weeks, I
began to realise once more that I was in the world of the living.
Listen to it, I say, and you will not be surprised that I thirsted
for vengeance. Up above the valley of Paraúna was a wild, bar-
ren, sun-scorched plateau which, after some three leagues or
so, dipped abruptly into a gorge of great extent filled with virgin
forest. Just where the plateau joined this belt of vegetation, the
searchers found the bodies of Juliette and Jocelino. They were
lying on their backs, and between them was a huge dead coral
snake, one of the most deadly reptiles found in the Brazils. As
it is not unusual for those who are bitten by this hideous creature to die almost immediately, so virulent and powerful is the
venom it injects into the blood of its victims, that it was not an
unnatural thought that both Juliette and the old servant had
been bitten by the reptile. But two things served to almost
instantly dispel this belief. The head of the snake was crushed,
and on the bosom of sweet Juliette's dress, as well as on the
shirt of the man, was a great patch of blood. And when the bodies were brought down and examined by a doctor it was discovered that both had died by being stabbed to the heart with a
long thin knife, and there was no sign or symptom of snake-
bite.

The dead coral snake lying between them, therefore, only
added to the mystery. The horses they had ridden returned after
many days by themselves. They had evidently wandered far and
suffered much, but they were dumb and could tell nothing of
the awful tale. They still carried their saddles and trappings.
Nothing had been stolen. The mystery deepened, but about the
mode of death there was no mystery. It was murder. Murder,
cruel, revolting, damnable. Where the bodies were found a diligent search was made for the weapon with which the crime was
committed, but it was not discovered. Jocelino, like all Brazilians
who live in the country, carried a hunting knife, but it was long

and broad, and it was resting unstained in its sheath attached to his belt.

Again I say it was murder—cruel, fiendish, deliberate murder. A crime so foul that it must have made the angels weep, and yet no angel in heaven stretched forth his hand to save my beloved from her awful end.

Bowed and broken though he was, Senhor Souza thirsted for vengeance on the slayer of his child, whom he loved with a tenderness passing words, and he offered a lavish reward to any one who would track the murderer down. To any individual of the people of the region the reward would have been a fortune, and Brazilian and Indian alike were stimulated to almost superhuman exertion. But the mystery defied their solving. The bodies lying side by side and the dead snake between them were elements in the puzzle to which no brain in that community seemed capable of finding an answer. As days went by and there was no result the reward was increased. The authorities themselves, usually lethargic and indifferent in Brazil, bestirred themselves in an unusual manner; but nothing came of it all. And as I began to drift back slowly to the living world, the old Senhor took to his bed, for his heart was broken. And it was decreed that he should rise no more as a man amongst men, for after lingering helpless and imbecile for many months, they carried him forth one golden day amidst the lamentations of his people, and laid him to rest beside his daughter.

And now what of myself? I have that still to tell which, for ghastly horror, has scarcely any parallel.

When I was able to realise the full measure of my sorrow, I knew that my beloved wife had been foully slain, and the motive for the crime was hard to define. But it seemed to me as I examined into the matter that probably she and the old servant had fallen victims to some strange superstition, and that might account for the dead snake being found between them. But whatever the motive that led to this diabolical destruction of two human beings, it was exceedingly desirable that the criminal should be discovered, so that he might be made an example of, as a terror to others who were inclined to evil-doing. In Brazil, unhappily, crime is common, but detection rare; at least, it is so in the wilder parts of the country. Money, however, is so greed-ily coveted by Brazilian and Indian alike that I watched with feverish yet hopeful anxiety the result of my father-in-law's large reward. And when I found there were no results, I added to it considerably myself, and I sent to Rio for a man who bore a high reputation as a detective. He was a half-breed in the Government employ, but he was just as much a failure as any one else. He learnt nothing. The mystery remained a mystery.

After this it seemed to me that further effort would be use-less, for weeks had passed since the commission of the deed, and every day that went by only served to increase the difficulty. Around us was an immense tract of country consisting of valley, mountain, and virgin forest. Most of the tract was sparsely populated. There were no telegraph wires, no railways.

As may be supposed, I felt reluctant to tear myself away from the spot where my sweet one slept—notwithstanding that the place was hateful to me, for it was associated with her mysteri-ous death. But duty called, and I had already been too long absent from my post. Everything, however, seemed hateful to me. Life itself had lost its savour, for the light of my life had gone out. No man could have been happier than I when I arrived in Paraúna. A few short weeks and that happiness had been turned to a sorrow so deep, so overwhelming that I sol-emnly declare I would have faced death with the most perfect resignation, and with the sure and certain hope that I should meet my darling in a world where there is neither sorrow nor sighing. But my departure could no longer be delayed, and my preparations being completed I had arranged to start on the morrow.

That night, after my evening meal, I sat alone, feeling miser-able, dejected, broken-hearted, when there came to me old José, one of the station hands. He had been born and brought up in the Paraúna district, and had never travelled fifty leagues away from his birthplace. He was intensely superstitious, intensely devout, and no less intensely bigoted; but he had been a faithful servitor, and though he was then bowed and frail he was still retained in the service.

"Senhor," he began, making a profound obeisance, "truly it is sad that the mystery of your sweet lady's and Jocelino's death has not been solved. But what money has failed to accomplish devilry may do."

He looked so strange that I thought he must have been indulging too freely in the native wine, and I asked sharply, "What do you mean?"

"Let not your anger fall on me, Senhor. I do not practise devilry myself; the saints guard me from it." Here he shuddered and crossed himself. "But I have heard some wonderful stories of Anita, though, God be praised, I have given her a wide berth." He crossed himself again.

"Anita! who is Anita?" I exclaimed impatiently.

"The devil's agent, Senhor," he answered, "as all the country knows for miles round; but few can look upon her and live."

"Do not befool me with this nonsense," I said. "I am sick at heart, and weary. Go. Leave me. I am in no mood to listen to silly stories."

"Nay, Senhor, I have no desire to befool you. But Anita—may the Virgin guard us from evil—is a witch, and they do say she has power over life and death. Perhaps—I only say perhaps— she might help you to bring the murderer to justice."

Although I was irritated and annoyed, and inclined to peremptorily order the old fellow out of my presence, I restrained myself, he seemed so earnest, so sincere. So I was induced to question him further, and I learnt that somewhere up in the mountains an old and withered woman dwelt in a cavern, and consorted with snakes and wild animals, but was shunned by human beings as a rule, for she was said to possess the evil eye, and it was generally believed that she could assume any shape, and drive men mad with fear. Anyway she was accredited with superhuman powers, and could show you your future as well as read your past.

I suppose that the frame of mind I was then in, coupled with a remembrance of the extraordinary incidents in Rio, had something to do with my desire to know more of this witch woman, and I asked José if he could take me to her. But he seemed startled by the bare suggestion, and again made the sign of the cross on his breast and forehead. No, he could not, and would not, though I poured gold in sackfuls at his feet; but there was Torquato, the negro in the village, he might for a consideration conduct me to Anita. Torquato was a dissolute, drunken fellow; by calling, a hunter, and used to making long and lonely journeys over the prairies and into the depths of the virgin forests. He was daring withal, and he had boasted in his cups that he had often sat with Anita, and she had shown him wonders. But of course no one believed him. They called him braggart and liar. Anxious to test if there was any truth in José's wonderful stories of Anita's power, I bade him fetch Torquato to me. What I had witnessed in Rio and what had happened since had removed my scepticism, if ever I had been sceptical, and now I was disposed to clutch at any desperate chance that promised to solve the mystery. In about an hour Torquato was introduced to me. He was a pure negro of powerful build, but beyond that was not remarkable. He was ignorant, but intelligent, and had the instincts of the born hunter. I questioned him closely. Yes, he knew Anita, he assured me, and could guide me to her. She was undoubtedly in league with the Evil One, he averred, and could perform miracles. The only way I could propitiate her would be by taking her an offering of tobacco and rum, for which she had a great partiality. My curiosity being aroused, I resolved to postpone my journey, and start off at daybreak, with Torquato as guide, to visit Anita, for he undertook to guide me, and said that as he had always propitiated the witch-woman he did not fear her, but he would not be answerable for me. I must take all risk. The weather, which up to then had been exceptionally fine, changed in the night, and the morning broke with a threatening and lowering sky. The natives predicted a great storm, but in that region a storm threatens long before it breaks, so I started off with Torquato, for I could not restrain my impatience; he carrying on his broad shoulders a knapsack containing, amongst other things, a quantity of rum and tobacco, in accordance with his advice. I had taken the precaution to fully arm myself. I had a double-barrelled hunting rifle, a six-chambered revolver, and a formidable hunting knife, as well as a plentiful supply of ammunition. Our road lay by a rough track that wound up precipitous slopes; then across a strip of prairie and forest; and finally we had to toil up a sun-smitten, weather-scarred mountain side. But during our journey we had caught no glimpse of the sun. The overcast sky had been growing blacker and blacker, and when we reached the mountain heavy drops of rain began to patter down, and from out the darkened heavens there leapt a blinding flash of fire that seemed to extend from horizon to horizon; it was followed instantly by a peal of thunder that crashed and reverberated until one could almost have imagined that the end of all things had come. So terrific are these storms in the highlands of Brazil that they are very alarming to any one unaccustomed to them; moreover, the deluge of rain that falls makes a shelter not only desirable but necessary. Fortunately, the rain was only spitting then, but Torquato began to look round anxiously for shelter, when, with quite startling suddenness, and as if she had risen from the earth, a woman stood before us, and demanded to know what we wanted there. She was the wildest, weirdest, strangest looking woman I have ever set eyes upon. She was almost a dwarf in stature, with misshapen limbs, and long skinny arms out of all proportion to the rest of her body. Her face—I declare it solemnly—was hardly human. It was more like a gargoyle from some old cathedral. A few scant grey hairs covered her head; and her chin and lips were also covered with a growth of wiry grey hair. Curiously enough, she had excellent teeth, which were in striking contrast to the rest of her appearance, and her eyes, deep sunk in their sockets and overhung with a pent-house fringe of wiry hair, were keen and brilliant as a hawk's, and seemed to look not at you but through you. The upper part of her body was clothed with a blanket, tied with a piece of rope at the waist, but her arms, legs, and feet were bare.

This singular-looking being was the woman we were seeking. Torquato recognised and saluted her, and spoke some words in the Indian language which I did not understand. She then addressed me in Portuguese, and as I marvelled at her perfect teeth and brilliant eyes, I marvelled still more at the clearness of her voice. Its tones were the dulcet tones of a young girl's. Indeed, I am not sure if that is a right description, for a girl's voice is often harsh, whereas Anita's was sweet and mellow. But in general appearance no more repulsive being could be imagined, and it was easy to understand how great an influence she could exert over the minds of superstitious people; nor am I ashamed to confess that I myself regarded her with a mixture of curiosity and fear.

"The Senhor seeks me?" she said.

"Yes."

"Follow then, and I will give you shelter from the storm."

She turned and led the way up the mountain. Although her feet were bare, the rocks made no impression upon her, and yet my feet were hurt, well shod as I was. Suddenly we came upon a sort of rocky platform before the entrance to a cave. It was on the very edge of a deep ravine—a rent in the earth, caused probably by an earthquake in the first instance, and gradually widened and deepened by the action of water. The sides of this ravine went down in broken precipices for thousands of feet, and were clothed with dense undergrowth and monstrous ferns, the home, as one could well imagine, of every reptile and loathsome insect to be found in Brazil. At the bottom of the ravine was a brawling river.

We had scarcely gained the shelter of the cave, at the mouth of which some wood ashes still smouldered, when the storm burst with appalling fury. We could see the lightning occasionally smite the rocks, tearing off great masses and hurling them into the dark depths of the ravine, where probably human foot had never yet trod; while the roll of the thunder was so awful that it seemed like the bursting up of the universe. Anita appeared to delight in the storm, and now and again she raised her long skinny arms straight up above her head and laughed like one demented. Presently she turned and motioned us to follow her, and led the way into the depths of the cavern, having first lighted a pine torch which she drew from a recess in the rocks, and plunged it into the glowing ashes. We went along a kind of corridor, but had to stoop low to avoid battering our skulls against the jagged roof. The floor was wet and soft, and Anita, in answer to my inquiries, said it was due to a natural spring of water which gave her a supply all the year round.

When we had traversed about a dozen yards, the roof got

higher in the passage, and after another few yards we found ourselves in a spacious chamber, with an almost perfectly level floor. Looking up, one could see nothing but darkness, so high was the roof, and beyond was what appeared to be another passage. The cavern, according to Anita, penetrated into the bowels of the mountains for more than a league, but she alone knew the secrets of those inner passages and chambers, and would reveal them to no one. I was led to inquire the cause of a strange rumbling noise I heard, and she told me it was due to a subterranean river.

In the chamber in which we found ourselves a hammock was stretched from two opposite points of rock, and afforded the witch good sleeping quarters, no doubt. There were also two or three wooden stools about, and on the floor, arranged on what appeared to be a square of carpet, was a miscellaneous collection of articles, including an old-fashioned sword, some peculiarly shaped goblets, a large wooden bowl, some human bones, several knives, including a hunting knife, an old gun, and various boxes. In another corner of the chamber I noticed a quantity of cooking utensils, which seemed to indicate that there was a good deal of the human about the old witch after all, and that if she loved solitude she also liked a certain amount of comfort. In such a country a woman of that kind was sure to get an evil reputation, whether she deserved it or not.

At my bidding Torquato unpacked his knapsack, and I presented my peace-offering of tobacco and rum, which the hag accepted with every sign of gratification, and filling a wooden cup with some of the rum, tossed it off at a draught. She had stuck the torch in a niche or hole in the rock, and its flickering, dancing flame threw a Rembrandt weirdness over the scene; and every time the woman's eyes caught the flame they glowed and glistened with such an unnatural light that I experienced a sense of creepiness which is hard to describe. The woman's whole appearance was so uncanny that while the hammock and the cooking utensils proclaimed her human, she seemed altogether unnatural, and, I am bound to add, devilish. She squatted on the floor while I and Torquato occupied stools. I told her the purpose of my errand; and the whole of the time while I was speaking she fixed her glowing eyes upon me, but they did not look at me, but through me. When I had finished my story she drew her knees up, rested her chin on them, and became very thoughtful; and though I spoke to her several times, she made no reply, and Torquato said she was in a trance. Whether that was really so or not I don't know. But when the silence had remained unbroken for nearly half an hour, she rose up slowly, and not without a certain dignity and grace, and turning her glowing eyes on me, said:

"In three days the Senhor will come here again when the sun is declining, and I will talk with him."

"But why not now," I asked, beginning to regard her as a humbug whose strange and uncouth appearance helped her to pass as a witch-woman.

"I have spoken. In three days," she replied, in such a decisive, commanding manner that I felt further parley would be use-less.

"And can Torquato come with me?" I asked.

"Yes. 'Tis well he should. Go."

There was no mistaking that peremptory order to depart; and, led by the negro, I groped my way back along the corridor, and was thankful to get into the open air. The rain had ceased, but the thunder still growled, the lightning still flashed; the air was delightful and refreshing after the rain. We stood for a few min-utes at the entrance to the cavern drinking in pure draughts of the cool fresh air, when suddenly there issued from the cave an eldritch scream, so piercing, so agonising that it seemed to indi-cate suffering beyond human endurance, so startling that I instinctively made a movement to rush back into the interior of the cavern with a view to ascertaining the cause of that awful cry. But Torquato gripped my arm like a vice, and drew me forc-ibly away. His eyes were filled with a scared expression, and his face told of the deadly fear working within.

"Come away, come," he whispered with suppressed expressed excitement. "Anita is quarrelling with her master the Devil, and he is scourging her."

I could hardly refrain from bursting into laughter at this state-ment; but Torquato looked so serious, so terribly in earnest, and evidently so firmly believed in what he said that I refrained. He continued to drag me along for some distance before he released my arm. He was then breathless and agitated, and sat down on a rock, and removing his large grass hat, he scraped the beads of perspiration from his forehead.

I was sorry, when I came to think of it, that I had allowed myself to be baulked in my intention to learn the cause of the strange wild cry which presumably came from Anita's lips; and for an instant I was tempted to reascend the mountain and enter the cavern again. But a glance at Torquato's scared face caused me to alter my mind, and in a few minutes we recommenced the descent, and in due time got back to the station. I had then come to feel a conviction that Anita was a humbug, and the scream was part of her imposition.

It was with something like feverish anxiety that I waited for the three days to pass. I really had no faith at that time in Anita's powers to tell me what I wished to know; but she was a remarkable creature, so uncanny and weird and wild in her aspects, so interesting as a study of abnormality that I was anxious to know more of her. I think I may safely say curiosity prompted me more than anything else, though I thought there was a bare possibility she *might* be able to clear up the mystery. When the morning of the third day came I found that Torquato was reluctant to again visit Anita, but at last I overcame his reluctance and scruples by the medium of silver dollars liberally bestowed, and without making known the objects of our journey we set off, well armed as before, and well provided with food in case of need. We hadn't the advantage of a clouded sky as on the previous visit, and the sun beat down with pitiless rays from the clear blue heavens. The heat was intense and tried my powers of endurance very much, but Torquato, being a child of the sun, was indifferent to the heat. As I suffered a good deal our progress was necessarily slow. Moreover, we had to exercise extreme caution on account of the numerous deadly snakes that lay in our path basking in the broiling sun, amongst them being the brilliant dazzling coral snake, one of the most beautiful but most deadly of the serpent tribe. It is a very vicious brute, and is said to be the only snake in Brazil that will attack a man without provocation—though in some districts the same thing is said about the Sorocotinga, which is also terribly deadly, and with no beauty to fascinate as in the case of the coral.

So slow was our progress that the sun was far down towards the western horizon when we reached our destination. We were startled by suddenly and unexpectedly coming upon Anita squatted on her haunches before the entrance to the cavern, while round her right arm was coiled a coral snake, its head moving backwards and forwards with a rhythmical sway. Instinctively I drew back, for the sight was so repulsive, but Anita rose and told us to follow her, and when I expressed my dislike of the snake, she waved her left hand before it, and its head and neck dropped straight down as if it were dead. I was amazed, for this power over the deadly reptile proved in itself that she was no ordinary being, although she might be an impostor in other respects.

Both Torquato and myself hesitated to follow the hag, when noticing this she turned angrily and cried:

"Why come you here if you are afraid? You seek knowledge which I alone can give you. If you are cowards, go at once and come here no more."

The taunt had its effect. I did my best to overcome the repugnance and even horror that I felt and entered the cavern with boldness, or at any rate assumed boldness, and Torquato followed. We reached the inner chamber where we had been on the previous visit. A burning torch was stuck in the rock, and threw a blood-red glare over the scene. I noted that the carpet was no longer there, but in its place stood a peculiarly shaped brazier containing living charcoal that gave off unpleasant fumes.

The old woman uncoiled the snake from her arm. It offered no resistance. It appeared to be perfectly passive. Then she coiled it into the figure of 8 at her feet, and told us to sit cross-legged on the ground as she did.

"You seek to know the past," she said, fixing her awful eyes upon me.

"Yes."

"But not the future?"

"No."

"'Tis well."

She began to make eccentric movements with both her hands before our eyes, and what followed was as a dream. I was conscious of a peculiar sense of languor stealing over me that was far from unpleasant. Presently I saw the woman snatch the burning torch from the niche in the rock and extinguish it, and we were plunged in Cimmerian gloom. A few minutes, as it seemed to me, passed, when a startling and peculiar light permeated the cavern. It proceeded from the brazier, from which rose a slender blue column of vapour that gave off apparently a phosphorescent glow. Anita was still standing, the snake was hanging from her neck, its head darting backwards and forwards viciously as if it were attacking its prey, while the woman with her long skinny arms described figures in the air. The blue, flowing column of smoke or vapour rose slowly, for it was dense and spread out mushroom shape until it filled every corner and crevice, and I seemed at last to be gazing through the medium of blue glass at a rolling prairieland over which the sun was shining brightly. The woman, the snake, the brazier, had faded away now, and only that vast stretch of sun-scorched prairie was visible. But presently, afar off, I saw two people on horseback. They gradually came nearer, and I recognised my sweet wife and Jocelino. Juliette was laughing merrily and seemed blithe and happy. They halted in the shadow of a rock, and hobbling their horses partook of their midday meal. That finished, and after a short siesta, they mounted their steeds and rode at a gallop towards a belt of virgin forest which they entered and were lost to my view. Presently they emerged, each bearing a mass of a peculiar orchid with flowers of the most brilliant colours. They dismounted again and knelt down on the ground to arrange the flowers in a more convenient way for carrying. From out of the forest, and all unobserved by them, a tall, powerful Indian hunter stole, and crept stealthily towards them. I wanted to cry out, to warn them, but I couldn't; I was spell-bound. The Indian reached them, and with an extraordinarily rapid sweep of his arm he plunged a long knife into my loved one's bosom. Jocelino half started up, but before he could offer resistance the arm swept around and the knife was plunged into his breast. With a grim sardonic grin on his features, the murderer wiped his dripping blade, and returned to the forest, reappearing after some lapse of time grasping a writhing coral snake, which he suddenly flung high into the air, and when it fell with a dull thud at his feet he struck it on the head with the handle of his knife.

He next dropped upon his knees and seemed to go through some form of incantation, throwing dirt upon his head, bowing his forehead to the ground, and raising his hand to heaven alternately, until at last he rose, laid the bodies side by side on their backs, and placed the snake at full length between them. Then the whole scene faded, and there was a blank.

Once more the same scene came before my eyes, but this time it was moonlight. The soft silver light threw a mysterious sheen over the landscape. I saw a man come out of the forest. It was the murderer. His face was filled with a look of concentrated horror, and he began to move slowly across the prairie, glancing about him in a nervous, agitated way. I became conscious at last that he was coming towards me, and I was filled with a fierce joy at the thought that when he came within reach I could strangle where he stood. The strangeness of it all is I could not move; I appeared to be rooted to the spot, but the Indian ever approached nearer to me, drawn by some power which he tried to resist, but against which he was helpless. And so nearer and nearer he came, and all the while that expression of concentrated horror was on his face. Although I could not move from the spot where I seemed to be rooted, fiercer and fiercer grew my joy, and I waved my hands about in expectant eagerness at the thought of being able at last to crush the worthless life out of the murderer of my sainted wife. On he came. I got frantic, I tugged and strained, but could not break away from the power that held me; my eyes ached with the strain put upon them, my pulses beat with a loud, audible noise, so it seemed to me; there was a burring and buzzing in my ears, an awful burning sensation was in my brain. I felt as if I were going mad with the horror of suspense.

At length the murderer came within my reach. I flung out my hands to seize him, when suddenly the moonlight faded, and there was total darkness. How long this darkness lasted I know not, but gradually light began to spread over the landscape again; the moon shone full once more. At my feet the Indian lay on his back. One knee was drawn up; one arm was bent under his body the other was raised up as if he were appealing to Heaven; his face was twisted and contorted with agony. He made no motion; he was stark and dead. Some strange irresistible fascination caused me to fix my gaze upon him, and as I watched I saw the face wither, the eyes fall into the sockets. Then the flesh of the arm turned green, and blue, and yellow, and gradually dropped rotten from the bones. Next the rest of the body began to rot away leaving the bones bare. Loathsome crawling things fed upon the decaying flesh, and cobras twisted themselves round his legs and arms.

The maddening, ghastly, gruesome horror of the scene was more than human brain could stand; and when a huge vulture suddenly descended and tore out the entrails and began to gorge upon them the climax was reached. With a mighty effort I burst the spell that enthralled me; uttered a great cry, and fell prone upon the ground.

What happened after that I know not. What I do know is I seemed suddenly to awake from a deep sleep. Above me the stars and moon were shining. From somewhere, far below, came the sound of falling water. The air was deliciously cool. I was covered with the skin of an animal, and squatted near me was Anita waving a palm leaf to keep the insects from my face. I glanced round and recognised that I was lying at the entrance to the cave.

"What does all this mean?" I asked.

"You have dreamed dreams," she answered. "You have seen that which is. Seek to know no more. But sleep, sleep, sleep." She repeated the word "sleep" with a sort of drowsy croon that seemed to lull and soothe me.

There was another blank. When I next awoke it was broad daylight and the sun was already high. I was lying on a bed of skins at the entrance to the cave. I sat up, and the sound of the falling water far below in the ravine sounded pleasantly. I called "Anita, Anita!" but there was no response. Presently I saw a figure crawling from the cavern. It was Torquato. He suddenly flung himself upon me, and wept and moaned like one distraught.

"Oh, master, master, what horrors!" he cried.

"Of what do you speak?" I asked. "Tell me all."

Gradually he regained control of himself. Then he recited to me all he had witnessed. It was identical with what I had seen. The murder, the mystery of the snake, the rotting corpse, the loathsome maggots, the vulture gnawing the entrails. Again I called Anita, but there was no response. I bade Torquato go into the cave and seek her, but he flatly refused. I struggled to my feet. I felt strangely ill and weak, and every now and then I shuddered as a remembrance of the horror came back. Still I was anxious to see Anita again and question her. I entered the cavern, but all was dark and silent. I groped my way forward for some distance and called once more. Only the echoes answered me. It was all so solemn, so awe-inspiring, so mysterious that I was glad to return to the fresh air again and to hear the voice of my companion. It was evident Anita did not intend to come to us, and so we slowly made our way down the mountain and reached the station at midday. And I had resolved by that time to make another visit to Anita. For several days, however, I had to keep my bed as I was feverish and ill. Then I summoned Torquato. He had also been ill, and when I asked him if he would go with me to Anita once more, he said, "No, not for a ton of gold"; so I sent to the little town for a notary. When he came I requested Torquato to tell the notary his marvellous experience and what he had seen. The notary wrote it down; Torquato signed it, and I appended a note over my own signature to the effect that I had witnessed the same scene. We next went before the Mayor of Paraúna and testified on oath to the correctness of our narrative, and that done, the strange document was deposited in the municipal archives of the town, where no doubt it can still be seen by the curious. My next step was to send out a party of trained hunters to the place where the bodies had been found, with the instructions to search for miles round for any indications of a human skeleton. They returned after many days, and reported that two leagues or so from the spot where the crime was committed, in a sandy sun-smitten waste, where only a few cacti grew, they came across the bleached skeleton of a man. The bones were falling apart, but it seemed as if one leg had been drawn up, one arm bent under the body, the other raised. Beside the body lay a long, rusty knife. Who the man was we never discovered. Even the knife was unlike those in use in that part of the country. That the skeleton was the skeleton of my wife's murderer I haven't a shadow of a doubt. Why he murdered her must remain a mystery until the secrets of all hearts be known. Who Anita was, and by what marvellous power she was able to show me the horrors she did, I have no knowledge. There are mysteries of the earth which the human brain cannot comprehend. It is given to only a few to see as I have seen and live.

For many years I have kept the awful secrets to myself, but the sands of my life are running low, and I resolved to give to the world the story of my strange experiences. To those who may be inclined to scoff I would repeat, "There are more things in heaven and earth than are dreamt of in your philosophy."

NOTE TO "THE MYSTIC SPELL."—Although Signor Roderick, who supplies the material for the foregoing remarkable story, suggests no theory for the murder of his wife and her attendant, any one who has travelled in the interior of Brazil will have no difficulty in doing so. The Indians are exceedingly superstitious, resentful, and blood-thirsty, as they are in many parts of Mexico. In the case of the Brazilians who inhabit the wild parts of the country, they regard certain parts of the virgin forests as their own special domains. As mentioned in the story, it is very unusual for a lady of good social position to be seen abroad, and the freedom which Juliette enjoyed in this respect was an innovation. Now if the vision that Signor Roderick saw, and which was conjured up by the mystic power of the witch-woman, was an accurate representation of the crime, it is easy to understand that some savage Indian, who had seen Juliette and Jocelino enter the forest and carry off the orchid bloom, resented it. Moreover, he may have regarded Juliette as an unnatural being, for probably he had never seen a white woman before. No women—save Indian women, and they but rarely—ever entered those deadly forests, the haunts and homes of the most venomous reptiles and the most savage animals, where there are plants exuding so virulent a poison that if but one drop falls on the flesh gangrene ensues; where loathsome insects fall upon the intruder from the trees and eat their way into his body; where the very air is deadly to those who breathe it, other than the native born. Juliette's presence, therefore, in such a place must have filled the Indian with dire alarm, and inflamed him with a desire to slay her. To him, no doubt, the crime would appear as a justifiable one. Anyway, with the stealth and cunning of his kind he crept after her, and his cruel knife drank her blood, and having killed her, it followed as a matter of course that he should kill her companion.

Now these Indians worship strange gods and sacrifice to them, and snake sacrifice is common, not only in the interior of Brazil, but in Mexico. The slaying of the coral snake was therefore a sacrifice on the part of the murderer. How he met his own death must ever remain a mystery. Probably he himself perished from snake bite, for though these Indians show an extraordinary fearlessness of poisonous reptiles, and will catch them and handle them in a way that makes a stranger shudder, they are not proof against their bites, although they boast that they possess infallible antidotes against the venom of the serpent. This, however, may be regarded as no more than a boast. In the forests of Brazil are to be found some of the most horrible snakes the world produces. Apart from the Cobra coral, or to give it its scientific name, *Elaps maregravii,* rattle snakes of the most virulent kind are found, and then there is the hideous Cascavel. It is said that death follows the bite of this snake almost immediately. The victim goes suddenly blind, and the flesh commences to peel off his bones through gangrene even before the breath is out of his body. The annual death roll from snake bite in all parts of South America is appalling; and, as might be supposed, the Indians who roam the forests and prairies, either as animal or orchid hunters, furnish a large percentage of the victims. It is a feasible theory, therefore, that the cruel murderer of Juliette and Jocelino lost his life through snake bite, probably the bite of the Cascavel.

As regards Anita, one can only suppose that she was possessed of some strange mesmeric or hypnotic power; but even if that were so, one is puzzled to understand how she was able to show her subjects the scene and incidents of that crime unless she herself knew them. The theory that suggests itself here is that during the three days' interval between Signor Roderick consulting her and his second visit, she had learned the story of the crime from some of the wandering Indians. She herself was an Indian and would be regarded by her tribe as "a wise woman." But whatever theory one likes to accept, it is a well-known fact attested over and over again by travellers that some of the Indian women of South America, especially in the neighbourhood of the Amazon, are gifted with the power of second sight and of forecasting the future. Such women are held in veneration by their own people, but Christians believe that they have an unholy alliance with the common enemy of mankind.

Lafcadio Hearn

Many authors at the turn of the century felt the pull of the Orient; however, precious few plunged into the Eastern cauldron with the fervour of Lafcadio Hearn (1850–1904), who spent the last years of his life as a Japanese citizen.

Hearn came from a tangled line of descent: born in Greece of a Greek mother and Irish father, he was raised in England and Ireland and ended up in America at the age of twenty.

He started work as a newspaper reporter, and by all accounts not a well-paid one, as he is widely described as having slept on the streets of New York for a while. He gained a fearsome reputation in America for digging up and writing the most lurid and repellent stories (something he continued to do when in Japan).

In 1890 he was sent to Japan on an assignment, fell in love with the country and stayed there for good. He delved into Japanese culture and literature, and wrote several books of stories and articles about the country and its folklore. Prominent among them are *In Ghostly Japan* (1899), *A Japanese Miscellany* (1901) and a really odd volume, *Shadowings* (1900).

When he died, Hearn had risen to become a lecturer in English literature at the Imperial University, Tokyo. His students must have found him an odd customer, especially if he spent his lessons musing on subjects like that of "Nightmare-Touch." This essay, taken from *Shadowings,* deals with a little-considered but nonetheless very true aspect of the fear of ghosts.

Nightmare-Touch

I

What *is* the fear of ghosts among those who believe in ghosts?

All fear is the result of experience—experience of the individual or of the race—experience either of the present life or of lives forgotten. Even the fear of the unknown can have no other origin. And the fear of ghosts must be a product of past pain.

Probably the fear of ghosts, as well as the belief in them, had its beginning in dreams. It is a peculiar fear. No other fear is so intense; yet none is so vague. Feelings thus voluminous and dim are super-individual mostly—feelings inherited—feelings made within us by the experience of the dead.

What experience?

Nowhere do I remember reading a plain statement of the reason why ghosts are feared. Ask any ten intelligent persons of your acquaintance, who remember having once been afraid of ghosts, to tell you exactly why they were afraid—to define the fancy behind the fear—and I doubt whether even one will be able to answer the question. The literature of folklore—oral and written—throws no clear light upon the subject. We find, indeed, various legends of men torn asunder by phantoms; but such gross imaginings could not explain the peculiar quality of ghostly fear. It is not a fear of bodily violence. It is not even a reasoning fear—not a fear that can readily explain itself—which would not be the case if it were founded upon definite ideas of physical danger. Furthermore, although primitive ghosts may have been imagined as capable of tearing and devouring, the common idea of a ghost is certainly that of a being intangible and imponderable.*

Now I venture to state boldly that the common fear of ghosts is *the fear of being touched by ghosts*—or, in other words, that the imagined Supernatural is dreaded mainly because of its imagined power to touch. Only to *touch*, remember!—not to wound or to kill.

But this dread of the touch would itself be the result of experience—chiefly, I think of prenatal experience stored up in the individual by inheritance, like the child's fear of darkness. And who can ever have had the sensation of being touched by ghosts? The answer is simple:—*Everybody who has been seized by phantoms in a dream.*

Elements of primeval fears—fears older than humanity—doubtless enter into the child-terror of darkness. But the more definite fears of ghosts may very possibly be composed with inherited results of dream-pain—ancestral experience of night-mare. And the intuitive terror of supernatural touch can thus be evolutionally explained.

Let me now try to illustrate my theory by relating some typical experiences.

II

When about five years old I was condemned to sleep by myself in a certain isolated room, thereafter always called the Child's Room. (At that time I was scarcely ever mentioned by name, but only referred to as "the Child.") The room was narrow, but very high, and, in spite of one tall window, very gloomy. It contained a fire-place wherein no fire was ever kindled; and the Child suspected that the chimney was haunted.

---

*I may remark there that in many old Japanese legends and ballads, ghosts are represented as having power to *pull off* people's heads. But so far as the origin of the fear of ghosts is concerned, such stories explain nothing—since the experiences that evolved the fear must have been real, not imaginary, experiences.

A law was made that no light should be left in the Child's Room at night—simply because the Child was afraid of the dark. His fear of the dark was judged to be a mental disorder requiring severe treatment. But the treatment aggravated the disorder. Previously I had been accustomed to sleep in a well-lighted room, with a nurse to take care of me. I thought that I should die of fright when sentenced to lie alone in the dark, and—what seemed to me then abominably cruel—actually *locked* into my room, the most dismal room of the house. Night after night when I had been warmly tucked into bed, the lamp was removed; the key clicked in the lock; the protecting light and the footsteps of my guardian receded together. Then an agony of fear would come upon me. Something in the black air would seem to gather and grow—(I thought that I could even *hear* it grow)—till I had to scream. Screaming regularly brought punishment; but it also brought back the light, which more than consoled for the punishment. This fact being at last found out, orders were given to pay no further heed to the screams of the Child.

Why was I thus insanely afraid? Partly because the dark had always been peopled for me with shapes of terror. So far back as memory extended, I had suffered from ugly dreams; and when aroused from them I could always *see* the forms dreamed of, lurking in the shadows of the room. They would soon fade out; but for several moments they would appear like tangible realities. And they were always the same figures . . . Sometimes, without any preface of dreams, I used to see them at twilight-time—following me about from room to room, or reaching long dim hands after me, from storey to storey, up through the interspaces of the deep stairways.

I had complained of these haunters only to be told that I must never speak of them, and that they did not exist. I had complained to everybody in the house; and everybody in the house had told me the very same thing. But there was the evidence of my eyes! The denial of that evidence I could explain only in two ways:—Either the shapes were afraid of big people, and showed themselves to me alone, because I was little and weak; or else the entire household had agreed, for some ghastly reason, to say what was not true. This latter theory seemed to me the more probable one, because I had several times perceived the shapes when I was not unattended;—and the consequent appearance of secrecy frightened me scarcely less than the visions did. Why was I forbidden to talk about what I saw, and even heard—on creaking stairways—behind waving curtains?

"Nothing will hurt you,"—this was the merciless answer to all my pleadings not to be left alone at night. But the haunters *did* hurt me. Only—they would wait until after I had fallen asleep, and so into their power—for they possessed occult means of preventing me from rising or moving or crying out.

Needless to comment upon the policy of locking me up alone with these fears in a black room. Unutterably was I tormented in that room—for years! Therefore I felt relatively happy when sent away at last to a children's boarding-school, where the haunters very seldom ventured to show themselves.

They were not like any people that I had ever known. They were shadowy dark-robed figures, capable of atrocious self-distortion—capable, for instance, of growing up to the ceiling, and then across it, and then lengthening themselves, head-downwards, along the opposite wall. Only their faces were distinct; and I tried not to look at their faces. I tried also in my dreams—or thought that I tried—to awaken myself from the sight of them by pulling at my eyelids with my fingers; but the eyelids would remain closed, as if sealed. . . . Many years afterwards, the frightful plates in Orfila's *Traité des Exhumés*, beheld for the first time, recalled to me with a sickening start the dream-terrors of childhood. But to understand the Child's experience, you must imagine Orfila's drawings intensely alive, and continually elongating or distorting, as in some monstrous anamorphosis.

Nevertheless the mere sight of those nightmare-faces was not the worst of the experiences in the Child's Room. The dreams always began with a suspicion, or sensation of something heavy in the air—slowly quenching will,—slowly numb-

ing my power to move. At such times I usually found myself
alone in a large unlighted apartment; and, almost simultane-
ously with the first sensation of fear, the atmosphere of the
room would become suffused, half-way to the ceiling, with a
sombre-yellowish glow, making objects dimly visible—though
the ceiling itself remained pitch-black. This was not a true
appearance of light: rather it seemed as if the black air were
changing colour from beneath. . . . Certain terrible aspects of
sunset, on the eve of storm, offer like effects of sinister colour.
. . . Forthwith I would try to escape—(feeling at every step a
sensation *as of wading*)—and would sometimes succeed in
struggling half-way across the room;—but there I would always
find myself brought to a standstill—paralyzed by some innom-
inable opposition. Happy voices I could hear in the next
room—I could see light through the transom over the door that
I had vainly endeavoured to reach—I knew that one loud cry
would save me. But not even by the most frantic effort could I
raise my voice above a whisper. . . . And all this signified only
that the Nameless was coming—was nearing—was mounting
the stairs. I could hear the step—booming like the sound of a
muffled drum—and I wondered why nobody else heard it. A
long, long time the haunter would take to come—malevolently
pausing after each ghastly footfall. Then, without a creak, the
bolted door would open—slowly, slowly—and the thing would
enter, gibbering soundlessly—and put out hands—and clutch
me—and toss me to the black ceiling—and catch me descending to toss me up again, and again, and again. . . . In those
moments the feeling was not fear: fear itself had been torpified
by the first seizure. It was a sensation that has no name in the
language of the living. For every touch brought a shock of
something infinitely worse than pain—something that thrilled
into the innermost secret being of me—a sort of abominable
electricity, discovering unimagined capacities of suffering in
totally unfamiliar regions of sentiency. . . . This was commonly
the work of a single tormentor; but I can also remember having
been caught by a group, and tossed from one to another—
seemingly for a time of many minutes.

III

Whence the fancy of those shapes? I do not know. Possibly from some impression of fear in earliest infancy; possibly from some experience of fear in other lives than mine. That mystery is forever insoluble. But the mystery of the shock of the touch admits of a definite hypothesis.

First, allow me to observe that the experience of the sensation itself cannot be dismissed as "mere imagination." Imagination means cerebral activity: its pains and its pleasures are alike inseparable from nervous operation, and their physical importance is sufficiently proved by their physiological effects. Dream-fear may kill as well as other fear; and no emotion thus powerful can be reasonably deemed undeserving of study.

One remarkable fact in the problem to be considered is that the sensation of seizure in dreams differs totally from all sensations familiar to ordinary walking life. Why this differentiation? How interpret the extraordinary massiveness and depth of the thrill?

I have already suggested that the dreamer's fear is most probably not a reflection of relative experience, but represents the incalculable total of ancestral experience of dream-fear. If the sum of the experience of active life be transmitted by inheritance, so must likewise be transmitted the summed experience of the life of sleep. And in normal heredity either class of transmissions would probably remain distinct.

Now, granting this hypothesis, the sensation of dream-seizure would have had its beginnings in the earliest phases of dream-consciousness—long prior to the apparition of man. The first creatures capable of thought and fear must often have dreamed of being caught by their natural enemies. There could not have been much imagining of pain in these primal dreams. But higher nervous development in later forms of being would have been accompanied with larger susceptibility to dream-pain. Still later, with the growth of reasoning-power, ideas of the supernatural would have changed and intensified the character of dream-fear. Furthermore, through all the course of evolution, heredity would have been accumulating the experience of such feeling. Under those forms of imaginative pain evolved through reaction of religious beliefs, there would persist some dim survival of savage primitive fears, and again, under this, a dimmer but incomparably deeper substratum of ancient animal-terrors. In the dreams of the modern child all these latencies might quicken—one below another—unfathomably—with the coming and the growing of nightmare.

It may be doubted whether the phantasms of any particular nightmare have a history older than the brain in which they move. But the shock of the touch would seem to indicate *some point of dream-contact with the total race-experience of shadowy seizure.* It may be that profundities of Self—abysses never reached by any ray from the life of sun—are strangely stirred in slumber, and that out of their blackness immediately responds a shuddering of memory, measureless even by millions of years.

Robert W. Chambers

Like many of the writers in this book, Robert W. Chambers (1865–1933) stumbled on his writing talent by accident and made his living at it thereafter.

Born in New York, he trained to be an artist and went to Paris to study art in 1886, with his friend the portrait painter Charles Dana Gibson. He studied and exhibited in Paris for seven years, but, on his return to New York in 1893, found it hard to get decent work. He did some magazine illustrations but at the same time tried writing a book based on his Paris experiences. The book, *In the Quarter* (1894), was published, perhaps much to his surprise, and he followed it up with an even more success- ful work, *The King in Yellow* (1895).

Chambers is remembered by macabre fiction enthusiasts for that second book. It has been reprinted steadily over the years and remains one of the finest, if somewhat erratic in quality, works in this genre. One story in particular, "The Yellow Sign," has been rightly included in many anthologies.

Sadly, Chambers only seldom returned to the macabre vein he had so richly mined in *The King in Yellow*. Throughout his writing career, which spanned forty years and encompassed over seventy books, he concentrated on detective and thriller novels, and society comedies and dramas. Just occasionally he wrote some more creepy stuff. There was a novel, *The Slayer of Souls* (1902) and some items in later books of short stories.

Happily, this one seems to have escaped reprinting since its original appearance. It comes from Chambers' 1915 book

Police!, a semi-humorous collection of fantasies, described by the author as "a few deathless truths concerning several mysteries recently and scientifically unravelled by a modest servant of science." Perhaps fittingly, it deals with an artist, though the problems encountered by this poor painter would be enough to deter the entire Royal Academy.

Un Peu d'Amour

When I returned to the plateau from my investigation of the crater, I realized that I had descended the grassy pit as far as any human being could descend. No living creature could pass that barrier of flame and vapour. Of that I was convinced.

Now, not only the crater but its steaming effluvia was utterly unlike anything I had ever before beheld. There was no trace of lava to be seen, or of pumice, ashes, or of volcanic rejecta in any form whatever. There were no sulphuric odours, no pungent fumes, nothing to teach the olfactory nerves what might be the nature of the silvery steam rising from the crater incessantly in a vast circle, ringing its circumference halfway down the slope.

Under this thin curtain of steam a ring of pale yellow flames played and sparkled, completely encircling the slope.

The crater was about half a mile deep; the sides sloped gently to the bottom.

But the odd feature of the entire phenomenon was this: the bottom of the crater seemed to be entirely free from fire and vapour. It was disk-shaped, sandy, and flat, about a quarter of a mile in diameter. Through my field-glasses I could see patches of grass and wild flowers growing in the sand here and there, and the sparkle of water, and a crow or two, feeding and walking about.

I looked at the girl who was standing beside me, then cast a glance around at the very unusual landscape.

We were standing on the summit of a mountain some two thousand feet high, looking into a cup-shaped depression or crater, on the edges of which we stood.

This low, flat-topped mountain, as I say, was grassy and quite treeless, although it rose like a truncated sugar-cone out of a wilderness of trees which stretched for miles below us, north, south, east, and west, bordered on the horizon by towering blue mountains, their distant ranges enclosing the forests as in a vast amphitheatre.

From the centre of this enormous green floor of foliage rose our grassy hill, and it appeared to be the only irregularity which broke the level wilderness as far as the base of the dim blue ranges encircling the horizon.

Except for the log bungalow of Mr. Blythe on the eastern edge of this grassy plateau, there was not a human habitation in sight, nor a trace of man's devastating presence in the wilderness around us.

Again I looked questioningly at the girl beside me and she looked back at me rather seriously.

"Shall we seat ourselves here in the sun?" she asked.

I nodded.

Very gravely we settled down side by side on the thick green grass.

"Now," she said, "I shall tell you why I wrote you to come out here. Shall I?"

"By all means, Miss Blythe."

Sitting cross-legged, she gathered her ankles into her hands, settling herself as snugly on the grass as a bird settles on its nest.

"The phenomena of nature," she said, "have always interested me intensely, not only from the artistic angle but from the scientific point of view.

"It is different with Father. He is a painter; he cares only for the artistic aspects of nature. Phenomena of a scientific nature bore him. Also, you may have noticed that he is of a—a slightly impatient disposition."

I had noticed it. He had been anything but civil to me when I arrived the night before, after a five-hundred mile trip on a mule, from the nearest railroad—a journey performed entirely alone and by compass, there being no trail after the first fifty miles.

To characterize Blythe as slightly impatient was letting him down easy. He was a selfish, bad-tempered old pig.

"Yes," I said, answering her, "I did notice a negligible trace of impatience about your father."

She flushed.

"You see I did not inform my father that I had written to you. He doesn't like strangers; he doesn't like scientists. I did not dare tell him that I had asked you to come out here. It was entirely my own idea. I felt that I *must* write you because I am positive that what is happening in this wilderness is of vital scientific importance."

"How did you get a letter out of this distant and desolate place?" I asked.

"Every two months the storekeeper at Windflower Station sends in a man and a string of mules with staples for us. The man takes our further orders and our letters back to civilization."

I nodded.

"He took my letter to you—among one or two others I sent—"

A charming colour came into her cheeks. She was really extremely pretty. I liked that girl. When a girl blushes when she speaks to a man he immediately accepts her heightened colour as a personal tribute. This is not vanity: it is merely a proper sense of personal worthiness.

She said thoughtfully:

"The mail bag which that man brought to us last week contained a letter which, had I received it earlier, would have made my invitation to you unnecessary. I'm sorry I disturbed you."

"*I* am not," said I, looking into her beautiful eyes.

I twisted my mustache into two attractive points, shot my cuffs, and glanced at her again, receptively.

She had a far-away expression in her eyes. I straightened my necktie. A man, without being vain, ought to be conscious of his own worth.

"And now," she continued, "I am going to tell you the various reasons why I asked so celebrated a scientist as yourself to come here."

I thanked her for her encomium.

"Ever since my father retired from Boston to purchase this hill and the wilderness surrounding it," she went on, "ever since he came here to live a hermit's life—a life devoted solely to painting landscapes—I also have lived here all alone with him.

"That is three years, now. And from the very beginning— from the very first day of our arrival, somehow or other I was conscious that there was something abnormal about this corner of the world."

She bent forward, lowering her voice a trifle:

"Have you noticed," she asked, "that so many things seem to be *circular* out here?"

"Circular?" I repeated, surprised.

"Yes. That crater is circular; so is the bottom of it; so is this plateau, and the hill; and the forests surrounding us; and the mountain ranges on the horizon."

"But all this is natural."

"Perhaps. But in those woods, down there, there are, here and there, great circles of crumbling soil—*perfect* circles a mile in diameter."

"Mounds built by prehistoric man, no doubt."

She shook her head:

"These are not prehistoric mounds."

"Why not?"

"Because they have been freshly made."

"How do you know?"

"The earth is freshly upheaved; great trees, partly uprooted, slant at every angle from the sides of the enormous piles of newly upturned earth; sand and stones are still sliding from the raw ridges."

She leaned nearer and dropped her voice still lower:

"More than that," she said, "my father and I both have seen one of these huge circles *in the making!*"

"What!" I exclaimed, incredulously.

"It is true. We have seen several. And it enrages Father."

"Enrages?"

"Yes, because it upsets the trees where he is painting land-scapes, and tilts them in every direction. Which, of course, ruins his picture; and he is obliged to start another, which vexes him dreadfully."

I think I must have gaped at her in sheer astonishment.

"But there is something more singular than that for you to investigate," she said calmly. "Look down at that circle of steam which makes a perfect ring around the bowl of the crater, halfway down. Do you see the flicker of fire under the vapour?"

"Yes."

She leaned so near and spoke in such a low voice that her fragrant breath fell upon my cheek:

"In the fire, under the vapours, there are little animals."

"What!"

"Little beasts live in the fire—slim, furry creatures, smaller than a weasel. I've seen them peep out of the fire and scurry back into it. . . . *Now* are you sorry that I wrote you to come? And will you forgive me for bringing you out here?"

An indescribable excitement seized me, endowing me with a fluency and eloquence unusual:

"I thank you from the bottom of my heart!" I cried; "—from the depths of a heart the emotions of which are entirely and exclusively of scientific origin!"

In the impulse of the moment I held out my hand; she laid hers in it with charming diffidence.

"Yours is the discovery," I said. "Yours shall be the glory. Fame shall crown you; and perhaps if there remains any reflected light in the form of a by-product, some modest and negligible little ray may chance to illuminate me."

Surprised and deeply moved by my eloquence, I bent over her hand and saluted it with my lips.

She thanked me. Her pretty face was rosy.

It appeared that she had three cows to milk, new-laid eggs to gather, and the construction of some fresh butter to be accomplished.

At the bars of the grassy pasture slope she dropped me a curtsey, declining very shyly to let me carry her lacteal paraphernalia.

So I continued on to the bungalow garden, where Blythe sat

on a camp stool under a green umbrella, painting a picture of something or other.

"Mr. Blythe!" I cried, striving to subdue my enthusiasm. "The eyes of the scientific world are now open upon this house! The searchlight of Fame is about to be turned upon you—"

"I prefer privacy," he interrupted. "That's why I came here. I'll be obliged if you'll turn off that searchlight."

"But, my dear Mr. Blythe—"

"I want to be let alone," he repeated irritably. "I came out here to paint and to enjoy privately my own paintings."

If what stood on his easel was a sample of his pictures, nobody was likely to share his enjoyment.

"Your work," said I, politely, "is—is—"

"Is what!" he snapped. "*What* is it—if you think you know?"

"It is entirely, so to speak, *per se*—by itself—"

"What the devil do you mean by that?"

I looked at his picture, appalled. The entire canvas was one monotonous vermilion conflagration. I examined it with my head on one side, then on the other side; I made a funnel with both hands and peered intently through it at the picture. A menacing murmuring sound came from him.

"Satisfying—exquisitely satisfying," I concluded. "I have often seen such sunsets—"

"What!"

"I mean such prairie fires—"

"Damnation!" he exclaimed. "I'm painting a bowl of nasturtiums!"

"I was speaking purely in metaphor," said I with a sickly smile. "To me a nasturtium by the river brink is more than a simple flower. It is a broader, grander, more magnificent, more stupendous symbol. It may mean anything, everything—such as sunsets and conflagrations and Götterdämmerungs! Or—" and my voice was subtly modulated to an appealing and persuasive softness—"it may mean nothing at all—chaos, void, vacuum, negation, the exquisite annihilation of what has never even existed."

He glared at me over his shoulder. If he was infected by Cubist tendencies he evidently had not understood what I said.

"If you won't talk about my pictures I don't mind your investigating this district," he grunted, dabbing at his palette and plastering a wad of vermilion upon his canvas; "but I object to any public invasion of my artistic privacy until I am ready for it."

"When will that be?"

He pointed with one vermilion-soaked brush towards a long, low, log building.

"In that structure," he said, "are packed one thousand and ninety-five paintings—all signed by me. I have executed one or two every day since I came here. When I have painted exactly ten thousand pictures, no more, no less, I shall erect here a gallery large enough to contain them all.

"Only real lovers of art will ever come here to study them. It is five hundred miles from the railroad. Therefore, I shall never have to endure the praises of the dilettante, the patronage of the idler, the vapid rhapsodies of the vulgar. Only those who understand will care to make the pilgrimage."

He waved his brushes at me:

"The conservation of national resources is all well enough—the setting aside of timber reserves, game preserves, bird refuges, all these projects are very good in a way. But I have dedicated this wilderness as a last and only refuge in all the world for true Art! Because true Art, except for my pictures, is, I believe, now practically extinct! . . . You're in my way. Would you mind getting out?"

I had sidled around between him and his bowl of nasturtiums, and I hastily stepped aside. He squinted at the flowers, mixed up a flamboyant mess of colour on his palette, and daubed away with unfeigned satisfaction, no longer noticing me until I started to go. Then:

"What is it you're here for, anyway?" he demanded abruptly. I said with dignity:

"I am here to investigate those huge rings of earth thrown up in the forest as by a gigantic mole." He continued to paint for a few moments: "Well, go and investigate 'em," he snapped. "I'm not infatuated with your society."

"What do you think they are?" I asked, mildly ignoring his wretched manners.

"I don't know and I don't care, except, that sometimes when I begin to paint several trees, the very trees I'm painting are suddenly heaved up and tilted in every direction, and all my work goes for nothing. *That* makes me mad! Otherwise, the matter has no interest for me."

"But what in the world could cause—"

"I don't know and I don't care!" he shouted, waving palette and brushes angrily. "Maybe it's an army of moles working all together under the ground; maybe it's some species of circular earthquake. I don't know! I don't care! But it annoys me. And if you can devise any scientific means to stop it, I'll be much obliged to you. Otherwise, to be perfectly frank, you bore me."

"The mission of Science," said I solemnly, "is to alleviate the inconveniences of mundane existence. Science, therefore, shall extend a helping hand to her frailer sister, Art—"

"Science can't patronize Art while I'm around!" he retorted. "I won't have it!"

"But, my dear Mr. Blythe—"

"I won't dispute with you, either! I don't like to dispute!" he shouted. "Don't try to make me. Don't attempt to inveigle me into discussion! I know all I want to know. I don't want to know anything you want me to know, either!"

I looked at the old pig in haughty silence, nauseated by his conceit.

After he had plastered a few more tubes of vermilion over his canvas he quieted down, and presently gave me an oblique glance over his shoulder.

"Well," he said, "what else are you intending to investigate?"

"Those little animals that live in the crater fires," I said bluntly.

"Yes," he nodded, indifferently, "there are creatures that live somewhere in the fires of that crater."

"Do you realize what an astounding statement you are making?" I asked.

"It doesn't astound *me*. What do I care whether it astounds you or anybody else? Nothing interests me except Art."

"But—"

"I tell you nothing interests me except Art!" he yelled. "Don't dispute it! Don't answer me! Don't irritate me! I don't care whether anything lives in the fire or not! Let it live there!"

"But have you actually seen live creatures in the flames?"

"Plenty! *Plenty!* What of it? What about it? Let 'em live there, for all I care. I've painted pictures of 'em, too. That's all that interests me."

"What do they look like, Mr. Blythe?"

"Look like? I don't know! They look like weasels or rats or bats or cats or—stop asking me questions! It irritates me! It depresses me! Don't ask any more! Why don't you go in to lunch? And—tell my daughter to bring me a bowl of salad out here. *I've* no time to stuff myself. Some people have. I haven't. You'd better go in to lunch. . . . And tell my daughter to bring me seven tubes of Chinese vermilion with my salad!"

"You don't mean to mix—" I began, then checked myself before his fury.

"I'd rather eat vermilion paint on my salad than sit here talking to *you!*" he shouted.

I cast a pitying glance at this impossible man, and went into the house. After all, he was *her* father. I *had* to endure him.

After Miss Blythe had carried to her father a large bucket of lettuce leaves, she returned to the veranda of the bungalow.

A delightful luncheon awaited us; I seated her, then took the chair opposite.

A delicious omelette, fresh biscuit, salad, and strawberry preserves, and a tall tumbler of iced tea imbued me with a sort of mild exhilaration.

Out of the corner of my eye I could see Blythe down in the garden, munching his lettuce leaves like an ill-tempered rabbit, and daubing away at his picture while he munched.

"Your father," said I politely, "is something of a genius."

"I am so glad you think so," she said gratefully. "But don't tell him so. He has been surfeited with praise in Boston. That is why we came out here."

"Art," said I, "is like Science, or tobacco, or toothwash. Every man to his own brand. Personally, I don't care for his kind. But who can say which is the best kind of anything? Only the consumer. Your father is his own consumer. He is the best judge of what he likes. And that is the only true test of art, or anything else."

"How delightfully you reason!" she said. "How logically, how generously!"

"Reason is the handmaid of Science, Miss Blythe."

She seemed to understand me. Her quick intelligence surprised me, because I myself was not perfectly sure whether I had emitted piffle or an epigram.

As we ate our strawberry preserves we discussed ways and means of capturing a specimen of the little fire creatures which, as she explained, so frequently peeped out at her from the crater fires, and, at her slightest movement, scurried back again into the flames. Of course I believed that this was only her imagination. Yet, for years I had entertained a theory that fire supported certain unknown forms of life.

"I have long believed," said I, "that fire is inhabited by living organisms which require the elements and temperature of active combustion for their existence—micro-organisms, but not," I added smilingly, "any higher type of life."

"In the fireplace," she ventured diffidently, "I sometimes see curious things—dragons and snakes and creatures of grotesque and peculiar shapes."

I smiled indulgently, charmed by this innocently offered contribution to science. Then she rose, and I rose and took her hand in mine, and we wandered over the grass towards the crater, while I explained to her the difference between what we imagine we see in the glowing coals of a grate fire and my own theory that fire is the abode of living animalculae.

On the grassy edge of the crater we paused and looked down the slope, where the circle of steam rose, partly veiling the pale flash of fire underneath.

"How near can we go?" I inquired.

"Quite near. Come; I'll guide you."

Leading me by the hand, she stepped over the brink and we began to descend the easy grass slope together.

There was no difficulty about it at all. Down we went, nearer and nearer to the wall of steam, until at last, when but fifteen feet away from it, I felt the heat from the flames which sparkled below the wall of vapour.

Here we seated ourselves upon the grass, and I knitted my brows and fixed my eyes upon this curious phenomenon, striving to discover some reason for it.

Except for the vapour and the fires, there was nothing whatever volcanic about this spectacle, or in the surroundings.

From where I sat I could see that the bed of fire which encircled the crater, and the wall of vapour which crowned the flames, were about three hundred feet wide. Of course this barrier was absolutely impassable. There was no way of getting through it into the bottom of the crater.

A slight pressure from Miss Blythe's fingers engaged my attention; I turned towards her, and she said:

"There is one more thing about which I have not told you. I feel a little guilty, because *that* is the real reason I asked you to come here."

"What is it?"

"I think there are emeralds on the floor of that crater."

"Emeralds!"

"I *think* so." She felt in the ruffled pocket of her apron, drew out a fragment of mineral, and passed it to me.

I screwed a jeweller's glass into my eye and examined it in astonished silence. It was an emerald; a fine, large, immensely valuable stone, if my experience counted for anything. One side of it was thickly coated with vermilion paint.

"Where did this come from?" I asked in an agitated voice.

"From the floor of the crater. Is it *really* an emerald?"

I lifted my head and stared at the girl incredulously.

"It happened this way," she said excitedly. "Father was painting a picture up there by the edge of the crater. He left his palette on the grass to go to the bungalow for some more tubes of colour. While he was in the house, hunting for the colours which he wanted, I stepped out on the veranda, and I saw some crows alight near the palette and begin to stalk about in the grass. One bird walked right over his wet palette; I stepped out and waved my sun-bonnet to frighten him off, but he had both feet in a sticky mass of Chinese vermilion, and for a moment was unable to free himself.

"I almost caught him, but he flapped away over the edge of the crater, high above the wall of vapour, sailed down onto the crater floor, and alighted.

"But his feet bothered him; he kept hopping about on the bottom of the crater, half running, half flying; and finally he took wing and rose up over the hill.

"As he flew above me, and while I was looking up at his vermilion feet, something dropped from his claws and nearly struck me. It was that emerald."

When I had recovered sufficient composure to speak steadily, I took her beautiful little hand in mine.

"This," said I, "is the most exciting locality I have ever visited for purposes of scientific research. Within this crater may lie millions of value in emeralds. You are probably, today, the wealthiest heiress upon the face of the globe!"

I gave her a winning glance. She smiled, shyly, and blushingly withdrew her hand.

For several exquisite minutes I sat there beside her in a sort of heavenly trance. How beautiful she was! How engaging—how sweet—how modestly appreciative of the man beside her, who had little beside his scientific learning, his fame, and a kind heart to appeal to such youth and loveliness as hers!

There was something about her that delicately appealed to me. Sometimes I pondered what this might be; sometimes I wondered how many emeralds lay on that floor of sandy gravel below us.

Yes, I loved her. I realised it now. I could even endure her father for her sake. I should make a good husband. I was quite certain of that.

I turned and gazed upon her, meltingly. But I did not wish to startle her, so I remained silent, permitting the chaste language of my eyes to interpret for her what my lips had not yet murmured. It was a brief but beautiful moment in my life.

"The way to do," said I, "is to trap several dozen crows, smear their feet with glue, tie a ball of Indian twine to the ankle of every bird, then liberate them. Some are certain to fly into the crater and try to scrape the glue off in the sand. Then," I added, triumphantly, "all we have to do is to haul in our birds and detach the wealth of Midas from their sticky claws!"

"That is an excellent suggestion," she said gratefully, "but I can do that after you have gone. All I wanted you to tell me was whether the stone is a genuine emerald."

I gazed at her blankly.

"You are here for purposes of scientific investigation," she added, sweetly. "I should not think of taking your time for the mere sake of accumulating wealth for my father and me."

There didn't seem to be anything for me to say at that moment. Chilled, I gazed at the flashing ring of fire.

And, as I gazed, suddenly I became aware of a little, pointed muzzle, two pricked-up ears, and two ruby-red eyes gazing intently out at me from the mass of flames.

The girl beside me saw it, too.

"Don't move!" she whispered. "That is one of the flame creatures. It may venture out if you keep perfectly still."

Rigid with amazement, I sat like a stone image, staring at the most astonishing sight I had ever beheld.

For several minutes the ferret-like creature never stirred from where it crouched in the crater fire; the alert head remained pointed towards us; I could even see that its thick fur must have possessed the qualities of asbestos, because here and there a hair or two glimmered incandescent; and its eyes, nose, and whiskers glowed and glowed as the flames pulsated around it.

After a long while it began to move out of the fire, slowly, cautiously, cunning eyes fixed on us—a small, slim, wiry, weasel-like creature on which the sunlight fell with a vitreous glitter as it crept forward into the grass.

Then, from the fire behind, another creature of the same sort appeared, another, others, then dozens of eager, lithe, little animals appeared everywhere from the flames and began to frisk and play and run about in the grass and nibble the fresh, green, succulent herbage with a snipping sound quite audible to us.

One came so near my feet that I could examine it minutely.

Its fur and whiskers seemed heavy and dense and like asbestos fibre, yet so fine as to appear silky. Its eyes, nose, and claws were scarlet, and seemed to possess a glassy surface.

I waited my opportunity, and when the little thing came nosing along within reach, I seized it.

Instantly it emitted a bewildering series of whistling shrieks, and twisted around to bite me. Its body was icy.

"Don't let it bite!" cried the girl. "Be careful, Mr. Smith!"

But its jaws were toothless; only soft, cold gums pinched me, and I held it twisting and writhing, while the icy temperature of its body began to benumb my fingers and creep up my wrist, paralyzing my arm; and its incessant and piercing shrieks deafened me.

In vain I transferred it to the other hand, and then passed it from one hand to the other, as one shifts a lump of ice or a hot potato, in an attempt to endure the temperature: it shrieked and squirmed and doubled, and finally wriggled out of my stiffened and useless hands, and scuttled away into the fire.

It was an overwhelming disappointment. For a moment it seemed unendurable.

"Never mind," I said, huskily, "if I caught one in my hands, I can surely catch another in a trap."

"I am so sorry for your disappointment," she said, pitifully.

"Do *you* care, Miss Blythe?" I asked.

She blushed.

"Of course I care," she murmured.

My hands were too badly frost-nipped to become eloquent. I merely sighed and thrust them into my pockets. Even my arm was too stiff to encircle her shapeful waist. Devotion to Science had temporarily crippled me. Love must wait. But, as we ascended the grassy slope together, I promised myself that I would make her a good husband, and that I should spend at least part of every day of my life in trapping crows and smearing their claws with glue.

That evening I was seated on the veranda beside Wilna—Miss Blythe's name was Wilna—and what with gazing at her and fitting together some of the folding box-traps which I always carried with me—and what with trying to realise the pecuniary magnificence of our future existence together, I was exceedingly busy when Blythe came in to display, as I supposed, his most recent daub to me.

The canvas he carried presented a series of crimson speckles, out of which burst an eruption of green streaks—and it made me think of stepping on a caterpillar.

My instinct was to placate this impossible man. He was *her* father. I meant to honour him if I had to assault him to do it.

"Supremely satisfying!" I nodded, chary of naming the subject. "It is a stride beyond the art of the future: it is a flying leap out of the Not Yet into the Possibly Perhaps! I thank you for enlightening me, Mr. Blythe. I am your debtor."

He fairly snarled at me:

"What are *you* talking about!" he demanded.

I remained modestly mute.

To Wilna he said, pointing passionately at his canvas:

"The crows have been walking all over it again! I'm going to paint in the woods after this, earthquakes or no earthquakes. Have the trees been heaved up anywhere recently?"

"Not since last week," she said, soothingly. "It usually happens after a rain."

"I think I'll risk it then—although it did rain early this morning. I'll do a moonlight down there this evening." And, turning to me: "If you know as much about science as you do about art you won't have to remain here long—I trust."

"What?" said I, very red.

He laughed a highly disagreeable laugh, and marched into the house. Presently he bawled for dinner, and Wilna went away. For her sake I had remained calm and dignified, but presently I went out and kicked up the turf two or three times; and, having foozled my wrath, I went back to dinner, realising that I might as well begin to accustom myself to my future father-in-law.

It seemed that he had a mania for prunes, and that's all he permitted anybody to have for dinner.

Disgusted, I attempted to swallow the loathly stewed fruit, watching Blythe askance as he hurriedly stuffed himself, using a tablespoon, with every symptom of relish.

"Now," he cried, shoving back his chair, "I'm going to paint a moonlight by moonlight. Wilna, if Billy arrives, make him comfortable, and tell him I'll return by midnight." And without taking the trouble to notice me at all, he strode away towards the veranda, chewing vigorously upon his last prune.

"Your father," said I, "is eccentric. Genius usually is. But he is a most interesting and estimable man. I revere him."

"It is kind of you to say so," said the girl, in a low voice.

I thought deeply for a few moments, then:

"Who is 'Billy?'" I inquired, casually.

I couldn't tell whether it was a sudden gleam of sunset light on her face, or whether she blushed.

"Billy," she said softly, "is a friend of Father's. His name is William Green."

"Oh."

"He is coming out here to visit—Father—I believe."

"Oh. An artist; and doubtless of mature years."

"He is a mineralogist by profession," she said, "—and somewhat young."

"Oh."

"Twenty-four years old," she added. Upon her pretty face was an absent expression, vaguely pleasant. Her blue eyes became dreamy and exquisitely remote.

I pondered deeply for a while:

"Wilna?" I said.

"Yes, Mr. Smith?" as though aroused from agreeable meditation.

But I didn't know exactly what to say, and I remained uneasily silent, thinking about that man Green and his twenty-four years, and his profession, and the bottom of the crater, and Wilna—and striving to satisfy myself that there was no logical connection between any of these.

"I think," said I, "that I'll take a bucket of salad to your father."

Why I should have so suddenly determined to ingratiate myself with the old grouch I scarcely understood: for the construction of a salad was my very best accomplishment.

Wilna looked at me in a peculiar manner, almost as though

she were controlling a sudden and not unpleasant inward desire to laugh.

Evidently the finer and more delicate instincts of a woman were divining my motive and sympathizing with my mental and sentimental perplexity.

So when she said: "I don't think you had better go near my father," I was convinced of her gentle solicitude in my behalf.

"With a bucket of salad," I whispered softly, "much may be accomplished, Wilna." And I took her little hand and pressed it gently and respectfully. "Trust all to me," I murmured.

She stood with her head turned away from me, her slim hand resting limply in mine. From the slight tremor of her shoulders I became aware how deeply her emotion was now swaying her. Evidently she was nearly ready to become mine.

But I remained calm and alert. The time was not yet. Her father had had his prunes, in which he delighted. And when pleasantly approached with a bucket of salad he could not listen otherwise than politely to what I had to say to him. Quick action was necessary—quick but diplomatic action—in view of the imminence of this young man Green, who evidently was *persona grata* at the bungalow of this irritable old dodo.

Tenderly pressing the pretty hand which I held, and saluting the finger-tips with a gesture which was, perhaps, not wholly ungraceful, I stepped into the kitchen, washed out several heads of lettuce, deftly chopped up some youthful onions, constructed a seductive French dressing, and, stirring together the crisp ingredients, set the savoury masterpiece away in the ice-box, after tasting it. It was delicious enough to draw sobs from any pig.

When I went out to the veranda, Wilna had disappeared. So I unfolded and set up some more box-traps, determined to lose no time.

Sunset still lingered beyond the chain of western mountains as I went out across the grassy plateau to the cornfield.

Here I set and baited several dozen aluminium crow-traps, padding the jaws so that no injury could be done to the birds when the springs snapped on their legs.

Then I went over to the crater and descended its gentle,

grassy slope. And there, all along the borders of the vapoury wall, I set box-traps for the lithe little denizens of the fire, baiting every trap with a handful of fresh, sweet clover which I had pulled up from the pasture beyond the cornfield.

My task ended, I ascended the slope again, and for a while stood there immersed in pleasurable premonitions.

Everything had been accomplished swiftly and methodically within the few hours in which I had first set eyes upon this extraordinary place—everything!—love at first sight, the delightfully lightning-like wooing and winning of an incomparable maiden and heiress; the discovery of the fire creatures; the solving of the emerald problem.

And now everything was ready, crow-traps, fire-traps, a bucket of irresistible salad for Blythe, a modest and tremulous avowal for Wilna as soon as her father tasted the salad and I had pleasantly notified him of my intentions concerning his lovely offspring.

Daylight faded from rose to lilac; already the mountains were growing fairy-like under that vague, diffuse lustre which heralds the rise of the full moon. It rose, enormous, yellow, unreal, becoming imperceptibly silvery as it climbed the sky and hung aloft like a stupendous arc-light flooding the world with a radiance so white and clear that I could very easily have written verses by it, if I wrote verses.

Down on the edge of the forest I could see Blythe on his camp-stool, madly besmearing his moonlit canvas, but I could not see Wilna anywhere. Maybe she had shyly retired somewhere by herself to think of me.

So I went back to the house, filled a bucket with my salad, and started towards the edge of the woods, singing happily as I sped on feet so light and frolicsome that they seemed to skim the ground. How wonderful is the power of love!

When I approached Blythe he heard me coming and turned around.

"What the devil do *you* want?" he asked with characteristic civility.

"I have brought you," said I gaily, "a bucket of salad."

"I don't want any salad!"

"W-what?"

"I never eat it at night."

I said confidently:

"Mr. Blythe, if you will taste this salad I am sure you will not regret it." And with hideous cunning I set the bucket beside him on the grass and seated myself near it. The old dodo grunted and continued to daub the canvas; but presently, as though forgetfully, and from sheer instinct, he reached down into the bucket, pulled out a leaf of lettuce, and shoved it into his mouth.

My heart leaped exultantly. I had him!

"Mr. Blythe," I began in a winningly modulated voice, and, at the same instant, he sprang from his camp-chair, his face distorted.

"There are onions in this salad!" he yelled. "What the devil do you mean! Are you trying to poison me! What are you following me about for, anyway? Why are you running about under foot every minute?"

"My dear Mr. Blythe," I protested—but he barked at me, kicked over the bucket of salad, and began to dance with rage.

"What's the matter with you, anyway!" he bawled. "Why are you trying to feed me? What do you mean by trying to be attentive to me!"

"I—I admire and revere you—"

"No you don't!" he shouted. "I don't want you to admire me! I don't desire to be revered! I don't like attention and politeness! Do you hear! It's artificial—out of date—ridiculous! The only thing that recommends a man to me is his bad manners, bad temper, and violent habits. There's some meaning to such a man, none at all to men like you!"

He ran at the salad bucket and kicked it again.

"They all fawned on me in Boston!" he panted. "They ran about under foot! They bought my pictures! And they made me sick! I came out here to be rid of 'em!"

I rose from the grass, pale and determined.

"You listen to me, you old grouch!" I hissed. "I'll go. But before I go I'll tell you why I've been civil to you. There's only one reason in the world: I want to marry your daughter! And I'm going to do it!"

I stepped nearer him, menacing him with outstretched hand:

"As for you, you pitiable old dodo, with your bad manners and your worse pictures, and your degraded mania for prunes, you are a necessary evil, that's all, and I haven't the slightest respect for either you or your art!"

"Is that true?" he said in an altered voice.

"True?" I laughed bitterly. "Of course it's true, you miserable dauber!"

"D-dauber!" he stammered.

"Certainly! I said 'dauber,' and I mean it. Why, your work would shame the pictures on a child's slate!"

"Smith," he said unsteadily, "I believe I have utterly mis-judged you. I believe you are a good deal of man, after all—"

"I'm man enough," said I, fiercely, "to go back, saddle my mule, kidnap your daughter, and start for home. And I'm going to do it!"

"Wait!" he cried. "I don't want you to go. If you'll remain I'll be very glad. I'll do anything you like. I'll quarrel with you, and you can insult my pictures. It will agreeably stimulate us both. Don't go, Smith—"

"If I stay, may I marry Wilna?"

"If you ask me I won't let you!"

"Very well!" I retorted, angrily. "Then I'll marry her any-way!"

"That's the way to talk! Don't go, Smith. I'm really beginning to like you. And when Billy Green arrives you and he will have a delightfully violent scene—"

"What!"

He rubbed his hands gleefully.

"He's in love with Wilna. You and he won't get on. It is going to be very stimulating for me—I can see that! You and he are going to behave most disagreeably to each other. And I shall be exceedingly unpleasant to you both! Come, Smith, promise me that you'll stay!"

Profoundly worried, I stood staring at him in the moonlight, gnawing my mustache.

"Very well," I said, "I'll remain if—"

Something checked me, I did not quite know what for a moment. Blythe, too, was staring at me in an odd, apprehensive way. Suddenly I realised that under my feet the ground was stirring.

"Look out!" I cried; but speech froze on my lips as beneath me the solid earth began to rock and crack and billow up into a high, crumbling ridge, moving continually, as the sod cracks, heaves up, and crumbles above the subterranean progress of a mole.

Up into the air we were slowly pushed on the ever-growing ridge; and with us were carried rocks and bushes and sod, and even forest trees.

I could hear their tap-roots part with pistol-like reports; see great pines and hemlocks and oaks moving, slanting, settling, tilting crazily in every direction as they were heaved upward in this gigantic disturbance.

Blythe caught me by the arm; we clutched each other, balancing on the crest of the steadily rising mound.

"W-what is it?" he stammered. "Look! It's circular. The woods are rising in a huge circle. What's happening? Do you know?"

Over me crept a horrible certainty that *something living* was moving under us through the depths of the earth—something that, as it progressed, was heaping up the surface of the world above its unseen and burrowing course—something dreadful, enormous, sinister, and *alive!*

"Look out!" screamed Blythe; and at the same instant the crumbling summit of the ridge opened under our feet and a fissure hundreds of yards long yawned ahead of us.

And along it, shining slimily in the moonlight, a vast, viscous, ringed surface was moving, retracting, undulating, elongating, writhing, squirming, shuddering.

"It's a worm!" shrieked Blythe. "Oh, God! It's a mile long!"

As in a nightmare we clutched each other, struggling frantically to avoid the fissure; but the soft earth slid and gave way under us, and we fell heavily upon that ghastly, living surface.

Instantly a violent convulsion hurled us upwards; we fell on it again, rebounding from the rubbery thing, strove to regain our feet and scramble up the edges of the fissure, strove madly

while the mammoth worm slid more rapidly through the rock-
ing forests, carrying us forward with a speed increasing.

Through the forest we tore, reeling about on the slippery
back of the thing, as though riding on a ploughshare, while trees
clashed and tilted and fell from the enormous furrow on every
side; then, suddenly out of the woods into the moonlight, far
ahead of us we could see the grassy upland heave up, cake,
break, and crumble above the burrowing course of the monster.

"It's making for the crater!" gasped Blythe; and horror
spurred us on, and we scrambled and slipped and clawed the
billowing sides of the furrow until we gained the heaving top
of it.

As one runs in a bad dream, heavily, half-paralyzed, so ran
Blythe and I, toiling over the undulating, tumbling upheaval
until, half-fainting, we fell and rolled down the shifting slope
onto solid and unvexed sod on the very edges of the crater.

Below us we saw, with sickened eyes, the entire circumference of the crater agitated, saw it rise and fall as avalanches of
rock and earth slid into it, tons and thousands of tons rushing
down the slope, blotting from our sight the flickering ring of
flame, and extinguishing the last filmy jet of vapour.

Suddenly the entire crater caved in and filled up under my
anguished eyes, quenching for all eternity the vapour wall, the
fire, and burying the little denizens of the flames, and perhaps
a billion dollars' worth of emeralds under as many billion tons of
earth.

Quieter and quieter grew the earth as the gigantic worm
bored straight down into depths immeasurable. And at last the
moon shone upon a world that lay without a tremor in its milky
lustre.

"I shall name it *Verma gigantica*," said I, with a hysterical sob;
"but nobody will ever believe me when I tell this story!"

Still terribly shaken, we turned towards the house. And, as we
approached the lamplit veranda, I saw a horse standing there
and a young man hastily dismounting.

And then a terrible thing occurred; for, before I could even shriek, Wilna had put both arms around that young man's neck, and both of his arms were clasping her waist.

Blythe was kind to me. He took me around the back way and put me to bed.

And there I lay through the most awful night I ever experienced, listening to the piano below, where Wilna and William Green were singing *Un Peu d'Amour*.

John C. Shannon

John C. Shannon, alas, is shrouded in mystery. All that is known about him is that he lived in Walsall, where he published several stories in the *Walsall Advertiser* in the 1890s, and later collected them into two volumes, *Who Shall Condemn* (1894), published in Walsall, and the later *Zylgrahof* (1901).

He also published a novel, *D'Aubise* (1900) and that seems to have been his total output. He never made enough of a mark to have been included in any directory of the day, so who he was and what he did for a living remains a puzzle.

"The Spirit of the Fjord" comes from *Zylgrahof* and is a neat little story in an unusual locale.

The Spirit of the Fjord

The S.S. *Valda* was steaming slowly over the broad expanse of one of the largest of the Norwegian Fjords. So slow was her progress that the lazy parting of the water at her prow was almost invisible.

Dinner was just over. Her passengers were seated in small groups about her spacious deck. Some talked, their conversation punctuated by frequent laughter; others passed the time indulging in the various amusements available on such a trip. Two or three of the men were pacing the deck arm-in-arm, smoking.

The sun was setting, flooding the water with dazzling glory. On the horizon the hills lay low and black. Nearer were a few solitary islands, their every detail clearly visible in the departing blaze. Afar was a solitary, tiny sail—the only sign of life, except the graceful steamship *Valda,* whose masts and rigging shewed blackly-delicate against the golden sky.

The sun sank swiftly till its lower edge disappeared behind the hills, and the distant mountains glowed blood-red. The light crept stealthily over the water, enveloped the vessel, passed over it, and finally outlined the lonely islands with a band of liquid fire. Then there succeeded that mysterious, purple twilight peculiar to those latitudes.

As the sun disappeared, a young man, who had been leaning alone over the vessel's stern contemplating the scene, turned from the rail and walked along the deck into the smoking-room. He was tall, well-proportioned, had a well-knit, athletic figure, and handsome, debonair face.

During the few days he had been aboard the *Valda,* Gilbert

Amyn had succeeded in making himself extremely popular. Of a sunny disposition, prone to see the ludicrous side of most things, he was an ideal shipmate. Ever willing to join in any amusement, he was in universal request, and his appearance was hailed with delight. Immediately half-a-dozen voices invited him to join in one or other of the various games in progress.

Soon, as the deck became deserted, cards were abandoned, and the men strolled out to seat themselves in the vacated deck-chairs for a final smoke in the cool night air before going below.

As they smoked, the Captain joined the circle. Wishing his passengers "Good evening," he sat down and lighted a cigar.

Taking advantage of a lull in the conversation, Amyn addressed the company in general.

"As I was leaning over the stern about an hour ago," he remarked, "a most extraordinary thing happened. I don't know whether it was what you would call an optical illusion or not. At any rate, it has puzzled me considerably. If it won't bore you, I will tell you what I saw. Perhaps between us we may evolve a solution of the mystery."

It is curious how small a thing awakens interest aboard ship. The men gathered on the *Valda*'s deck immediately evinced their eagerness to hear what Amyn had to say. The Doctor, acting as spokesman, and lighting a fresh cigar, replied for all:—

"Fire away, Amyn, by all means let us hear your experience."

Thus adjured, Amyn told his story:—

"I was watching the sunset from the stern of the vessel. I confess to a weakness for sunsets, and this evening's was passing beautiful. Over yonder the hills were intensely black, presenting a vivid contrast to the luminous yellow radiance cast by the setting sun. Overhead the sky was a beautiful tinge midway between crimson and gold. The whole scene was lovely in the extreme. I was watching more particularly the long trail made by our propellor, noting the varied tints the foam assumed as it danced in the brilliant light, when suddenly, a short distance away, I saw a skiff. Now, I can swear that a moment before the Fjord was absolutely deserted, except for our own vessel and a solitary fishing-boat over by the distant mountains. Whence, then, came the skiff?

"As I watched it drew swiftly nearer, and I saw that it was occupied by a girl. She was quite alone, standing erect in the boat, her hands loosely clasped before her. The skiff moved rapidly towards me, though the girl had no oar, and did not appear, so far as I could see, to make any movement which would account for its progress. How it advanced, therefore, was as much a mystery as it coming.

"These questions, however, faded into insignificance beside the amazing beauty of the girl. I have seen many beautiful women, but never so lovely a face.

"Its colouring was fresh and delicate. The skin was tinged with a dainty rose-flush. The mouth was small; the eyes large and blue, their half-shy, half-tender, wholly trusting glance making them dangerously fascinating. But her hair was her crowning glory. It fell around her in rich, wavy masses, completely enveloping the upper part of her form. The colour of molten gold, it flamed about her like some gorgeous aureole as the waning sunlight kissed it.

"Clad in white from head to foot, her simple robe was exquisitely broidered, and was confined at her waist by a curiously wrought silver girdle. The skiff in which she stood was of ancient shape and very small.

"Such was the vision. To say that I was astonished is but feebly to express my feelings. Whither the girl and boat had come was beyond my power to fathom.

"As she approached I obtained a clearer view of her, but the nearer she came the more beautiful she seemed. It was the type of face for love of which men commit crimes; the dangerous beauty of a Circe; the witching countenance of a Siren.

"Soon she drew abreast of our vessel, but as she came within a stone's throw the skiff turned aside and shot away towards the mountains. As it receded I strained my eyes in my eagerness to catch the last glimpse of that lovely form. When some little distance away she turned her head and smiled at me; and, smiling, I think she looked more beautiful than before. Then, as I watched, though I am not conscious of having removed my eyes for a moment, she vanished. It was most mysterious."

"A very curious occurrence altogether, Amyn. You are quite

sure, old fellow, that you were not enjoying an afternoon siesta?" laughingly remarked the Doctor.

"Spare me your chaff, if you please, Doctor. I was most certainly not asleep, though I was almost tempted to think I was the victim of a waking dream."

"I think I can give Mr. Amyn some explanation of the phenomenon," interjected the Captain.

Every man settled himself to listen. Amyn's story had evidently excited their imaginations.

"First of all, are you superstitious?"

"Not the least," replied Amyn, somewhat surprised.

"I only ask because if you are, what I am about to say may affect your nerves and considerably startle you. In short, are you a believer in omens or presentiments?"

"No, Captain, I'm not," answered Amyn, emphatically.

"Good. Then I'll tell you as briefly as possible the story of the 'Spirit of the Fjord.'"

Clearing his throat, and flicking the ash from his cigar, the Captain related the following legend:—

"Many years ago there stood on the brow of a cliff over yonder," pointing to the distant mountains, "a Castle. It was strongly fortified, and occupied a position practically impregnable.

"It was the home of a warrior Norseman, of whose life-history the legend does not speak. He does not seem to have been of the slightest importance to the story.

"He had a beautiful wife, but unfortunately, up to a certain point in their lives, children had been denied them. Sorely troubled, the woman prayed to the Norwegian Fates to give her a child. Pitying her, they promised that she should have a daughter. In process of time the child was born, and the mother's heart rejoiced.

"Norwa grew and throve as the years passed, ever increasing in beauty. Gradually, however, the mother forgot the kindness of the Norns. Her heart grew arrogant because of the loveliness which had been entrusted to her, till at last her pride became so great that it burst all bounds. She openly boasted to her kinsfolk concerning the exceeding beauty of her child, asserting that nothing could surpass it. In extravagant language she eulogized it, saying that to her, and to her only, had been born one so lovely. The Fates grew angry at the vain-glorious boasting of the woman, and one night, as she slept, they appeared to her in a dream to upbraid her for her folly.

"In fear, the mother prayed to be forgiven. Willingly the Norns extended their forgiveness, but as the penalty of her boasting they decreed that henceforth the child's beauty should be accursed and the death of many. Humbly the mother pleaded, but they would not relent, and as the morning broke they left her weeping.

"Years passed. Norwa's beauty increased exceedingly, till the fame of it spread throughout the length and breadth of Norway. From far and near came knights and warriors eager to win her hand. The mother's heart was heavy as she saw these things, for the words of the Fates echoed continually in her memory.

"Men of noble blood, of mighty deeds—the greatest the land could boast—sought Norwa's love. But the girl's heart seemed formed of ice. She laughed at their words, sending them away sorrowing or gnashing their teeth at the bitterness of her speech. Then came the fulfilment of the curse the Norns had laid upon her. Of all those who came, confident of success, few were heard of more. Many vanished as though the earth had opened and swallowed them. Others were found dead on the path leading to the Castle gate, a look of nameless terror on their faces. Others, missing their way in the darkness, fell over the precipice and were either drowned in the sea or dashed to pieces on the rocks below.

"Awesome tales began to be whispered concerning these things, and Frelda, Norwa's mother, sorrowed over the terrible thing her folly had brought to pass. As for the beautiful Norwa, she did but laugh, singing softly to herself as she stood by the edge of the cliff looking out over the sea. What were the lives of men to her? Of their own free will they sought her. If her beauty slew them, what mattered it?

"So time passed, till the Castle of Geiranger came to be regarded as a haunted place, and dark stories were recounted concerning Norwa, Maiden of the Ice Heart.

"Then came a noble knight. His manner was winsome, his

words pleasing. He had come, he said, to woo and win the lady Norwa, and for many days he sojourned at the Castle.

"At this time, Frelda, Norwa's mother, wearied by much sorrow, died, and was buried by the edge of the cliff, in sight of the great Fjord, whose constant murmur sighed plaintively above her grave.

"At last the knight told his love to Norwa. With a radiant smile she listened to his impassioned words. As he ceased, she laughed in his face, a silvery, rippling laugh which maddened him. Fiercely he demanded if she loved him. Gaily the maiden answered "Nay," and laughed again.

"In silence he turned on his heel and left her. His face was not good to see. He strode to the brow of the precipice, and descending a steep and dangerous path reached the shore. There he entered a boat and rowed out over the waters of the Fjord.

"Dark clouds gathered, lightning flashed, thunder rolled; great waves rose and threatened to engulf the slender craft in which he rode.

"Seeing from the Castle battlements the peril her knight endured, love came into the Ice Heart of the maiden. With a wild cry she dashed down the path to the shore and, entering her own tiny skiff, followed her lover out into the storm. Nearer, nearer she approached, till at last, when only a few boat-lengths separated them, a huge wave swept over his craft and he sank from sight. A blinding flash of lightning split the heavens; a deafening crash of thunder rent the air; darkness covered the sea. Again the lightning blazed forth. The maiden and her craft had also vanished. Afar on the cliff the Castle, struck by the electric fluid, was burning fiercely.

"Such gentlemen, is the legend of the 'Spirit of the Fjord.' It is a typical Norwegian myth, but at the same time one little known. Now comes the most extraordinary part of the story. The spirit of Norwa is still supposed to haunt the Fjords, and so the legend runs, whoever sees her dies suddenly within a short time. Now, I hope what I have just said does not make you feel uneasy."

"Not the least," answered Amyn, nonchalantly, "it would

require considerably more than an old legend of that description to affect me. Nevertheless, it is all very interesting. I am
infinitely obliged to you. Of course I presume, after what I have
just heard, that I have actually seen Norwa, 'Spirit of the
Fjord.'"

"Don't you think, Captain, that it is most ludicrous to hear
members of the civilization of the twentieth century gravely
discussing the ghosts of people who lived so long ago?" asked
one of the men present.

"It certainly does," replied the Captain, "but I am a superstitious man, and must confess, though you may laugh, that I fully
believe Amyn has seen the 'Spirit of the Fjord.'"

Silence fell on the group as the Captain ceased speaking.
Presently he remarked:—

"I don't wish to appear a 'croaker,' or in any way to alarm you,
but I happen to have had aboard the *Valda* three other passengers who have, at various times and under similar circumstances
to those Mr. Amyn has just described, seen the 'Spirit of the
Fjord.' One, going ashore, fell between the companion-ladder
and the launch. Striking his head violently, he became unconscious, and never came to the surface again. The second was
thrown from a *stolkjaerre* over a precipice and instantly killed.
The third died suddenly in the smoking-room whilst playing
cards. Of course, these may simply have been startling coincidences, but to a superstitious man like myself they appeal
strongly."

"It is, indeed, strange," commented Amyn, "that such things
should have happened at such times, but after all, one often
hears of similar coincidences. You will pardon me saying so, but
personally, I attach no importance whatever to facts like these."

The Captain's other listeners seemed far more impressed
than Amyn.

Two days afterwards a fellow-passenger was pacing the deck
with him. The two men were smoking and chatting confiden-
tially.

Again the sun was setting, lighting up the scene with golden
glory. Suddenly Amyn gripped his companion tightly by the
arm. Pointing out over the water, he exclaimed, excitedly:—

"There is precisely what I saw the other evening. The 'Spirit of the Fjord' the Captain calls her. Can't you see her—yonder in that skiff?"

His friend looked in the direction indicated, but could see nothing.

"That is very strange," said Amyn, thoughtfully, "I certainly saw her a moment ago, but now she has vanished."

Three days afterwards, in the evening, it being somewhat cold, the male section of the passengers was in the smoking-room. Presently the Captain joined them. Someone introduced the subject of the legend he had told them a night or two previously. As he answered he glanced quickly round the room.

"By the way," he asked, "where is our friend Amyn?"

Scarcely were the words spoken than the door opened and the scared face of the man who had been walking with Amyn appeared.

"Will you come with me at once, Doctor?" he asked, directly addressing that gentleman. "Something very serious has happened."

The Doctor immediately complied with the request. The Captain, signing to the others, remained seated to await his report.

The two men soon reappeared. Their faces wore a grave, awe-stricken expression. The Doctor addressed the Captain:—

"Sir," said he, "it is my painful duty to inform you that an hour ago Mr. Amyn died very suddenly." His words created a profound sensation. "Of course I shall have to make a post-mortem examination, but at present his death is a mystery. Mr. Winterton, will you please explain to the Captain under what circumstances you found Mr. Amyn?"

"Not feeling very well, I did not go down to dinner this evening, thinking that a walk would relieve the headache and depression from which I was suffering. I had taken three or four turns up and down the deck when I noticed that someone was leaning over the stern-rail. Seeing that it was neither one of the crew, nor yet an officer, I was curious to know who was omitting dinner from the day's programme.

"I walked aft. As I approached I recognized poor Amyn. He

was standing in an attitude of strained attention, evidently watching something intently. I might say that last evening I was walking with him when, pointing over the water he asked me if I could see a girl in a skiff. Thinking he was again under the impression that he saw the vision, I went up to him and laughingly remarked, 'Are you receiving another visit from the Spirit of the Fjord, Amyn?'"

"He did not answer, nor, indeed, did he appear to have heard me. Going nearer I said, 'You seem very much absorbed in your dreams, old fellow. Are you not going down to dinner?'"

"Still he took no notice. I saw that his eyes were staring fixedly out over the water, that his face was pale as though from intense excitement. For a minute or two I looked at him in silence. Then a curious feeling came over me—a feeling of dread I never wish to experience again. I tapped him on the shoulder. My touch disturbed the perfect balance of his body. He fell full length upon the deck. He was quite dead."

An ejaculation of horror escaped Winterton's listeners. After a moment, he added:—

"For a minute or two I was too overcome to move. I did not wish to make a scene during dinner, or unnecessarily to alarm the other passengers, so obtaining assistance, we carried him down to his cabin and laid him in his bunk. Then I sat by him, dazed and horror-stricken, till I came up here to ask the Doctor to come and see him. I tell you, gentlemen, the shock was very terrible."

The Captain listened in silence, then beckoning to the Doctor and muttering some words under his breath, he rose and, followed by his brother-officer, left the room.

For some time after he had gone no one spoke. Winterton, who had been sitting next to the Captain, broke the silence.

"Did any of you hear what the Captain said just before he went out?" he asked.

No one had.

"My God, the Spirit of the Fjord again," repeated Winterton, gravely.

Frank Frankfort Moore

Here is a grand piece of Edwardian terror from one of the era's most prolific writers—who was also Bram Stoker's brother-in-law.

Frank Frankfort Moore (1855–1931) was born in Limerick and became a journalist when he was twenty. He travelled all over the world—India, the West Indies, South America and Africa—and in his spare time turned out fiction, plays and poetry.

His first book, the poetry collection *Flying from a Shadow* (1872) was published when he was seventeen but his first big success was the novel *I Forbid the Banns* (1893).

He published over eighty books, including novels, short story collections, verse, westerns, biographies (including books on Byron, Fanny Burney and Goldsmith), as well as books for the Christian Knowledge Society and even a book on collecting antique furniture! His last book, *The Awakening of Helen*, was published in 1929.

Moore and Stoker were friends; both settled in London and they married the Balcombe sisters. Moore's wife Grace died in 1901.

Like Stoker, Moore tried his hand at the occasional ghost story and this one comes from his 1904 collection *The Other World*. It certainly deserves a second chance but it warrants careful reading.

The Strange Story
of Northavon Priory

When Arthur Jephson wrote to me to join his Christmas party at Northavon Priory, I was set wondering where I had heard the name of this particular establishment. I felt certain that I had heard the name before, but I could not recollect for the moment whether I had come upon it in a newspaper report of a breach of promise of marriage or in a Blue-Book bearing upon Inland Fisheries: I rather inclined to the belief that it was in a Blue-Book of some sort. I had been devoting myself some years previously to an exhaustive study of this form of literature; for being very young, I had had a notion that a Blue-Book education was essential to any one with parliamentary aspirations. Yes, I had, I repeat, been very young at that time, and I had not found out that a Blue-Book is the *oubliette* of inconvenient facts.

It was not until I had promised Arthur to be with him on Christmas Eve that I recollected where I had read something about Northavon Priory, and in a moment I understood how it was I had acquired the notion that the name had appeared in an official document. I had read a good deal about this Priory in a curious manuscript which I had unearthed at Sir Dennis le Warden's place in Norfolk, known as Marsh Towers. The document, which, with many others, I found stowed away in a wall-cupboard in the great library, purported to be a draft of the evidence taken before one of the Commissions appointed by King Henry VIII to inquire into the abuses alleged to be associated with certain religious houses throughout England. An ancestor of Sir Dennis's had, it appeared, been a member of one of these Commissions, and he had taken a note of the evidence which he had in the course of his duties handed to the King.

The parchments had, I learned, been preserved in an iron coffer with double padlocks, but the keys had been lost at some remote period, and then the coffer had been covered over with lumber in a room in the east tower overlooking the moat, until an outbreak of fire had resulted in an overturning of the rubbish and a discovery of the coffer. A blacksmith had been employed to pick the locks, which he did with a sledge-hammer; but it was generally admitted that his energy had been wasted when the contents of the box were made known. Sir Dennis cared about nothing except the improvement of the breed of horses through the agency of race meetings, so the manuscripts of his painstaking ancestor were bundled into one of the presses in the library, some, however, being reserved by the intelligent housekeeper in the still-room to make jam-pot covers—a purpose for which, as she explained to me at considerable length, they were extremely well adapted.

I had no great difficulty in deciphering those that came under my hand, for I had had considerable experience of the tricks of early English writers; and as I read I became greatly interested in all the original "trustie and well-beelou'd Sir Denice le Warden" had written. The frankness of the evidence which he had collected on certain points took away my breath, although I had been long accustomed to the directness with which some of the fifteenth-century people expressed themselves.

Northavon Priory was among the religious houses whose practices had formed the subject of the inquiry, and it was the summary of Sir Denice's notes regarding the Black Masses alleged to have been celebrated within its walls that proved so absorbing to me. The bald account of the nature of these orgies would of itself have been sufficient, if substantiated, to bring about the dissolution of all the order in England. The Black Mass was a pagan revel, the details of which were unspeakable, though their nature was more than hinted at by the King's Commissioner. Anything so monstrously blasphemous could not be imagined by the mind of man, for with the pagan orgie there was mixed up the most solemn rite of the Mass. It ws celebrated on the night of Christmas Eve, and at the hour of midnight the celebration culminated in an invocation to the devil, written so as to parody an office of the Church, and, according to the accounts of some witnesses, in a human sacrifice. Upon this latter point, however, Sir Denice admitted there was a diversity of opinion.

One of the witnesses examined was a man who had entered the Priory grounds from the river during a fearful tempest, on one Christmas Eve, and had, he said, witnessed the revel through a window to which he had climbed. He declared that at the hour of midnight the candles had been extinguished, but that a moment afterwards an awful red light had floated through the room, followed by the shrieks of a human being at the point of strangulation, and then by horrible yells of laughter. Another man who was examined had been a wood-cutter in the service of the Priory, and he had upon one occasion witnessed the celebration of a Black Mass; but he averred that no life was sacrificed, though he admitted that in the strange red light, which had flashed through the room, he had seen what appeared to be two men struggling on the floor. In the general particulars of the orgie there was, however, no diversity of opinion, and had the old Sir Denice le Warden been anything of a comparative mythologist, he could scarcely fail to have been greatly interested in being brought face to face with so striking an example of the survival of an ancient superstition within the walls of a holy building.

During a rainy week I amused myself among the parchments dealing with Northavon Priory, and although what I read impressed me greatly at the time, yet three years of pretty hard work in various parts of the world had so dulled my memory of any incident so unimportant as the deciphering of a mouldy document that, as I have already stated, it was not until I had posted my letter to Arthur Jephson agreeing to spend a day or two with his party, that I succeeded in recalling something of what I had read regarding Northavon Priory.

I had taken it for granted that the Priory had been demolished when Henry had superintended the dissolution of the religious establishments throughout the country: I did not think it likely that one with such a record as was embodied in the notes would be allowed to remain with a single stone on another. A moment's additional reflection admitted of my perceiving how extremely unlikely it was that, even if Northavon Priory had been spared by the King, it would still be available for visitors during the latter years of the nineteenth century. I had seen many red-brick "abbeys" and "priories" in various parts of the country, not more than ten years old, inhabited mostly by gentlemen who had made fortunes in iron, or perhaps lard, which constitutes, I understand, an excellent foundation for a fortune. There might be, for all I knew, a score of Northavon Priories in England. Arthur Jephson's father had made his money by the judicious advertising of a certain oriental rug manufactured in the Midlands, and I thought it very likely that he had built a mansion for himself which he had called Northavon Priory.

A letter which I received from Arthur set my mind at rest. He explained to me very fully that Northavon Priory was a hotel built within the walls of an ancient religious house. He had spent a delightful month fishing in the river during the summer—I had been fishing in the Amazon at that time—and had sojourned at the hotel, which he had found to be a marvel of comfort in spite of its picturesqueness. This was why, he said, he had thought how jolly it would be to entertain a party of his friends at the place during the Christmas week.

That explanation was quite good enough for me. I had a week or two to myself in England before going to India, and so soon as I recalled what I had read regarding Northavon Priory, I felt glad that my liking for Jephson had induced me to accept his invitation.

It was not until we were travelling together to the station nearest to the Priory that he mentioned to me, quite incidentally, that during the summer he had been fortunate enough to make the acquaintance of a young woman who resided in a spacious mansion within easy distance of the Priory Hotel, and who was, so far as he was capable of judging—and he considered that in such matters his judgment was worth something—the most charming girl in England.

"I see," I remarked, before his preliminary panegyric had quite come to a legitimate conclusion—"I see all now: you haven't the courage—to be more exact, the impudence—to come down alone to the hotel—she has probably a brother who is a bit of an athlete—but you think that Tom Singleton and I will form a good enough excuse for an act on your part which parents and guardians can construe in one way only."

"Well, perhaps—Hang it all, man, you needn't attribute to me any motives but those of the purest hospitality," laughed my companion. "Isn't the prospect of a genuine old English Christmas—the Yule log, and that sort of thing—good enough for you without going any further?"

"It's quite good enough for me," I replied. "I only regret that it is not good enough for you. You expect to see her every day?"

"Every day? Don't be a fool, Jim. If I see her more than four times in the course of the week—I think I should manage to see her four times—I will consider myself exceptionally lucky."

"And if you see her less than four times you will reckon yourself uncommonly unlucky?"

"O, I think I have arranged for four times all right: I'll have to trust to luck for the rest."

"What! You mean to say that the business has gone as far as that?"

"As what?"

"As making arrangements for meeting with her?"

My friend laughed complacently.

"Well, you see, old chap, I couldn't very well give you this treat without letting her know that I should be in the neighbourhood," said he.

"Oh, indeed. I don't see, however, what the—."

"Great heavens! You mean to say that you don't see—Oh, you will have your joke."

"I hope I will have one eventually; I can't say that I perceive much chance of one at present, however. You'll not give us much of your interesting society during the week of our treat, as you call it."

"I'll give you as much of it as I can spare—more than you'll be likely to relish, perhaps. A week's a long time, Jim."

"'Time travels at divers paces with divers persons,' my friend. I suppose she's as lovely as any of the others of past years?"

"As lovely! Jim, she's just the—"

"Don't trouble yourself over the description. I have a vivid recollection of the phrases you employed in regard to the others. There was Lily, and Gwen, and Bee, and—yes, by George! there was a fourth; her name was Nelly, or—"

"All flashes in the pan, my friend. I didn't know my own mind in those old days; but now, thank heaven!—Oh, you'll agree with me when you see her. This is the real thing and no mistake."

He was good enough to give me a genuine lover's description of the young woman, whose name was, he said, Sylvia St. Leger; but it did not differ materially from the descriptions which had come from him in past days, of certainly four other girls for whom he had, he imagined, entertained a devotion strong as death itself. Alas! his devotion had not survived a single year in any case.

When we arrived at the hotel, after a drive of eight miles from the railway station, we found Tom Singleton waiting for us rather impatiently, and in a quarter of an hour we were facing an excellent dinner. We were the only guests at the hotel, for though it was picturesquely situated on the high bank of the river, and was doubtless a delightful place for a sojourn in summer, yet in winter it possessed few attractions to casual visitors.

After dinner I strolled over the house, and found, to my surprise, that the old walls of the Priory were practically intact. The kitchen was also unchanged, but the great refectory was now divided into four rooms. The apartments upstairs had plainly been divided in the same way by brick partitions; but the outer walls, pierced with narrow windows, were those of the original Priory.

In the morning I made further explorations, only outside the building, and came upon the ruins of the old Priory tower; and then I perceived that only a small portion of the original building had been utilised for the hotel. The landlord, who accompanied me, was certainly no antiquarian. He told me that he had been "let in" so far as the hotel was concerned. He had been given to understand that the receipts for the summer months were sufficiently great to compensate for the absence of visitors during the winter; but his experience of one year had not confirmed this statement, made by the people from whom he had bought the place, and he had come to the conclusion that, as he had been taken in in the transaction, it was his duty to try to take in some one else in the same way.

"I only hope that I may succeed, sir," he said, "but I'm doubtful about it. People are getting more suspicious every day."

"You weren't suspicious, at any rate," said I.

"That I weren't—more's the pity, sir," said he. "But it'll take me all my time to get the place off my hands, I know. Ah, yes; it's hard to get people to take your word for anything nowadays."

For the next two days Tom Singleton and I were left a good deal together, the fact being that our friend Arthur parted from us after lunch and only returned in time for dinner, declaring upon each occasion that he had just passed the pleasantest day of his life. On Christmas Eve he came to us in high spirits, bearing with him an invitation from a lady who had attained distinction, through being the mother of Miss St. Leger, for us to spend Christmas Day at her house—it had already been pointed out to us by Arthur: it was a fine Georgian country house, named The Grange.

"I've accepted for you both," said Arthur. "Mrs. St. Leger is a most charming woman, and her daughter—I don't know if I mentioned that she had a daughter—well, if I omitted, I am now in a position to assure you that her daughter—her name is Sylvia—is possibly the most beautiful—But there's no use trying to describe her; you'll see her for yourselves tomorrow, and judge if I've exaggerated in the least when I say that the world does not contain a more exquisite creature."

"Yes, one hour with her will be quite sufficient to enable us to pronounce an opinion on that point," laughed Tom.

We remained smoking in front of the log fire that blazed in the great hearth, until about eleven o'clock, and then went to our rooms upstairs, after some horse-play in the hall.

My room was a small one at the beginning of the corridor, Arthur Jephson's was alongside it, and at the very end of the corridor was Tom Singleton's. All had at one time been one apartment.

Having walked a good deal during the day, I was very tired, and had scarcely got into bed before I fell asleep.

When I awoke it was with a start and a consciousness that something was burning. A curious red light streamed into the room from outside. I sprang from my bed in a moment and ran to the window. But before I had reached it the room was in darkness once more, and there came a yell of laughter, apparently from the next room.

For a moment I was paralyzed. But the next instant I had recovered my presence of mind. I believed that Arthur and Tom had been playing some of their tricks upon me. They had burnt a red light outside my window, and were roaring with laughter as they heard me spring out of bed.

That was the explanation of what I had seen and heard which first suggested itself to me; and I was about to return to bed when my door was knocked at and then opened.

"What on earth have you been up to?" came the voice of Arthur Jephson. "Have you set the bed-curtains on fire? If you have, that's nothing to laugh at."

"Get out of this room with your larking," said I. "It's a very poor joke that of yours, Arthur. Go back to your bed."

He struck a light—he had a match-box in his hand—and went to my candle without a word. In a moment the room was faintly illuminated.

"Do you mean to say that you hadn't a light here just now—a red light?" he cried.

"I had no light: a red light floated through the room, but it seemed to come from outside," said I.

"And who was it laughed in that wild way?"

"I took it for granted that it was you and Tom who were about your usual larks."

"Larks! No, I was about no larks, I can promise you. Good Lord! man, that laugh was something beyond a lark." He seated himself on my bed. "Do you fancy it may have been some of the servants going about the stables with a carriage-lamp?" he continued. "There may have been a late arrival at the hotel, you know."

"That's not at all unlikely," said I. "Yes, it may have been that, and the laughter may have been between the grooms."

"I don't hear any sound of bustle through the house or outside," said he.

"The stables are not at this angle of the building," said I. "We must merely have seen the light and heard that laughter as the carriage passed our angle. Anyhow, we'll only catch cold if we lounge about in our pyjamas like this. You'd best get back to bed and let me do the same."

"I don't feel much inclined to sleep, but I'll not prevent your having your night's rest," said he, resting. "I wonder is it near morning?"

I held the candle before the dial of my watch that hung above my bed.

"It's exactly five minutes past twelve," said I. "We've slept barely an hour."

"Then the sooner I clear out the better it will be for both of us," said he.

He went away slowly, and I heard him strike a match in his own room. He evidently meant to light his candle.

Some hours had passed before I fell into an uneasy sleep, and once more I was awakened by Arthur Jephson, who stood by my bedside. The morning light was in the room.

"For God's sake, come into Tom's room!" he whispered. "He's dead!—Tom is dead!"

I tried to realize his words. Some moments had elapsed before I succeeded in doing so. I sprang from my bed and ran down the corridor to the room occupied by Tom Singleton. The landlord and a couple of servants were already there. They had burst in the door.

It was but too true: our poor friend lay on his bed with his body bent and his arms twisted as though he had been struggling desperately with someone at his last moment. His face, too, was horribly contorted, and his eyes were wide open.

"A doctor," I managed to say.

"He's already sent for, sir," said the landlord.

In a few moments the doctor arrived.

"Cardiac attack," said he. "Was he alone in the room? No, he can't have been alone."

"He was quite alone," said Arthur. "I knocked at the door a quarter of an hour ago, but getting no answer, I tried to force the lock. It was too strong for me; but the landlord and the man-servant who was bringing us our hot water burst in the door at my request."

"And the window—was it fastened?" asked the doctor.

"It was secure, sir," said the landlord.

"Ah, a sudden cardiac attack," said the doctor.

There was, of course, an inquest, but as no evidence of foul play was forthcoming, the doctor's phrase "cardiac attack" satisfied the jury, and a verdict of "death from natural causes" was returned.

Before I went back to town I examined the room in which our poor friend had died. On the side of one of the window-shutters there were four curious burnt marks. They gave one the impression that the shutter had at one time been grasped by a man wearing a red-hot gauntlet.

I started for India before the end of the year and remained there for eight months. Then I thought I would pay a visit to a sister of mine in Queensland. On my return at the end of the year I meant to stop at Cairo for a few weeks. On entering Shepheard's Hotel I found myself face to face with Arthur Jephson and his wife—he called her Sylvia. They had been married in August, but their honeymoon seemed still to be in its first quarter. It was after Mrs. Jephson had retired, and when Arthur was sitting with me enjoying the cool of the night by the aid of a pretty strong cigar or two, that we ventured to allude to the tragic occurrence which marked our last time of meeting.

"I wish to beg of you not to make any allusion to that awful business in the hearing of my wife," said Arthur. "In fact I must ask you not to allude to that fearful room in the Priory in any way."

"I will be careful not to do so," said I. "You have your own reasons, I suppose, for giving me this warning."

"I have the best of reasons, Jim. She too had her experience of that room, and it was as terrible as ours."

"Good heavens! I heard nothing of that. She did not sleep in that room?"

"Thank God, she didn't. I arrived in time to save her."

I need scarcely say that my interest was now fully aroused.

"Tell me what happened—if you dare tell it," I said.

"You were abroad, and so you wouldn't be likely to hear of the fire at The Grange," said my friend, after a pause.

"I heard nothing of it."

"It took place only two days before last Christmas. I had been in the south of France, where I had spent a month or two with my mother—she cannot stand a winter at home—and I had promised Sylvia to return to The Grange for Christmas. When I got to Northavon I found her and her mother and their servants at the Priory Hotel. The fire had taken place the previous night, and they found the hotel very handy when they hadn't a roof of their own over their heads. Well, we dined together, and were as jolly as was possible under the circumstances until bedtime. I had actually said "Good night" to Sylvia before I recollected what had taken place the previous Christmas Eve in the same house. I rushed upstairs, and found Sylvia in the act of entering the room—that fatal room. When I implored of her to choose some other apartment, she only laughed at first, and assured me that she wasn't superstitious; but when she saw that I was serious—I was deadly serious, as you can believe, Jim—"

"I can—I can."

"Well she agreed to sleep in her mother's room, and I went away relieved. So soon as I returned to the fire in the dining-room I began to think of poor Tom Singleton. I felt curiously excited, and I knew that it would be useless for me to go to bed—in fact, I made up my mind not to leave the dining-room for some hours, at any rate, and when the landlord came to turn out the lights I told him he might trust me to do that duty for him. He left me alone in the room about half-past eleven o'clock. When the sound of his feet upon the oaken stairs died away I felt as fearful as a child in the dark. I lit another cigar and walked about the room for some time. I went to the window that opened upon the old Priory ground, and, seeing that the night was a fine one, I opened the door and strolled out, hoping that the cool air would do me good. I had not gone many yards across the little patch of green before I turned and looked up at the house—at the last window, the window of that room. A fire had been lighted in the room early in the evening, and its glow shone through the white blind. Suddenly that faint glow increased to a terrific glare—a red glare, Jim—and then there came before my eyes for a moment the shadow of two figures upon the blind—one the figure of a woman, the other—God knows what it was. I rushed back to the room, but before I had reached the door I heard the horrible laughter once again. It seemed to come from that room and to pass on through the air into the distance across the river. I ran upstairs with a light, and found Sylvia and her mother standing together with wraps around them at the door of the room. "Thank God, you are safe!" I managed to cry. "I feared that you had returned to the room." "You heard it—that awful laughter?" she whispered. "You heard it, and you saw something—what was it?" I gently forced her and her mother back to their room, for the servants and the landlord's family were now crowding into the corridor. They, too, had heard enough to alarm them."

"You went to the room?"

"The scene of that dreadful morning was repeated. The door was locked on the inside. We broke it in and found a girl lying dead on the floor, her face contorted just as poor Singleton's was. She was Sylvia's maid, and it was thought that, on hearing that her mistress was not going to occupy the room, she had gone into it herself on account of the fire which had been lighted there."

"And the doctor said—?"

"Cardiac attack—the same as before—singular coincidence! I need scarcely say that we never slept again under that accursed roof. Poor Sylvia! She was overwhelmed at the thought of how narrow her escape had been."

"Did you notice anything remarkable about the room—about the shutters of the windows?" I asked.

He looked at me curiously for a moment. Then he bent forward and said—

"On the edge of the shutter there were some curious marks where the wood had been charred."

"As if a hand with a red-hot gauntlet had been laid upon it?"

"There were the marks of two such hands," said my friend slowly.

We remained for an hour in the garden; then we threw away the ends of our cigars and went into the hotel without another word.

William Hope Hodgson

Few horror authors have been strong enough to lift a man over their head with one arm, but William Hope Hodgson (1877–1918) managed it. In addition to writing some of the most highly regarded works in this field, he was a physical fitness enthusiast and remarkable athlete.

Born in Weathersfield, Essex, Hodgson was the son of a clergyman and one of twelve children. Samuel Hodgson, his father, moved round the country a lot, even spending some time in Ireland, and friction between Hodgson and his father ended in William running away to sea in 1891 (it also left him a lifelong atheist). He joined the merchant navy, sailed round the world three times and won a medal from the Royal Humane Society for saving the life of a shipmate in New Zealand. He should have held on a bit longer, we now know; his father died the year after he left.

While in the merchant navy, Hodgson took up photography and body-building. He became an expert boxer into the bargain. His family, meanwhile, had fallen on hard times after Samuel's death, so William came home for good in 1899. The family had moved to Blackburn and here he set up a school of physical culture in 1901.

Around this time, he encountered Harry Houdini, the great magician and escapologist, who was then on a tour of northern theatres. Hodgson almost defeated the great man by challenging him to escape from a pair of handcuffs. It took Houdini an hour: he was not happy by all accounts!

Hodgson began his writing career in 1902, with a mixture of fitness articles and the short stories that would one day make his name. Very quickly, this led to him writing the brilliant novels that are now classics: *The Boats of the Glen Carrig* (1907), *The House on the Borderland* (1908), *The Ghost Pirates* (1909) and *The Night Land* (1912).

Hodgson moved to London in 1910 and married Bessie Farnworth, a girl from his home town, in 1913. They moved to France but Hodgson's dreams of a quiet married life were rudely shattered the next year with the outbreak of the First World War.

He returned to Britain and joined the Royal Artillery as a lieutenant. An injury in training forced him out of the RA for a while but he could not stay away from the war and what he saw as his duty. He re-enlisted in 1917 and was sent to France.

On 19 April 1918, after fighting in the battle of Ypres, he was manning an observation post at Mont Kemmel in Belgium. A German shell landed straight on the post and Hodgson was blown apart.

It was as much a tragedy for those who enjoy his writings as it was for his family. We are left with a small output in book form and a steady uncovering, as years pass, of more of his short stories by diligent researchers.

Such a tale is "A Tropical Horror." It was first published in the *Grand Magazine,* June 1905, and never saw book form in Hodgson's lifetime. It was resurrected in an American edition of his stories in the mid-1970s but is still not widely known.

Hodgson enthusiasts will relish a little more of what they know to be Hodgson's speciality: horrors that come in the night for unfortunate seamen . . .

A Tropical Horror

We are a hundred and thirty days out from Melbourne, and for three weeks we have lain in this sweltering calm.

It is midnight, and our watch on deck until four A.M. I go out and sit on the hatch. A minute later, Joky, our youngest 'prentice, joins me for a chatter. Many are the hours we have sat thus and talked in the night watches; though, to be sure, it is Joky who does the talking. I am content to smoke and listen, giving an occasional grunt at seasons to show that I am attentive.

Joky has been silent for some time, his head bent in meditation. Suddenly he looks up, evidently with the intention of making some remark. As he does so, I see his face stiffen with a nameless horror. He crouches back, his eyes staring past me at some unseen fear. Then his mouth opens. He gives forth a strangulated cry and topples backwards off the hatch, striking his head against the deck. Fearing I know not what, I turn to look.

Great Heavens! Rising above the bulwarks, seen plainly in the bright moonlight, is a vast slobbering mouth a fathom across. From the huge dripping lips hang great tentacles. As I look the Thing comes further over the rail. It is rising, rising, higher and higher. There are no eyes visible; only that fearful slobbering mouth set on the tremendous trunk-like neck; which, even as I watch, is curling inboard with the stealthy celerity of an enormous eel. Over it comes in vast heaving folds. Will it never end? The ship gives a slow, sullen roll to starboard as she feels the weight. Then the tail, a broad, flat-shaped mass, slips over the teak rail and falls with a loud slump on to the deck.

For a few seconds the hideous creature lies heaped in writhing, slimy coils. Then, with quick, darting movements, the monstrous head travels along the deck. Close by the mainmast stand the harness casks, and alongside of these a freshly opened cask of salt beef with the top loosely replaced. The smell of the meat seems to attract the monster, and I can hear it sniffing with a vast indrawing breath. Then those lips open, displaying four huge fangs; there is a quick forward motion of the head, a sudden crashing, crunching sound, and beef and barrel have disappeared. The noise brings one of the ordinary seamen out of the fo'cas'le. Coming into the night, he can see nothing for a moment. Then, as he gets further aft, he sees, and with horrified cries rushes forward. Too late! From the mouth of the Thing there flashes forth a long, broad blade of glistening white, set with fierce teeth. I avert my eyes, but cannot shut out the sickening "Glut! Glut!" that follows.

The man on the "look-out," attracted by the disturbance, has witnessed the tragedy, and flies for refuge into the fo'cas'le, flinging to the heavy iron door after him.

The carpenter and sailmaker come running out from the half-deck in their drawers. Seeing the awful Thing, they rush aft to the cabin with shouts of fear. The second mate, after one glance over the break of the poop, runs down the companion-way with the helmsman after him. I can hear them barring the scuttle, and abruptly I realise that I am on the main deck alone.

So far I have forgotten my own danger. The past few minutes seem like a portion of an awful dream. Now, however, I comprehend my position and, shaking off the horror that has held me, turn to seek safety. As I do so my eyes fall upon Joky, lying huddled and senseless with fright where he has fallen. I cannot leave him there. Close by stands the empty half-deck—a little steel-built house with iron doors. The lee one is hooked open. Once inside I am safe.

Up to the present the Thing has seemed to be unconscious of my presence. Now, however, the huge barrel-like head sways in my direction; then comes a muffled bellow, and the great tongue flickers in and out as the brute turns and swirls aft to meet me. I know there is not a moment to lose, and, picking up the helpless lad, I make a run for the open door. It is only distant a few yards, but that awful shape is coming down the deck to me in great wreathing coils. I reach the house and tumble in with my burden; then out on deck again to unhook and close the door. Even as I do so something white curls round the end of the house. With a bound I am inside and the door is shut and bolted. Through the thick glass of the ports I see the Thing sweep round the house, in vain search for me.

Joky has not moved yet; so, kneeling down, I loosen his shirt collar and sprinkle some water from the breaker over his face. While I am doing this I hear Morgan shout something; then comes a great shriek of terror, and again that sickening "Glut! Glut!"

Joky stirs uneasily, rubs his eyes, and sits up suddenly.

"Was that Morgan shouting—?" He breaks off with a cry. "Where are we? I have had such awful dreams!"

At this instant there is a sound of running footsteps on the deck and I hear Morgan's voice at the door.

"Tom, open—!"

He stops abruptly and gives an awful cry of despair. Then I hear him rush forward. Through the porthole, I see him spring into the fore rigging and scramble madly aloft. Something steals up after him. It shows white in the moonlight. It wraps itself around his right ankle. Morgan stops dead, plucks out his sheath-knife, and hacks fiercely at the fiendish thing. It lets go, and in a second he is over the top and running for dear life up the t'gallant rigging.

A time of quietness follows, and presently I see that the day is breaking. Not a sound can be heard save the heavy gasping breathing of the Thing. As the sun rises higher the creature stretches itself out along the deck and seems to enjoy the warmth. Still no sound, either from the men forward or the officers aft. I can only suppose that they are afraid of attracting its attention. Yet, a little later, I hear the report of a pistol away aft, and looking out I see the serpent raise its huge head as though listening. As it does so I get a good view of the fore part, and in the daylight see what the night has hidden.

There, right about the mouth, is a pair of little pig-eyes, that seem to twinkle with a diabolical intelligence. It is swaying its head slowly from side to side; then, without warning, it turns quickly and looks right in through the port. I dodge out of sight; but not soon enough. It has seen me, and brings its great mouth up against the glass.

I hold my breath. My God! If it breaks the glass! I cower, horrified. From the direction of the port there comes a loud, harsh, scraping sound. I shiver. Then I remember that there are little iron doors to shut over the ports in bad weather. Without a moment's waste of time I rise to my feet and slam to the door over the port. Then I go round to the others and do the same. We are now in darkness, and I tell Joky in a whisper to light the lamp, which, after some fumbling, he does.

About an hour before midnight I fall asleep. I am awakened suddenly some hours later by a scream of agony and the rattle of a water-dipper. There is a slight scuffling sound; then that soul-revolting "Glut! Glut!"

I guess what has happened. One of the men forrad has slipped out of the fo'cas'le to try and get a little water. Evidently he has trusted to the darkness to hide his movements. Poor beggar! He has paid for his attempt with his life!

After this I cannot sleep, though the rest of the night passes quietly enough. Towards morning I doze a bit, but wake every few minutes with a start. Joky is sleeping peacefully; indeed, he seems worn out with the terrible strain of the past twenty-four hours. About eight A.M. I call him, and we make a light breakfast off the dry ship's biscuit and water. Of the latter happily we have a good supply. Joky seems more himself, and starts to talk a little—possibly somewhat louder than is safe; for, as he chatters on, wondering how it will end, there comes a tremendous blow against the side of the house, making it ring again. After this Joky is very silent. As we sit there I cannot but wonder what all the rest are doing, and how the poor beggars forrad are faring, cooped up without water, as the tragedy of the night has proved.

Towards noon, I hear a loud bang, followed by a terrific bellowing. Then comes a great smashing of woodwork, and the cries of men in pain. Vainly I ask myself what has happened. I begin to reason. By the sound of the report it was evidently something much heavier than a rifle or pistol, and judging from the mad roaring of the Thing, the shot must have done some execution. On thinking it over further, I become convinced that, by some means, those aft have got hold of the small signal cannon we carry, and though I know that some have been hurt, perhaps killed, yet a feeling of exultation seizes me as I listen to the roars of the Thing, and realise that it is badly wounded, perhaps mortally. After a while, however, the bellowing dies away, and only an occasional roar, denoting more of anger than aught else, is heard.

Presently I become aware, by the ship's canting over to starboard, that the creature has gone over to that side, and a great hope springs up within me that possibly it has had enough of us and is going over the rail into the sea. For a time all is silent and my hope grows stronger. I lean across and nudge Joky, who is sleeping with his head on the table. He starts up sharply with a loud cry.

"Hush!" I whisper hoarsely. "I'm not certain, but I do believe it's gone."

Joky's face brightens wonderfully, and he questions me eagerly. We wait another hour or so, with hope ever rising. Our confidence is returning fast. Not a sound can we hear, not even the breathing of the Beast. I get out some biscuits, and Joky, after rummaging in the locker, produces a small piece of pork and a bottle of ship's vinegar. We fall to with a relish. After our long abstinence from food the meal acts on us like wine, and what must Joky do but insist on opening the door, to make sure the Thing has gone. This I will not allow, telling him that at least it will be safer to open the iron port-covers first and have a look out. Joky argues, but I am immovable. He becomes excited. I believe the youngster is light-headed. Then, as I turn to unscrew one of the after-covers, Joky makes a dash at the door. Before he can undo the bolts I have him, and after a short struggle lead him back to the table. Even as I endeavour to quieten him there comes at the starboard door—the door that Joky has tried to open—a sharp, loud sniff, sniff, followed immediately by a thunderous grunting howl and a foul stench of putrid breath sweeps in under the door. A great trembling takes me, and were it not for the carpenter's tool-box I should fall. Joky turns very white and is violently sick, after which he is seized by a hopeless fit of sobbing.

Hour after hour passes, and, weary to death, I lie down on the chest upon which I have been sitting, and try to rest.

It must be about half past two in the morning, after a somewhat longer doze, that I am suddenly awakened by a most tremendous uproar away forrad—men's voices shrieking, cursing, praying; but in spite of the terror expressed, so weak and feeble; while in the midst, and at times broken off short with that hellishly suggestive "Glut! Glut!", is the unearthly bellowing of the Thing. Fear incarnate seizes me, and I can only fall on my knees and pray. Too well I know what is happening.

Joky has slept through it all, and I am thankful.

Presently, under the door there steals a narrow ribbon of light, and I know that the day has broken on the second morning of our imprisonment. I let Joky sleep on. I will let him have peace while he may. Time passes, but I take little notice. The Thing is quiet, probably sleeping. About midday I eat a little biscuit and drink some of the water. Joky still sleeps. It is best so.

A sound breaks the stillness. The ship gives a slight heave, and I know that once more the Thing is awake. Round the deck it moves, causing the ship to roll perceptibly. Once it goes forrad—I fancy to again explore the fo'cas'le. Evidently it finds nothing, for it returns almost immediately. It pauses a moment at the house, then goes on further aft. Up aloft, somewhere in the fore-rigging, there rings out a peal of wild laughter, though sounding very faint and far away. The Horror stops suddenly. I listen intently, but hear nothing save a sharp creaking beyond the after end of the house, as though a strain had come upon the rigging.

A minute later I hear a cry aloft, followed almost instantly by a loud crash on deck that seems to shake the ship. I wait in anxious fear. What is happening? The minutes pass slowly. Then comes another frightened shout. It ceases suddenly. The suspense has become terrible, and I am no longer able to bear it. Very cautiously I open one of the after port-covers, and peep out to see a fearful sight. There, with its tail upon the deck and its vast body curled round the mainmast, is the monster, its head above the topsail yard, and its great claw-armed tentacle waving in the air. It is the first proper sight that I have had of the Thing. Good Heavens! It must weigh a hundred tons! Knowing that I shall have time, I open the port itself, then crane my head out and look up. There on the extreme end of the lower topsail yard I see one of the able seamen. Even down here I note the staring horror of his face. At this moment he sees me and gives a weak, hoarse cry for help. I can do nothing for him. As I look the great tongue shoots out and licks him off the yard, much as might a dog a fly off the window-pane.

Higher still, but happily out of reach, are two more of the men. As far as I can judge they are lashed to the mast above the royal yard. The Thing attempts to reach them, but after a futile effort it ceases, and starts to slide down, coil on coil, to the deck. While doing this I notice a great gaping wound on its body some twenty feet above the tail.

I drop my gaze from aloft and look aft. The cabin door is torn from its hinges, and the bulkhead—which, unlike the half-deck, is of teak wood—is partly broken down. With a shudder I realise the cause of those cries after the cannon-shot. Turning I screw my head round and try to see the foremast, but cannot. The sun, I notice, is low, and the night is near. Then I draw in my head and fasten up both port and cover.

How will it end? Oh! how will it end?

After a while Joky wakes up. He is very restless, yet though he has eaten nothing during the day I cannot get him to touch anything.

Night draws on. We are too weary—too dispirited to talk. I lie down, but not to sleep . . . Time passes.

A ventilator rattles violently somewhere on the main deck, and there sounds constantly that slurring, gritty noise. Later I hear a cat's agonised howl, and then again all is quiet. Some time after comes a great splash alongside. Then, for some hours, all is silent as the grave. Occasionally I sit up on the chest and listen, yet never a whisper of noise comes to me. There is an absolute

silence, even the monotonous creak of the gear has died away
entirely, and at last a real hope is springing up within me. That
splash, this silence—surely I am justified in hoping. I do not
wake Joky this time. I will prove first for myself that all is safe.
Still I wait. I will run no unnecessary risks. After a time I creep
to the after-port and will listen; but there is no sound. I put up
my hand and feel at the screw, then again I hesitate, yet not for
long. Noiselessly I begin to unscrew the fastening of the heavy
shield. It swings loose on its hinge, and I pull it back and peer
out. My heart is beating madly. Everything seems strangely dark
outside. Perhaps the moon has gone behind a cloud. Suddenly a
beam of moonlight enters through the port, and goes as quickly.
I stare out. Something moves. Again the light streams in, and
now I seem to be looking into a great cavern, at the bottom of
which quivers and curls something palely white.

My heart seems to stand still! It is the Horror! I start back and
seize the iron port-flap to slam it to. As I do so, something
strikes the glass like a steam ram, shatters it to atoms, and flicks
past me into the berth. I scream and spring away. The port is
quite filled with it. The lamp shows it dimly. It is curling and
twisting here and there. It is as thick as a tree, and covered with
a smooth slimy skin. At the end is a great claw, like a lobster's,
only a thousand times larger. I cower down into the farthest
corner. . . . It has broken the tool-chest to pieces with one click
of those frightful mandibles. Joky has crawled under a bunk.
The Thing sweeps round in my direction. I feel a drop of sweat
trickle slowly down my face—it tastes salty. Nearer comes that
awful death . . . Crash! I roll over backwards. It has crushed the
water breaker against which I leant, and I am rolling in the
water across the floor. The claw drives up, then down, with a
quick uncertain movement, striking the deck a dull, heavy blow,
a foot from my head. Joky gives a little gasp of horror. Slowly the
Thing rises and starts feeling its way round the berth. It plunges
into a bunk and pulls out a bolster, nips it in half and drops it,
then moves on. It is feeling along the deck. As it does so it comes
across a half of the bolster. It seems to toy with it, then picks it
up and takes it out through the port. . . .

A wave of putrid air fills the berth. There is a grating sound, and something enters the port again—something white and tapering and set with teeth. Hither and thither it curls, rasping over the bunks, ceiling, and deck, with a noise like that of a great saw at work. Twice it flickers above my head, and I close my eyes. Then off it goes again. It sounds now on the opposite side of the berth and nearer to Joky. Suddenly the harsh, raspy noise becomes muffled, as though the teeth were passing across some soft substance. Joky gives a horrid little scream, that breaks off into a bubbling, whistling sound. I open my eyes. The tip of the vast tongue is curled tightly round something that drips, then is quickly withdrawn, allowing the moonbeams to steal again into the berth. I rise to my feet. Looking round, I note in a mechanical sort of way the wrecked state of the berth—the shattered chests, dismantled bunks, and something else—

"Joky!" I cry, and tingle all over.

There is that awful Thing again at the port. I glance round for a weapon. I will revenge Joky. Ah! there, right under the lamp, where the wreck of the carpenter's chest strews the floor, lies a small hatchet. I spring forward and seize it. It is small, but so keen—so keen! I feel its razor edge lovingly. Then I am back at the port. I stand to one side and raise my weapon. The great tongue is feeling its way to those fearsome remains. It reaches them. As it does so, with a scream of "Joky! Joky!" I strike savagely again and again and again, gasping as I strike; once more, and the monstrous mass falls to the deck, writhing like a hideous eel. A vast, warm flood rushes in through the porthole. There is a sound of breaking steel and an enormous bellowing. A singing comes in my ears and grows louder—louder. Then the berth grows indistinct and suddenly dark.

Extract from the log of the steamship *Hispaniola*.

June 24.—Lat.—N. Long.—W. 11 A.M.—Sighted four-masted barque about four points on the port bow, flying signal of distress. Ran down to her and sent a boat aboard. She proved to be the *Glen Doon*, homeward bound from Melbourne to London. Found things in a terrible state. Decks covered with blood and slime. Steel deck-house stove in. Broke open door, and discovered youth of about nineteen in last stage of inanition, also part remains of boy about fourteen years of age. There was a great quantity of blood in the place, and a huge curled-up mass of whitish flesh, weighing about half a ton, one end of which appeared to have been hacked through with a sharp instrument. Found forecastle door open and hanging from one hinge. Doorway bulged, as though something had been forced through. Went inside. Terrible state of affairs, blood everywhere, broken chests, smashed bunks, but no men nor remains. Went aft again and found youth showing signs of recovery. When he came round, gave the name of Thompson. Said they had been attacked by a huge serpent—thought it must have been sea-serpent. He was too weak to say much, but told us there were some men up the mainmast. Sent a hand aloft, who reported them lashed to the royal mast, and quite dead. Went aft to the cabin. Here we found the bulkhead smashed to pieces, and the cabin-door lying on the deck near the after-hatch. Found body of captain down lazarette, but no officers. Noticed amongst the wreckage part of the carriage of a small cannon. Came aboard again.

Have sent the second mate with six men to work her into port. Thompson is with us. He has written out his version of the affair. We certainly consider that the state of the ship, as we found her, bears out in every respect his story. (Signed)

William Norton (Master).
Tom Briggs (1st Mate).

W. Bourne Cooke

W. Bourne Cooke passed into obscurity after his death, despite being a prolific and popular writer of children's adventure stories.

Born in 1869, Cooke became a frequent contributor to many weeklies and dailies of his time, including the *Daily Chronicle, Tit Bits, Chums* and *Little Folk*. His serials were particularly popular, among them "The Black Box" which ran in *The Captain* in 1913 and the two-year long "Wreck Cove" in the same journal in 1915–16.

Cooke published fifteen books as well as his periodical work. The first was *The Canon's Daughter* (1902) and the last seems to have been *Red Feather* (1934). He published book forms of some of his serials, like *Grey Wizard* (1925) and the weird *The Curse of Amaris* (1924).

He specialized in historical fiction, and occasionally tried his hand at a creepy story, as in this one. Taken from his 1908 book *For King and Love,* a volume of stories mainly about the Civil War, this is one of a group of tales which first appeared in the author's native Nottinghamshire *Guardian.* Sub-titled "A Charnwood Forest Mystery," it is a straightforward good old ghost story, well worth a second airing.

The Woman with a Candle

In the autumn of the year 1900 I was staying at the isolated village of Knelby, which place, I need hardly inform the reader, is situated in the heart of the wild forest country known as Charnwood.

I have always had a decided weakness for antiquities, and it was, therefore, only natural that, on the day following my arrival at Knelby, I should take my way to the ancient church, which stands on a rocky eminence overlooking a precipitous and disused slate-quarry.

In the churchyard I found the sexton busily engaged in putting the final touches to a newly-dug grave. As I drew near, he came up the ladder from the depths where he had been working, and, after stretching himself, stood looking down at his handiwork with the air of one who has accomplished a hard task, and was satisfied.

He was a fine specimen of village manhood—tall, and broad in proportion; and although his white hair and beard indicated that he must be well advanced in years, his back was as straight as one of the spruce firs that fringed the churchyard in which he worked.

As he stood thus, gazing down into the grave at his feet, there was an expression of solemn thoughtfulness in his face, which betokened a mind not wholly engrossed with the doings of spade and pickaxe; while the height of his forehead and keenness of his eyes bespoke a more than ordinary intelligence.

Walking quietly over the grass, I reached the opposite side of the grave to the one on which he stood before he noticed my presence.

"Good-day, sir," said he, touching his cap.

"Good-day," I replied. "You are, or rather, have been busy, I see."

"Yes, sir," returned he. "I was just thinking, among other things, how many this one makes, and it's either sixty-eight or sixty-nine; but I can't be quite sure which, without referring to my figures at home."

"You allude, I suppose, to the number of graves you have dug?"

"Yes, sir."

"May I ask how long you have been sexton of Knelby?"

"It is forty years this very day, sir, since I was appointed."

"Strange, that you should have had a grave to dig on the anniversary."

"Very strange, sir; I have been thinking so, off and on, all the morning."

"And during the forty years you have been sexton, you have probably buried every person who has died in the parish?"

"All but one, sir," replied the sexton; and then, to my surprise, I noticed that he regarded me with an uneasy look, and evinced a desire to change the subject of our conversation.

"Perhaps you would like to look over the church, sir?" he said.

I replied that I was most anxious to do so, in fact, had come out with that intention; and so we moved off in the direction of the time-worn building, the sexton leading the way, while I followed, with the thought of the one parishoner, whose grave had not been dug by my guide, uppermost in my mind.

"You are staying at Knelby, pehaps, sir?" said the sexton, as he unlocked the ponderous door.

I replied that it was my intention to stay in the village for some weeks, in order that I might have perfect quietness and rest.

"You will certainly find our village quiet, sir," rejoined the old man, as he threw open the door and bowed me courteously in.

As we entered, the sun was shining brightly through the ivy-clad windows, the movement of the leaves in the wind breaking the light into a hundred fantastic shapes, which quivered on the walls.

The chancel was a large one in proportion to the church, and in it there reposed in stony watchfulness, two knights in armour, with their ladies beside them; for the Androvil family, who still lived at the Hall, had been lords of the manor far back in the Middle Ages.

After looking for some time on the cold, expectant faces of these effigies, trying, as I did so, to make them live again in my imagination, I raised my eyes and noticed a small brass plate on the north wall of the chancel. Following a habit I have, I read aloud the following inscription:—

Sacred to the Memory
of
DOROTHY LESLIE HOWARD,

Who disappeared mysteriously on the 18th of December, 1858. Her remains were found by a strange coincidence on the 5th day of March, 1865, and now rest in the churchyard.
"Until the day dawns, and the shadows flee away."

As I finished reading the inscription I turned round, and looking at the sexton, noticed the same half-fearful expression which had so impressed me at the side of the newly-made grave. I think as our eyes met, he saw the questioning look in mine, for, with a hasty remark about its being a long time ago, and best forgotten, he turned and led the way to another part of the church. But in spite of the interest I felt in a most perfect specimen of a cross-legged knight, I found my thoughts and eyes continually wandering to the brass tablet in the chancel, and I was not sorry when, after seeing everything worthy of notice, I found myself once more in the churchyard and the sunshine.

When we came to the grave I left the sexton to gather up his tools, and, walking across to the south side of the churchyard, seated myself on the low stone wall. It was then that I noticed for the first time a mournful-looking house, standing in somewhat extensive grounds, and surrounded by trees—most of which were ancient yews of gigantic growth.

Surely, thought I, this must be the rectory, and yet I marvelled to see that it was in a state of utter neglect and decay, as though it had been unoccupied for many years. The windows were close-shuttered, except in the case of one in the upper storey, where a shutter had in some way become loose and hung by a single hinge, creaking in the wind. One end of the house was covered with ivy, which, unchecked by the pruner's knife, had overgrown itself, and now waved its long tendrils above the chimney stack like the arms of some mighty octopus feeling for its prey. Truly this ancient and deserted house was the most eerie one I had ever seen.

I am of a decidedly imaginative temperament, and at once began to indulge in all sorts of wild fancies to account for the gloomy scene before me.

My reverie was broken by the sound of a footstep at my side, and, looking up, I found the sexton standing beside me, his spade and pickaxe over his shoulder, and his gaze fixed on the lifeless old house which had so fascinated me.

"Is that the rectory?" I asked.

"Yes, sir," replied the sexton, "or rather it still goes by that name, although no rector has lived there these thirty years."

"Indeed," replied I, "that is singular, for although the house has evidently fallen into great decay through neglect, it still bears evidence of having once been a pleasant and commodious residence; besides which, the grounds are extensive and beautiful, and the close situation of the rectory to the church must have been extremely convenient."

"Yes, sir," rejoined the sexton, "I daresay you're right in your way of looking at it, but I happen to know that there were good reasons for the rector refusing to live there."

"Reasons!" I exclaimed, my curiosity now thoroughly awakened by the mysterious tone of my informant's voice. "It must, indeed, have been a very strong reason that could drive a man from a spot like this to new surroundings and a new house."

The sexton seated himself on the wall beside me, and lowering his voice to a solemn whisper, said:—

"The reason, sir, was one that would have driven a man from any house, even though the surroundings were like Paradise. Sir, the house you are looking at is haunted."

"Haunted!" I exclaimed, in an incredulous and bantering tone. "By what?"

The sexton drew closer to me, and looking round with an air of one who was half-fearful of being overheard, whispered in my ear:—"By a woman, sir—an old and ghastly woman—who walks the house at dead of night with a lighted candle in her hand."

"But, surely," said I, "you do not believe in such a foolish tale as that. It must be one of those village superstitions, which one finds handed down from generation to generation in all remote country districts; and most probably the rector's reasons for removing to a new house was that he might have the benefit of more modern conveniences; for certainly yonder house is very ancient."

But the sexton passed over unheeded the latter part of my speech, and replied in even more set and solemn tones than before:—

"Sir, it is no foolish tale, for I, who now speak to you, have met the woman face to face."

Even had I felt so inclined, I could not, looking into the old man's face as he uttered these words, have made light of them.

"Pray tell me all about it," I said eagerly, placing my hand upon his arm.

"Sir," he replied, "I have told no one for many years, and even now when I think of it, all the horror of that night comes back upon me, making me tremble like an aspen leaf; but as you have shown such interest in the matter, I will do my best to tell you the story, asking you to excuse me if I am unable to finish it."

Having said this, the sexton sat for some moments gazing in absorbed silence on the eerie scene before us; then, with a shrug of his broad shoulders, as though bracing himself for a great effort, he thus began:—

"First of all, sir, I must tell you that my name is William Harness, and that I have lived in Knelby all my life, succeeding my father as sexton forty years ago. I was then a young man of about thirty-two, and had, up to the time of entering upon my new duties, been in the service of the rector for over ten years as coachman and gardener; but it was always an understood thing that I should follow my father in the sextonship, that office having been in our family for many generations; and though it may seem hard and strange to you, sir, I began my new duties by digging my father's grave; this, too, being an understood thing in our family, my father having done the same in the case of my grandfather, and so on right back for nearly one hundred and fifty years.

"In the year 1858, two years before I became sexton, a mysterious event happened which cast a gloom and horror over the whole district.

"There lived with the then rector, who was childless, his niece, a Miss Howard, the tablet to whose memory you saw in the church this morning. She was as good as she was beautiful, and was beloved by everyone in the parish, from the highest to the lowest. Her time was spent in doing good, and her sunny face and cheery voice brought happiness and gladness wherever she went. Needless to say that she was worshipped by the old rector and his wife, of whose home she was the life and light. Judge, then, of our dismay when the news spread one dark December morning that Miss Howard had disappeared. As she did not make her appearance at breakfast, a servant was sent to her room, when it was found that the door was open, and that she had evidently left her bed during the night.

"The old rector and his wife were nearly frantic, and I can truly say that I was hardly less affected, for Miss Howard had been my dearest friend, and many a long talk we had had together.

"During the whole day the rector and myself led search parties, beating every part of the country for miles around; but all to no purpose—we found not a trace of the missing one; and although the search was continued day after day for more than a week, all our efforts ended in failure and despair; so that we had, at last, to face the awful fact that our dear young friend had gone from us for ever. It was the rector's death-blow, and ere a year had passed away we laid him to rest in the churchyard, whither, within a few weeks, he was followed by his sorrowing wife.

"And here I must tell you that for some years a tale had been rife in the village—of the rectory being haunted by an old woman, who walked the house at night with a lighted candle in her hand. Several of the servants vowed that they had seen her, and had refused to stay in consequence; and, moreover, the rector, shortly before he died, had confided in me·that he had also met her, when one night, being unable to sleep, he had gone down to his study to read.

"I shall never forget how the old man's face went ashy pale as he told me how the woman came upon him suddenly as he sat reading; how hideous was her face, and how she beckoned to him to follow her. But at that sight he swooned away, and knew no more until he found himself in bed, with his wife bending anxiously over him.

"He, however, desired that I would not speak of this to anyone, for fear of strengthening a story that he had always ridiculed as foolish and superstitious. And, indeed, when I considered the shattered state of his health since the disappearance of his niece, and being moreover myself a decided disbeliever in ghosts of any kind—I say, when I considered these things, I readily came to the conclusion that the old man's senses had deceived him, and that he had seen nothing.

"I was, however, soon to find how greatly in error I had been in coming to this hasty conclusion.

"In the spring of the year 1860 our new rector settled among us, taking up his residence at the old rectory; and I continued to occupy the same position I had done in the time of his predecessor; for I knew well the ways of both house and garden, and could be relied upon to do my best for my new master.

"So the spring and summer ran on to autumn, when my father died, and, as I have already told you, the duties of sexton and grave-digger fell to my lot. But my new employment, though it occupied a great part of my time, did not take me wholly out of the rector's private service, and I continued to work a day or two each week on his garden. It was one morning in the early spring of 1865 that the rector came to me, as I was engaged in pruning some rose trees, and after greeting me as was his wont, said:—

"'William, you will be sorry to hear that Mrs. Rennard is so poorly that the doctor has ordered me to take her away at once for a complete change of scene. I have, therefore, decided to start tomorrow, and to close the rectory, taking the two children and servants with us.'

"I told him how sorry I was to hear it, but hoped the change and rest would soon pull Mrs. Rennard round again. Then, not knowing what more to say, I continued my work, thinking that the rector would pass on; but as he did not do so I looked round, and was surprised to find that he was eyeing me in an anxious way, and tapping the ground uneasily with his stick, as though there was something more which he wished to say, and yet did not know how to begin.

"At length, after an awkward pause, which I did my best to cover by the loud click of my pruning shears, he came close to where I stood, and said:—

"'William, you are not a superstitious man, are you?'

"'I don't think so, sir,' I answered, laughing.

"'I thought not,' went on the rector, still playing uneasily with his stick among the pebbles on the path. 'No doubt you have heard a tale about the rectory being haunted.'

"'Yes, sir,' I replied, 'I have heard it.'

"'But you don't believe it, of course, William?'

"'Not a bit of it, sir,' said I, laughing again.

"'Well,' went on the rector, looking down at the ground, 'the reason I mention it is that Mrs. Rennard declares that she last night saw this old woman, who is said to walk the house with a lighted candle in her hand; and I will tell you in strict confidence that it is this that has helped to make her so much worse.'

"'Indeed, sir,' I replied, 'I am very sorry to hear what you say, but no doubt Mrs. Rennard's health accounts for the delusion.'

"'Exactly, William; exactly what I think and believe; but the doctor insists on the necessity of taking her away at once, and so, as I have said, we start tomorrow. Now there is another thing I wish to ask you, and that is, if you will mind sleeping at the rectory during our absence, just as a kind of guard against burglary or anything of that sort. You will be about the grounds pretty often during the day, and if you do not mind sleeping in the house at night, we shall leave home more comfortably, for I know everything will be safe in your care. What do you say, William; do you mind?'

"'Not in the least, sir,' I replied, 'if it will make you and Mrs. Rennard more satisfied.'

"'Thank you,' said the rector. 'That is a great relief to me. You will, of course, have the free run of the place and come and go as you please. Good morning, William, I must be off.' And with that he left me and went towards the door which leads from the rectory garden to the churchyard. On reaching the door he turned, with his hand upon the latch, and said, laughing:

"'Remember, William, no tales of ghosts when we return.'

"'Aye, aye, sir,' I replied, and then fell to my work again; but I could not help thinking that the rector's laugh was of a forced kind, and my mind went back to what he had just told me concerning Mrs. Rennard.

"Also I thought of what the late rector had told me with regard to the same woman with the candle. But I persuaded myself that in both cases weakened nerves, the result of continued bad health, were responsible for the hallucination.

"On the following day I saw them drive off to the station which, as you know, is some five miles distant. The rector and children were in good spirits, but Mrs. Rennard looked old and broken, and I fancied that, as the carriage moved off, she shuddered on looking back quickly at the house. When they were out of sight I walked slowly back to my work in the garden.

"I was a young man in those days, sir, and not over troubled with nerves; still, when night came on and I found myself sitting alone in the rectory kitchen, I couldn't help my mind running on the mystery of poor Miss Howard's sudden disappearance and also on the creature who was said to haunt the house. However, I did my best to put these thoughts away from me, and even started a song (for I was a bit of a singer in those days); but my voice sounded so unnatural and hollow in the silence, that I was quiet again ere I had sung one verse; and after trying in vain to give my attention to reading, I rose as the church clock struck nine, and went upstairs to bed.

"The room I occupied was one of the upper row overlooking the churchyard, and was that which, as you may perhaps have noticed, has a shutter hanging loosely by a single hinge. I was a heavy sleeper, and little troubled by dreams, so that I soon fell into a heavy slumber, from which I awoke to find the sun streaming brightly into the room. Then I laughed at the idea of ghosts and springing out of bed, threw open the lattice, and took deep draughts of the pure morning air.

"Villagers who knew where I had passed the night, questioned me, with solemn faces, as to whether I had seen anything; but I returned one answer to them all, namely—that ghosts only show themselves to those who believe in them. And so the second night came on.

"Having had a heavy day, I retired to rest earlier than on the previous night, and hardly had my head touched the pillow before I fell into a deep sleep.

"How long I slept I cannot tell, but suddenly I awoke to find myself in utter darkness. I have heard it said that the sound of a footstep at dead of night, will, in some mysterious way, penetrate to the brain of the deepest sleeper, and cause sudden wakefulness, where a louder but more usual noise, such as the howling of the wind, will but lull him into heavier slumber. Whether it was so in my case, or whether what I had been told had so impressed itself on my brain as to make me dream of a footstep, I cannot say; but certain it is that I now found myself lying wide awake, listening with an intensity that was almost overpowering, to the sound of a stealthy tread in the passage outside my room. It was a halting step, as of one who was lame, and by the flap on the stone floor, I knew the feet were bare.

"The sound came nearer and nearer, and then I remembered, with sudden fright, that the door was not fastened. I could not move, but lay stark still, and listened.

"Presently the halting tread ceased, and the latch of my door clicked. A moment later the door was opened, and then such a sight met my horrified gaze as to think of, even after all these years, makes my blood run cold."

Here the sexton passed his hand over his brow, on which a cold sweat was plainly to be seen. After a short time he thus continued:

"As I was saying, the door slowly opened, and there appeared a bare and shrivelled arm, and in the hand a lighted candle. I could not move; a cold sweat broke out upon me, and although I tried to shout, all utterance was frozen on my lips. But if the candle-bearing hand and arm were terrible, a thousand times more so was the figure belonging to them, which now came slowly into the room. It was that of a woman, well advanced in years, whose haggard face and wild, staring eyes were now turned full upon me. Grizzled hair hung about a face of such diabolical ugliness as is impossible to describe in words.

"Her lips were parted in a horrid grin, exposing to view flaccid gums, studded with broken stumps of teeth; a loose, flowing garment of some ancient make was thrown about her shoulders, and reached to the ground; and at every step she went down on one side, as one afflicted with a shortened limb or stiffened knee-joint. Thus she came slowly towards me, her mouth twitching horribly the while. When within a few feet of my bed, she raised her left hand and beckoned to me as if to follow. But I could neither move nor speak, and my eyes felt as though they must roll from their sockets, so intense and fixed was my horrified gaze.

"Closer and closer she came, step by step, until with one frantic effort, born of the fear that she would touch me, my voice rushed from my lips, and I gave one loud, piercing scream.

"She stopped, and, regarding me with a look that I could pray might be blotted out from my memory for ever, again beckoned with her left hand, turning her body partly round as she did so, but still keeping her ghastly face towards me.

"Unable to resist the power of those wild, drawing eyes, I rose straightaway from my bed and followed her as one bereft of his senses. Perceiving this, she turned round and led the way from the room, ever and anon casting a hideous glance at me over her shoulder.

"Along the silent passages we passed; down the broad creaking stairs, and so out into the dark still night.

"I was as powerless as a child, and if, at any moment, a thought of turning back shot through my brain, one sight of that twitching face cast back upon its shoulder was sufficient to make me follow as though I were drawn along by some great mesmeric force.

"Across the rectory lawn she led the way—under the great yew trees, which looked like weird funeral plumes in their inky blackness. Not a breath of wind stirred the trees, and not a star relieved the frowning, clouded sky.

"So on and on we went, until we came to the little wood which stands upon the verge of one of the oldest slate pits. Skirting this wood, the old hag led the way to the further end of the pit, where the deep water may be approached, even to its very brink. There she stopped, and beckoned to me with her bony hand to come to her—for I was some yards behind.

"I had no power but to obey, and so, when I was within a yard of her, she moved on again, leading the way along a narrow and dangerous shelf of rock, which was in some parts under water. Suddenly I saw her stop, and bend down towards a chasm or small cave in the side of the pit, which, from the splash of a stone which fell from near her feet, I knew must contain water. Holding the candle to the opening, she motioned me to look in. At first I would not, but the fury of her face and gestures compelled me at last to do so, and stooping down I beheld, by the glittering light of the candle, a sight that froze me to the spot with horror; for there, lying in the water, which was three feet deep, lay a skeleton, with the face of the skull turned towards me, while round the neck there hung, by a chain, a metal cross, which told me at once whose remains they were I looked upon.

"I was as one turned to stone—without thought or feeling, or any sense of life; and for some time—I know not how long—I stood there, forgetful of everything, even of the scene before me. Then again, for a second time, I realized that in those bleaching bones beneath the water, I saw all that was left of my first rector's niece, and of our dear friend of years ago—Miss Howard.

"The flaring of the candle in its socket broke the spell, and looking quickly round I found the old hag's horrible face so close to mine that her grizzled locks nearly touched my cheek. That was the final straw to my already cracking nerves, and with a shriek that echoed round and round the pit, I sank down into a deep swoon.

"When I came to myself the dawn was breaking and I was alone. For some moments I lay dazed, but gradually the horrors of the night came back to me, and turning my head I looked into the cave, hoping, I believe, to find that it was all a dream; but to my horror I saw the skeleton, with the chain about its neck, lying beneath the water. The next moment I rushed wildly from the spot, never stopping until I reached the Hall, where the servants, who were just astir, doubtless took me for a madman.

"I insisted on seeing Lord Androvil, and presently he came to me in the study, in his dressing gown. To him I told my tale, he listening, I remember, with a pitying look; then, as I rose to go, I fell senseless at his feet.

"I remember no more until I awoke to consciousness, after a dangerous illness, some weeks later.

"When I was strong enough to bear it, I learned from Lord Androvil himself how, after bringing me home, he had organized and led a search party to the spot I had indicated; how they there found the skeleton, which was at once identified as Miss Howard's (for the metal cross bore the significant initials 'D.L.H.'), and how the remains had been buried in the churchyard, the sexton of a neighbouring village digging the grave.

"And that, sir," concluded the sexton, "ends my story of the woman with the candle, and of the one grave I did not dig: and if you are disposed to question it or put it down to a delusion of the senses, I can only point to the fact of the finding of the skeleton and ask you to account for that."

"I do not question it for one moment," I replied, "though it is the strangest tale I have ever listened to. But I would like to ask you one thing. How do you think Miss Howard met her death?"

The old man bent upon me a most serious look as he replied in a deep and solemn voice:—

"My only answer to that question, sir, is that I firmly believe Miss Howard was led from her room by the same hideous creature who led me; that she was taken along the same way; and that, coming to the cave, and being beckoned to look in, she saw there something—I cannot tell what—something that caused her to swoon and lose her life by falling into the water."

"One more question," said I. "Are you a believer in ghosts?"

"Yes, sir," replied the sexton, more solemnly than ever; "I am."

Perceval Landon

Perceval Landon (1869–1927) is one of those authors (lucky or unlucky, depending on your point of view) who is now only remembered for just one story. In his case, the story is a classic, "Thurnley Abbey," from his 1908 collection *Raw Edges*, one of the most reprinted tales in the genre.

But there was more to Landon than ghost stories. He was a barrister and journalist who gained his reputation as a war correspondent covering the Boer War. He knew Africa well, and travelled extensively in the Far East and India.

Landon's knowledge of Asia came to fruition when he joined the Younghusband expedition to Lhasa in 1903, at first as a special correspondent for *The Times* but eventually becoming the expedition's official recorder. His massive two volume (870 pages!) book *Lhasa: An Account of the Country and People of Central Tibet* was published in 1905.

Landon's first book was as editor of *Heliotropes* (1903), a revised edition of a seventeenth century work by John Parmenter. He put his knowledge of the East to good use again in a later book, *Under the Sun* (1906), a volume on Indian cities.

Though his book output was limited, Landon wrote for over twenty years as the *Daily Telegraph*'s eastern correspondent, and covered the First World War for all its four years.

Raw Edges and "Thurnley Abbey" is now all he is remembered for in the literary field. I thought it might be worth while having another look at *Raw Edges* to see if there were any further stories that merit revival.

"Mrs. Rivers's Journal," from that book, seems to have been overlooked for 100 years. For most of its length, an intriguing Victorian morality drama, right at the end it brings in the supernatural in a scene worthy of M. R. James. It is most definitely worth reprinting.

Mrs. Rivers's Journal

I

"*May 19th*. Two or three people to dinner and a play. Dennis, Mr. and Mrs. Richmond, Lady Alresford, and Colonel Wyke. D. saw me home after. I think something must be the matter. D. was very much upset last night, I'm sure. It all happened very suddenly, as he had been as delightful as ever all the evening. I can't think what it is. It was about midnight when he said something to himself, as he was looking out of the window, and changed completely."

Later in the day Mrs. Rivers added, almost in another hand, these notes:

"D. called here this afternoon. At first he was very silent, and I asked him what the matter was. He said that it was not my fault in any way, and that he would explain some day. Meanwhile he asked me not to worry. But I'm sure something is very wrong, and if it is not my fault I'm half afraid that it may be on my behalf that Dennis is so upset. But he won't say anything, and I can't think that there is anything really to be feared. He only stayed half an hour, and went away saying that he would like to see me tomorrow morning. I thought it was a pity that he should come too often to the house, and said that I would meet him in the National Gallery at twelve o'clock. I wonder what it all means."

Mrs. Rivers, whose locked journal is here quoted, was in herself a very ordinary kind of pretty woman. So far as the world knew, she was a widow, and a rich widow. Her husband had died about four years before this date, and it is unlikely that he was very seriously mourned. Colonel Rivers—his title was really a Volunteer distinction, but the man deserved no little credit for the way in which he worked up his battalion—was an inordinately jealous man, and though no one believed he had the least reason for suspecting his wife's acquaintance with Captain Dennis Cardyne, there is no doubt that, shortly before he died, it became almost a monomania with him, it may even have been a symptom of the trouble from which he must even then have been suffering acutely. Cardyne, a remarkably straight and loyal friend, with no brains, but a good sense of humour and principles which were at least as correct as those of his fellow-officers, was surprised one day by being peremptorily forbidden the house by Colonel Rivers. Human nature being what it is, it is possible that Cardyne then felt that the least impediment which friendship or loyalty could impose was removed, and there is no doubt that a general feeling of sympathy and affection for Mrs. Rivers took on quite another colouring by this idiotic proceeding on the part of Mrs. Rivers's husband. Cardyne's eyes were opened for the first time to the life that Mrs. Rivers must have led since her marriage four years before, though indeed she had previously taken some pains that he should quite understand her unhappiness at home. But Cardyne, who knew and liked the Colonel—in the patronizing way that the most junior of regular officers will regard a volunteer—unconsciously discounted a good deal, knowing that most women like to think that their husbands misunderstand them. Hitherto he had neither disbelieved nor believed what Mrs. Rivers was insinuating. Now, however, his pity was aroused, though nothing in his conduct showed it at the moment.

I do not suggest for a moment that Mrs. Rivers was either a very interesting or a very virtuous person. But she had the little fluffy pleading ways by which many men are strangely attracted, and even if Cardyne had made any advances, her respect for conventionality, which was far more sacred to her than she quite realized, fully supplied the place of morality during the few months that elapsed between Colonel Rivers's explosion of jealousy and his sudden death.

There were not many people, except the very nearest of kin,

who were aware of a curious clause which Colonel Rivers had inserted in his will about the time that he forbade Dennis Cardyne to come to the house. Personal references of an unpleasant kind are not copied into the volumes in Somerset House, which contain the wills to which probate has been granted. A proviso in the will that Mrs. Rivers, in the event of her marrying again, was to forfeit one-half of the somewhat large fortune bequeathed to her by her husband was public property, but only to those who were chiefly concerned it was allowed to be known that in the event of her marrying Captain Dennis Cardyne—whose name was preceded by an epithet— she was to forfeit every penny.

When Mrs. Rivers heard the terms of her husband's will, she lost the last tinge of respect she had ever had for her departed helpmeet. The prohibition certainly achieved its end, but it was not long before Cardyne and Mrs. Rivers settled down to a hole-and-corner flirtation, which probably brought far more terror than pleasure into the latter's life. Cardyne assured me that there was never anything more, and I am accustomed to believe that Dennis Cardyne speaks the truth. But the world thought otherwise and found many excuses for them. Mrs. Rivers could always justify to herself what she was doing by a remembrance of her husband's insane and ungenerous jealousy; but the fact remained that, however much this sufficed to quiet her own conscience, Mrs. Rivers was, to the very marrow of her, a common little thing, utterly afraid of the world's opinion, and quite unable to carry through the unconventionality of her affection for Cardyne without a burden of misery. And they did the silliest of things. After all, if a man will see a woman home from the play night after night and stay till two in the morning, he must be ready for a howl or two from the brute world. We have all done it, and done it most platonically, but at least we knew that it wasn't over wise.

I used to meet her at one time. She was always to be found in houses of a certain type. Her friends were women who took their views of life from one another, or from Society weekly papers. In the wake of Royalty they did no doubt achieve a certain amount of serviceable work for others, and at least it could

be said of them that none of them seemed likely to scandalize
the susceptibilities of their comfortable, if somewhat narrow,
circle. Never twice would you meet a clever man, or a brilliant
woman, at these feasts.

If you will take the names of those who were present at Mrs.
Rivers's small dinner-party on 18 March, you will see exactly
what I mean. Colonel Wyke was an old friend of her husband's.
He had a little place in the country in which he grew begonias
very well, and was, I believed, writing the history of the parish,
from such printed material as he could find in the library of the
country town. Lady Alresford lent her name to every charity
organization without discrimination or inquiry. She was a presi-
dent of a rescue home in London, which probably did much
harm to conventional morality. Mr. and Mrs. Richmond were a
quiet, and somewhat colourless, little couple of considerable
wealth, but without any real interest or purpose in life except
that, if the truth must be told, of gossiping about their neighbours. I have never known Richmond at a loss for an inaccurate
version of any scandal in London.

I have set out the circumstances in which Mrs. Rivers lived at
greater length than may be thought necessary. But I am inclined
to think that it was very largely the facts of her surroundings,
and the influence unconsciously exerted by her friends, that
eventually led Mrs. Rivers into the most awful trouble. As I have
said, I am a somewhat silent person, and I meditate more perhaps than talkative folk upon the reversals and eccentricities of
fate. I think I could safely affirm that though I did not then
know the real relations that existed between Mrs. Rivers and
Cardyne—who, by the way, for all his density, was head and
shoulders above this crowd—I still could never have dreamed
that fate would have whetted her heaviest shaft to bring down
such poor and uninteresting game as this. But, as a matter of
fact, I did not know that Mrs. Rivers was nothing more than a
close friend of Cardyne's. On the face of it I thought that
Cardyne could never be very long attracted by any one possessed of so little interest as Mrs. Rivers; but, against that, I
admitted that Cardyne's constancy was quite in keeping with his
general simple loyalty; and, on the other hand, I was not sure

that Mrs. Rivers might not be more interesting in that relation than she might have seemed likely to be to a mere outsider like myself. She might have been possessed, like many other women, of the two entirely distinct and mutually exclusive natures that Browning thanks God for.

I came to know Cardyne pretty well in those months, and if any feeling of anger should be caused by the story I am going to tell with the help of Mrs. Rivers's journal, it is only fair to say that Cardyne did all he could. It is a grim tale.

Cardyne, as he had promised, went to the National Gallery at twelve o'clock on 20 May. It was a Friday, and in consequence there were very few present, except the young ladies in brown holland over-alls, who were painting copies of deceased masters in the intervals of conversation. But in the central room there was one industrious figure labouring away at a really important copy of the Bronzino at the other end of the room. Mrs. Rivers was sitting in a chair opposite the Michael Angelo—a picture, by the way, which she would certainly have relegated to a housemaid's bedroom had she possessed it herself.

Cardyne was punctual. But it was clear from the moment he entered the gallery that the interview was going to be unpleasant. He walked listlessly, and with a white face, up to where Mrs. Rivers was sitting.

She was really alarmed at the sight of him, and, putting out a hand, said to him:

"Good gracious, Dennis, don't frighten me like this!"

Cardyne sat down and said:

"You've got to listen, Mary. It is a matter that concerns you."

Mrs. Rivers grew rather white, and said:

"Nobody knows, surely? Nobody would believe. We are perfectly safe if we deny it absolutely?"

Cardyne shook his head.

"Listen," he said wearily, "did you see the posters of the *Star* as you came along?"

Mrs. Rivers thought that he was going mad.

"Yes," she said; "there was a speech by Roosevelt and a West End murder, but what has that got to do with us?"

Dennis put his hand in front of his eyes for a moment, and then said:

"Everything—at least the murder has."

Mrs. Rivers grew rather cross.

"For Heaven's sake tell me what you mean!" she said; "I don't understand anything. What can this murder have to do with you and me?"

Cardyne said, in a dull and rather monotonous voice:

"A man called Harkness was murdered on the night of 18 May. He lived at No. 43 Addistone Place."

Mrs. Rivers began a remark, but Cardyne impatiently stopped her.

"That house, as you know, is exactly opposite yours. The old man was found murdered yesterday, the police were making inquiries all day, the newspapers have just got hold of it, and an arrest has been made. They have taken into custody a maidservant called Craik, who had apparently one of the best of reasons for hating Harkness."

Cardyne broke off. Mrs. Rivers breathed again.

"But what in the name of Heaven has all this to do with me or you?"

Cardyne paused for thirty seconds before he answered:

"The maidservant is innocent." His sentences fell slowly and heavily. "The murder was committed by the manservant."

Mrs. Rivers was not a person of very quick imagination, but she vaguely felt that there was something horrible impending over her, and, after an indrawn breath, she said quickly:

"Where did you see it from?"

Dennis turned round and looked at her straight in the eyes and did not say a word. Mrs. Rivers felt the whole gallery swinging and swirling round her. She seemed to be dropping through ˎ space, and the only certain things were Dennis Cardyne's two straight grey eyes fixed in mingled despair and misery upon her own. A moment later the girl at the other end of the room looked up with a start, and went quickly across the gallery to ask if she could be of any use. Mrs. Rivers, in a high falsetto that was almost a scream, had said, "What are you going to do?" and fallen forward out of her chair. She pulled herself together as the girl came up, and muttered a conventional excuse, but she hardly knows how it was that she got home and found herself lying on her own bed, vaguely conscious that Cardyne had just left the room after giving her the strictest instructions as to what she was to do to keep well, and assuring her that there might not be the slightest risk or trouble of any kind. And he added that he would return about six o'clock in the evening, and tell her all there was to be known.

II

I heard this story some time afterwards, but I remember, as if it were yesterday, the remark which some one made to me about Mrs. Rivers during the season of 1904.

"The woman's going mad. She goes to every lighted candle she can scrape up an invitation to, and last week, to my certain knowledge, she—she, poor dear!—went to two Primrose League dances."

Right enough this feverish activity was regarded as a sign and portent, for Mrs. Rivers was one of those people who thought that her social position was best secured by kicking down her ladders below her. I confess that a night or two later I was amazed indeed at finding her at my poor old friend Miss Frankie's evening party. Miss Frankie was the kindest and dullest soul in London. She was also the only real conscientious Christian I have ever known. She refrained from malicious criticism of those around her. This perhaps made her duller than ever, and I will admit that there was a curious species of mental exercise associated with visits to her house. As a rule, one found the earnest district visitor sitting next one at dinner, or it might be some well-intentioned faddist with elastic-sided boots, bent on the reformation of the butterflies of society, or the House of Lords. But among those who really understood things, there were many who used to put up with the eccentricities of a night out at Miss Frankie's if only because of the genuine pleasure that it obviously gave to the little lady to entertain her old friends. I twice met San Iguelo the painter there, and for the first time began to like the man, if only for going. Now this was particularly, I fancy, the social level from which Mrs. Rivers had herself risen; but precisely therefore was it the social level which she took particular pains now to ignore. A year ago Mrs. Rivers would have regarded an evening with Miss Frankie as an evening worse than wasted.

That night, I was sitting in a corner of the room. I was talking to a young artist who had not yet risen in the world, and probably never will; still, she had a sense of humour, and knew Mrs. Rivers by sight. She watched her entrance and, without a touch of malice, she turned to me and said:

"What on earth has made Mrs. Rivers honour us with her presence to-night?"

I did not know, and said so, but I watched Mrs. Rivers for some minutes. Of course it was Mrs. Rivers, but I doubt if any one who knew her in a merely casual way would have been quite sure. I am perfectly certain that the woman was painted. Now Mrs. Rivers never painted in old days. Moreover, she never stopped talking, which was also unlike her. (The woman had her good points, you see.) However, there she was. Once, our eyes met, and probably neither of us liked to define the uneasiness that I am sure we both felt.

She had a way of leaving her mouth open and allowing the tip of a very pink tongue to fill one corner of it. I knew it well in the old days. Somebody must have told her that it was arch. It was a touch of vulgarity of just that sort of which no one could very well break her after she had once started climbing the society ladder, and in time it grew to be a trick. At one moment, when Miss Frankie was occupied with a newcomer, Mrs. Rivers's face fell into a mask that convinced me that the woman was ill. As soon as her forced vivacity left her, the whole face fell away on to the bones, the eyes became unnaturally bright, and there was a quick, hunted look about them. She was evidently quite oblivious for the moment, and I saw her tongue go up into the corner of her mouth. It was a small matter, but the contrast between the expression of her face, and this silly little affectation no one could fail to notice.

She stayed for half an hour and went on somewhere, I suppose to a dance. She was alone, and as I happened to be at the foot of the stairs as she came down, I thought it was only civil, as I was myself hatted and coated for going away, to ask if she had her servant there to call the carriage. It was all rather awkward. I moved across the floor to her with the conventional offer so obviously on my lips and even in my gait, that I could not well be stopped going on with my part, even though at the last moment, almost after she might have recognized me, she shut her eyes and said in a tone of broken helplessness: "O my God, have mercy upon me!" She opened her eyes again a moment afterwards, saw me with a start, recovered herself, and pressed me almost hysterically to be dropped somewhere by her, she did not seem to care where. But I refused. I did not much want to be dropped by Mrs. Rivers, and I am quite sure that my humble diggings did not lie anywhere on the route to her next engagement that evening.

A few days after that I met Cardyne, and with the usual fatuity of any one who tries with all his might to keep off a subject, I said to him that I had seen Mrs. Rivers, and that she seemed to me to be strangely upset and unlike herself. He looked at me rather hard for a moment and said:

"Oh, I know all about that: she is worried about her people."

Now that is absurd, for nobody ever is worried to that extent about her people, or at least she doesn't say, "O my God, have mercy upon me!" if she is. However, it was no business of mine, and I went on in my humble way of life, though from time to time I heard some notice taken of Mrs. Rivers's hysterical behaviour during that season.

Cardyne told me afterwards that at the moment when I had noticed Mrs. Rivers's behaviour, she was almost determined to make the sacrifice by which alone, as it was now too clear, could the unfortunate maidservant at No. 43 be cleared from the charge against her. The excitement caused by the murder had died down somewhat since the middle of May when it had taken place, but every one was looking forward with gladiatorial interest to the trial. It was appointed to begin on 30 June at the Old Bailey, and though, as I have said, from a legal point of view the case looked very black against Martha Craik, the servant, it was still felt that something more was needed before the jury would accept as proved a crime which for some reasons a woman seemed hardly likely to carry out. Cardyne told me that, of course, his first duty was to reassure Mrs. Rivers. This he did at first with such effect that the woman regarded the likelihood of any serious issue to the trial as most improbable, and eagerly hugged to herself the relief which her lover thus held out to her.

"On Thursday afternoon," said Cardyne to me, "after our meeting in the National Gallery, the unhappy woman had so convinced herself that there was nothing really to fear, that she went down on her knees in her own drawing-room beside the tea-table and made me kneel with her." Cardyne's face, as he said this, almost made me smile, though it was hardly an occasion for mirth. "She rose, gave me tea, and all the time asked me to see in it the kindness and tenderness of God, and hoped it would be a warning to me." Of what, I really hardly think either Cardyne or myself knew. "But at any rate," said Cardyne, "I had cheered her up for the time being. But I lied like a trooper."

As a matter of fact, the case against Craik grew blacker and blacker every day. She was the only servant who slept alone in the house, and all the others were ready to swear, with unanimity, that neither they nor their stable-companions had left their rooms all night. To this I ought to have attached little importance, as servants, when frightened, are always ready to swear that they did not sleep a wink all night. But it made a very great impression on the public.

The knife with which the murder was done was found in rather a curious way. The police inspector was asking some questions of the manservant in the passage outside Mr. Harkness's bedroom door. Another servant came by, and both men took a step inwards to allow room for him to pass. The manservant, whose name was Steele, in taking a sharp pace up to the wall, actually cut his boot upon the knife, which was stuck upright in the floor, blade outwards, between the jamb of the door and the wainscoting, where it had escaped notice. It was an ordinary kitchen table-knife, worn and very sharp, and the fact that Steele cut his boot upon it was taken as proof beyond all hesitation or question that Steele at least was totally ignorant of everything connected with the crime. But Steele was the man whom Cardyne had seen in Harkness's room.

To return to Mrs. Rivers. Cardyne found that it was impossible to conceal from her much longer the fact that things were going badly indeed against Craik. One afternoon, about a fortnight before the trial opened, he found it his terrible duty to make Mrs. Rivers see that unless his evidence was forthcoming, an innocent woman might be condemned to death. For a long time Mrs. Rivers had understood that all was not well. Perhaps if all had been well she would have had just the same nervous breakdown. The woman was at her tether's end, and there is no doubt that in spite of her hysterical attempts to distract her thoughts, she was coming to realize what the position was.

Here are some extracts from her diary at different times:—

"*June 20th.* All going as well as possible. D. tells me that he still thinks there may be no real reason for alarm. He hears at the club that the verdict at the inquest is thought unreasonable by people in town."

(Let every woman remember that there is no more worthless authority for any statement than that a man has heard it at his club. As a rule, it is worth no more than her maid's opinion as she does her hair that evening.)

"*July 1st.* Lady Garrison came across this afternoon and upset me a good deal. D. never told me about the door of 43 having been chained all night. Will see him about this tomorrow.

"*June 10th.* [This was about the time when I saw Mrs. Rivers.] Worse and worse. Of course everything must go right, but I would give five years of my life to be over the next two months. All might be right. D. tells me so. The suspense is awful.

"*July 14th.* Sampson gave me warning this morning. I was horribly frightened when he actually told me, and I'm rather afraid that he noticed it. He says he is going to his brother in Canada, and of course he has always told me that he would go as soon as he could. He said nothing to make me uneasy, spoke very respectfully, and offered to suit his convenience to mine at any time. I don't know what to do. I must ask D. Perhaps it would be better if he left at once."

I am sure it passed through that wretched woman's brain that if her butler could, so to speak, be made to look as if he had bolted from the country a week before the trial took place, some suspicion would be aroused which might, perhaps, cause a post-ponement of the sentence, if the worst came to the worst. More than that, she was, of course, anxious to get rid thus easily of some one who, for all her precautions, might have known about Cardyne's visit, and finally, in the event of her having to go through a great nervous strain at the time of the trial, she hard-ly knew whether it would be better to have a new butler who might simply look upon her with unpleasant inquisitiveness as an hysterical subject, or the old one who, for all his discretion and sympathy, could hardly fail to see that something very new, very odd, and very wrong was going on in her life.

It was clear, in fact, that Mrs. Rivers was slowly realizing that there was actually a probability of the trial resulting in the con-viction of Craik, and when, a fortnight later, Cardyne took his courage in his hands and went to Addistone Terrace to break the news to her of Craik's conviction and sentence to death, I fancy she knew all before he opened his lips. Cardyne never intentionally told me much about that interview. Indirectly he let me know a good deal, and I am perfectly sure that any feel-ing of repugnance or horror that he ever felt against Mrs. Rivers was that afternoon changed into the deepest and most heartfelt pity. It was one of those interviews from which both parties emerge old and broken. Mrs. Rivers apparently saw what was going to be urged by Cardyne, rattled off his arguments one after the other, with horrible fluency, and then, while he sat in white silence on the sofa, flung at him:

"And you've come to tell me that as things have gone wrong, I'm to sacrifice my honour and my reputation for that wretched woman's life?"

All Cardyne could say was simply, "I have."

At this Mrs. Rivers leant against the mantelpiece and spoke clearly and monotonously for half a minute, as if she had been long conning the lesson, and drew out before Cardyne's dazed understanding a dramatic but unconvincing picture of what a woman's reputation means to her. She declaimed with pathos that, like any other woman, she would rather die than be disgraced in the eyes of the world. Poor Cardyne's one interruption was not a happy one, yet it is one which, from a man's standpoint, had a touch of nobility. He said:

"But it isn't a question of *your* dying."

When Mrs. Rivers said that she would rather die than suffer dishonour, his involuntary ejaculation told her plainly enough that, up to that moment, he had not conceived it possible that any woman could be so vile as to sacrifice the life of an innocent woman for her own social ambitions.

Ther was a silence of a quarter of a minute. Mrs. Rivers fidgeted with the fire-screen. Then she said:

"So you intend to betray me?"

At this poor Cardyne was more hopelessly bewildered than ever.

"Good God, no!" he said: "of course I can only do what you decide. The matter is entirely in your hands; but surely—"

Mrs. Rivers stopped him with a gesture.

"I absolutely forbid you to say a word. I will decide the matter, and I will let you know; but, understand me, except with my express permission, I rely upon your honour to keep the secret for ever, if I wish it."

This at least Cardyne could understand, and he gave the promise with unquestionable earnestness. But he was to realize that a man placed in such a position, with honour tearing him in two opposite ways, is condemned to the worst anguish which the devil knows how to inflict.

However, he had given his word—a quite unnecessary proceeding, if only Mrs. Rivers had known it—and it only remained for him to try and make her see the matter from the point of view from which he himself regarded it. He could not bring himself to believe that she would refuse. This continual appeal resulted in almost daily scenes. Cardyne, with the best of intentions, was not a tactful person, and in season and out of season he presented the case to Mrs. Rivers from a standpoint she never understood, and never could have understood. She in turn, driven to bay like an animal, wholly failed to see that in this matter Cardyne's secrecy might be trusted to his death, and shook with terror as the date for the execution drew on. These two wretched souls, during the last fortnight in July, fought out this dreary fight between themselves, until poor Cardyne came to wonder how it was that he had ever in the wildest moment of infatuation cared for such a woman as Mrs. Rivers daily proved herself to be.

All this while Mrs. Rivers was steadily going out to dinners and dances, and in the afternoons she attended more regularly than anyone the committee meetings presided over by Royalty with which her name had been so long and honourably connected.

III

It is strange in the light of after events to remember Cardyne's life among us during the days which followed the trial of Martha Craik. I have never supposed, nor do I now suppose, that Cardyne had in him many of the necessary constituents of an actor, but I am perfectly sure that there were few among us, his friends, who noticed at that time anything in him except perhaps a certain absentmindedness and irritability. Perhaps the man's simple nature was its own salvation. To his mind there could be no two views as to his own personal duty. He was clearly bound to adopt Mrs. Rivers's decision in this matter, just as on a doubtful field of battle he would not have dreamed of disobeying his colonel's most desperate order. What must have made it doubly hard for him, however, was the feeling that though he was thus bound he was obliged to use every fair argument in his power to make Mrs. Rivers see that she had adopted a course which, to him, and I believe to any man, was almost unthinkable. Here his plain, blunt tactlessness served him poorly indeed. One afternoon, after an hour's conversation—if any discussion between a man and a woman of such a topic can rightly be called conversation—it happened that he blurted out what, in his simple soul, he had imagined Mrs. Rivers had understood from the beginning. To her incessant argument that death was better than dishonour he opposed, as if it were the most natural thing in the world, the remark: "But there is not the least reason why we should survive. Provided this woman's life is saved you will have done everything that is necessary, and I think you would be right. I will gladly die with you."

Upon Mrs. Rivers's fevered brain and throbbing conscience this last suggestion had at least the effect of making the woman and the man understand each other at last. Disregarding, forgetting all that she had said, the haggard, red-eyed woman, dressed as it chanced in the most becoming of biscuit-coloured cloth gowns, turned upon Cardyne with a scream.

"Die!" she echoed. "Do you mean that I ought to get that woman off and then kill myself? Good God, what a brute you are!"

And then Cardyne understood what manner of woman wretched Mrs. Rivers was. Perhaps a clever man might have availed himself of her reaction, which set in the next day and which was necessarily great, but poor Cardyne had had neither the capacity nor the inclination to conceal from Mrs. Rivers, as he had left the house the previous day, that he detested and despised her. He never went back till the afternoon before the day set for Craik's execution.

Now and then, during the course of the next day, Mrs. Rivers saw things with Cardyne's eyes. So far, however, from this leading to any permanent change of her intentions, it merely made her suspect in abject cowardly terror that those considerations might, as the fatal day approached, prove too much for Cardyne, and that on his own initiative he would blurt out the story. The days went on. Mrs. Rivers still clung to the hope that though Craik had been sentenced to death, something would be done, something must happen to prevent the execution. What was God in His heaven for if not for this? She had a blind hope that somehow or other a wholly innocent person could not be allowed by God to suffer capital punishment in these days of modern civilization.

There had been a time in these miserable weeks when she

attempted to persuade Cardyne that what he had seen would
not, after all, make much difference to the fate of Martha Craik.
But upon his point he was as clear as the ablest of barristers. He
had seen the manservant in the house opposite, stripped to the
skin, with a knife in his hand, moving about in Mr. Harkness's
room at midnight. Cardyne was the only man in England who
knew why it was that so barbarous a murder could have taken
place without the murderer receiving even a splash or smear
upon his or her clothes. Mere proof of the presence of a naked
man moving about in the house that night would beyond all
question have saved the unhappy maidservant.

Martha Craik had been sentenced to be hanged at eight
o'clock on Monday morning, 30 July.

Cardyne spent Sunday afternoon with Mrs. Rivers.

Sunday evening he spent in his own rooms. He did not leave
them for three months. I suppose if ever a man had an excuse
for intentional and continuous self-intoxication, Cardyne was
that man. He had done his best. He had used every argument,
entreaty, and exhortation he knew of. He had failed completely,
and his sense of honour bound him with a band of iron. Few
men will dare to criticise him. He would have killed himself if
he had been sober, I think.

Mrs. Rivers was in a state that night which clearly bordered
on insanity. Twice over she wrote out a confession. Once she
actually rang the bell and gave the letter, which was addressed
to Cardyne, into her servant's hands, but she was at the door
calling for it again before he had reached the bottom of the
stairs. About one o'clock she got into a dressing-gown, and with
dry, hot eyes and scorching brain she watched the small hours
of the morning go by. She was up in her room alone. The servants had long gone to bed.

Daylight came small thin, and blue, between the crack of the
curtains. Six o'clock. Mrs. Rivers was kneeling by the side of her
bed with her face buried in the quilt. One hand dropped beside
her, the other was stretched out and clutched a prettily designed
Italian crucifix.

She had prayed at intervals all night long, and had even
denounced the injustice of God that no mercy or comfort was

extended to her in what she even then called her hour of trial. You will have grossly misunderstood the nature of Mrs. Rivers if you think that this was mere blasphemy. It was the solemn conviction in that poor little mind that God was treating her very hardly in not deadening the last appeals of her conscience against her own wickedness.

Dry-eyed and with aching brain she watched, with her chin on the quilt like a dog, the daylight grow. Seven o'clock. There was a clock on a church near which gave the chimes with astonishing clearness in the morning air. The milk-carts had ceased to rattle through the street. Vans took up their daily work, and the foot-passengers hurried by, sometimes with a low murmur of conversation, under the bright, ashy sky of a London July morning. She still knelt there unmoved. She could not have moved, I think, if she had wished; anyway she told herself that physically she could not do anything now, much as she wanted to. It was now too late.

In the curious half-light of her curtained room she could distinguish things pretty well, and one of the three slants of light fell upon herself. There was a glass between the windows, and as the light increased she could see herself in it. Even then she had time to pity the drawn and haggard misery which was stamped upon the face that met her own.

The first chime of eight o'clock struck from the church clock. With a shudder Mrs. Rivers drew her face down again and buried it in the side of the bed, convulsively clutching the crucifix. The four quarters tinkled out, and then the hour struck.

There was a light knock at the door.

Mrs. Rivers did not answer. With her face buried in the side of the bed, she was still trying to pray, but she heard it and she listened.

There was a step across the room, and someone was clearly standing at her side. She moved her eyes enough to look downwards, and she saw, three feet away from her, the end of a common skirt and two coarse boots. They did not belong either to her maid or to anyone else in the house. With a sudden icy hand at her heart, she turned back with shut eyes to the position she had occupied for so long. At last she let her eyes open. She fixed them horribly upon the reflection in the glass. And she has known little or nothing since.

Sometimes in sheer defence of Cardyne himself, I think that he *must* have lied to me about their relations. Sometimes I feel sure he did lie.